W9-CHT-415

All the
Numbers

Ballantine Books
New York

All the
Numbers

a novel

Judy Merrill Larsen

All the Numbers is a work of fiction. Names, characters, places, and incidents are the products of the author's imagination or are used fictitiously. Any resemblance to actual events, locales, or persons, living or dead, is entirely coincidental.

A Ballantine Books Trade Paperback Original

Copyright © 2006 by Judy Merrill Larsen
Reading group guide copyright © 2006 by Random House, Inc.

All rights reserved.

Published in the United States by Ballantine Books, an imprint of The Random House Publishing Group, a division of Random House, Inc., New York.

BALLANTINE and colophon are registered trademarks of Random House, Inc.
READER'S CIRCLE and colophon are trademarks of Random House, Inc.

Grateful acknowledgment is made to Alfred A. Knopf, a division of Random House, Inc., for permission to reprint an excerpt from *The Prophet* by Kahlil Gibran, copyright © 1923 by Kahlil Gibran and renewed 1951 by Administrators C.T.A. of Kahlil Gibran Estate and Mary G. Gibran. Reprinted by permission of Alfred A. Knopf, a division of Random House, Inc.

ISBN 978-0-7394-7284-2

Printed in the United States of America

www.thereaderscircle.com

Book design by Mercedes Everett

For my mother, Bev Merrill,
who set the standard for being a mom,
and for my sons, David and Eric,
who always forgave me when I fell short

Your children are not your children. . . .
They come through you but not from you,
And though they are with you, yet
   they belong not to you.
You may give them your love but not
   your thoughts,
For they have their own thoughts.
You may house their bodies but not
   their souls,
For their souls dwell in the house of
   tomorrow, which you cannot
   visit, not even in your dreams.

from "On Children," *The Prophet*
Kahlil Gibran

Acknowledgments

Seven summers ago, an offhand comment on a dock at Lake Ripley in Wisconsin became the germ of an idea for this novel. Six summers ago on my front porch in Kirkwood, Missouri, I wrote a first draft.

Through the intervening years, the number of people I am indebted to has grown exponentially.

To my agent, Marly Rusoff—if not for her, this would still be just a large document taking up space on my iMac. I never dreamed I would have the good fortune to find such a supportive, kind, insightful agent to introduce me to this wonderful world of publishing. To Marly's colleague, Michael Radulescu, whose voice on the phone always signals good news and whose calming, friendly manner makes me feel almost competent when transferring attachments. To my editor, Allison Dickens, whose uncanny understanding of the characters in this book made revisions easier than I had ever dreamed and the final product better than I had ever hoped. To Ingrid Powell, who handled all the details and my numerous questions with patience and humor. Thank you.

To my experts: Betsy DiFabio—almost twenty years ago we learned how to be new moms together, and even though we now live in different states and those firstborns are away at college, your ICU nursing wisdom flows through the hospital scenes. John Hansen, Biff LaTourette, and John Moticka—my uncle, my friend, and my soon-to-be husband—you answered all my legal questions, helped dig up intricacies about Wisconsin laws and procedures, and were great sounding boards and advisors in helping create the trial scenes and legal tension. Thank you for your expertise, and any mistakes are mine and mine alone.

To my family—John and Bev Merrill, Sue and Herb Benham, Dave and Karen Merrill, and David and Eric Larsen—thanks for your love, support, patience, and belief in me when I said I was going to write a novel.

To my Madison "family"—Patty and Mark Schweiger, Mary and Russ Evansen, David and Betsy Hovde, and Sarah and Paul Harari—thanks for all the years of love, laughter, and friendship. I hope you see yourselves all over these pages. To Jim and Muggy Schweiger, thanks for the lake house.

To Josh Kendall and the members of our 2004 Iowa Summer Writing Workshop class—thank you for taking my "first ten pages" to the next level. And Josh, I wouldn't be writing an acknowledgment page if not for your kindness and generosity.

To my friends who read various drafts over the years—Mark Autrey, Lorri Coates, Connie Copley, Kevin Hampton, Cathie Kane, Andrea Karban, Karen Kuehnle, Doug Lane, Barb McKone, Nancy Menchhofer, Renee Schenk, Ray Schoch, Debbie Shrout, Gayle Stratmann, and Karen Wentzel—thanks for your time, your honesty, and your eyes. Your questions and suggestions helped every step of the way.

To all my Kirkwood friends and students who have been excited with me and cheered me on, thanks.

And finally, to John, love of my life, who some days believed in this more than I dared to. Thanks for coming along and finding me. Everything is better when I can share it with you. It is what it is . . . and it's all good.

March 2005

All the
Numbers

Prologue

Ellen pulled into an empty parking space and turned off the car. She stared at the shoe box on the floor between the front seats.

I have to carry that in, she thought. And the bag of clothes. The effort seemed overwhelming. Is there a desk I take them to? she wondered. Should I have labeled this stuff like when the boys went to camp? Maybe I have a Sharpie in the glove compartment. She reached across in front of Liz, her sister-in-law, not even noticing her efforts to get out of the way.

How had her summer come to this? As she rummaged in the glove box, the receipt for her license renewal fell out. Was that just two months ago? Really? That was how my summer began? Okay, she told herself, they're just clothes. Nothing else. Block out where you are. And why. Just block it out. But then a hearse pulled into the long driveway next to her. She watched stunned family members leaving the funeral home and getting into limousines behind the hearse. So I'm not the only one. There are other people who have lost someone. This happens to everyone. This happens all the time.

"How come I never knew?" she said, more to herself than to Liz, who'd been sitting silently with her.

"Knew what, honey?"

"Knew that people died. Every damn day. Knew that families had to collect clothes and shoes for their dead children. Knew that there were all these details . . ." Ellen's voice trailed off.

"Because it hadn't happened to you."

Ellen shook her head. It was more than that. But she didn't know what. Add it to the list of things I don't understand anymore, she thought.

She went back to looking for a Sharpie; she hauled out all the papers and receipts and manuals crammed into the glove compartment, but even though she found two tire gauges and several straws from McDonald's, there were no markers. She dropped the mess on the floor and started to gather up the clothes and shoes instead, but when she reached for the door latch, she stopped.

"I can't," she whispered.

"I'll go with you," Liz offered.

"No. I can't do this. Not by myself. Not even with you or with anybody." Ellen hugged the clothes to her chest and inhaled deeply. She sniffed the shirt again, expecting the smell of fabric softener. Oh God, she thought, he must have worn this and put it away again rather than down the laundry chute. I smell him. I can't lose that. I won't. I can go home, she thought frantically. I can go through all his drawers and smell all his shirts. And I can seal up all the dirty ones in ziplock bags so years from now I'll still be able to smell him. She heard Liz gasp and realized she had said some of this out loud. First the new shoes, she thought, and now this. They'll be ordering me a straitjacket before sundown.

"Ellen, I'll take in the clothes. You stay here."

Ellen nodded but didn't loosen her grip on the clothes. Liz got out and came around to the driver's side and opened the door.

"Okay, honey, let go. I'll be right back. Stay here."

Ellen nodded and unclenched the clothes, but even so Liz glanced back as she opened the doors to the funeral home as if expecting Ellen to jump out of the car and take off running. I would if there were anyplace to go, Ellen thought. I'd run and run and run. But she knew that she could run for hours or weeks or years and never get back to where she wanted to be, where it was safe, four days ago on the dock at the lake right before the accident or maybe two months ago at the start of what had seemed like just another summer.

Chapter
One

"Good God," Ellen Banks said when she entered the drab, scuffed room that housed the west side Madison branch of the Wisconsin Department of Motor Vehicles. "Could they make this place any more unappealing?"

"What do you suppose they call this color? Sludge?"

Ellen turned to smile at the woman holding the door open for her and answered, "It definitely isn't in the Martha Stewart Collection."

The woman laughed in agreement and exited the building.

Ellen groaned as she wended her way to the line for renewing licenses. At first, she was too busy calculating how long it had been since these walls had last been repainted—she noted the decade-old cigarette smoke stains near the ceiling—to notice the length of the line she was standing in. Then she realized that only one person had left her line so she had barely moved in five minutes.

"I thought getting here early would prevent this kind of holdup," she muttered.

"No such luck."

Ellen was startled to have her complaint answered by the young man in front of her. She smiled back at him and took a sip of coffee from her Badger football travel mug. She looked at the clock on the wall, then at her wristwatch, convinced the time could not be right. Had she really been in line only eight minutes? Both timepieces must be lying. She started to tap her toes impatiently, then took another swig of coffee. Thank God for thermos mugs, she thought.

"Excuse me, ma'am," a deep voice barked at her from behind.

"Yes?" Ellen turned eagerly, hoping she was being summoned to a newly opened line.

A stern, uniformed woman with her hair pulled back tightly in a bun glared at her. "Didn't you see the sign?"

"What sign?" Crap, Ellen thought, if I've been wasting time in the wrong line I'll scream.

"The sign that says 'No food or drink allowed.'"

Oh, please, Ellen thought, you've got to be kidding. "I'm almost done with my coffee," she said to the woman, who seemed to see herself in the role of warden. "Don't worry."

"There are no drinks allowed. No exceptions. You'll have to give it to me to throw away or take it back to your car and then come back in."

"Look," Ellen pleaded, "I don't want to lose my place in line. My coffee's nearly gone, okay? I'm just here for my annual license renewal."

"You should have paid attention to the sign before you took your place in line." The warden didn't move. Ellen tried to summon up some friendly feelings. I guess if I had to work in this environment every day I'd be a little grumpy, too, she thought.

People around them had started to chuckle and stare. Ellen wasn't sure the best way to respond to the last statement, but she was pretty sure ignoring it wasn't going to work.

"You're so right. I should've noticed the sign. I'm sorry." Ellen tried to sound sheepish, but her words came out too heavily laced with sarcasm to buy her any leniency.

"I don't believe you're sorry at all. Return the mug to your car now."

The young man in front of her assured her he would save her place in line. Ellen thanked him and started to walk out but couldn't resist first saying to the woman, "Now that you've made the room safe from coffee spills, would it kill you to open up another line?"

Thirty coffeeless minutes later, Ellen neared the front of the line. All that stood between her and release was a heavyset middle-aged woman at the counter and the young man who had saved her place in line. The woman conversed seriously, but quietly, with the clerk. Ellen strained to hear what was holding the line up yet again.

"Oh," the woman whined, "I just don't know what to do. I'm never sure about this."

"It's gotta be your decision," the clerk responded. She appeared bored and tired as she looked back and forth between the woman and the long line stretching behind her.

"What do you suggest?" the woman asked the clerk again.

Ellen sighed and asked her newfound line friend, "What's her big quandary?"

"Organ donation."

Ellen shook her head and watched them talk quietly. Come on, lady, she pleaded silently, I've just lost thirty minutes of my life standing right here waiting. While the clerk nodded at the woman, popped her gum, and toyed with her hair, Ellen thought she heard the woman ask about being sure she was really gone before anyone started cutting her open to get at her heart. Again Ellen groaned, then said softly, "Jeez, it's not like it'll matter to you if they take anything. You'll be dead."

Apparently she had used too much volume—not only did this elicit laughter from those in line with her, but the woman at the counter turned to her, frowned, then said to the clerk, "Just forget it. I can't decide something this important when I am being pressured."

As the woman left, Ellen smiled at her in an effort to apologize for her rudeness. So far this morning, I've made at least two people angry in this room alone, and I've cost the organ donation program a future donor, she thought. Not a great start to my first day of summer vacation.

Ellen pushed her grocery cart through the produce section and stopped to add lettuce and peppers to her cart. She'd already selected peaches, plums, grapes, and strawberries. One of her goals was to eat more like an adult—she kept telling herself that by the time she was forty her diet should be more health-focused and less like a teenager's, but that deadline was now less than two years away and she hadn't made any major progress. She bought "healthy," but more often than not the vegetables turned to liquid in the crisper drawer before she'd eaten them.

"Mrs. Banks?"

Ellen glanced up to see one of her students shopping with her mom. "Hi, Melanie. Hi, Ms. Monroe."

"Actually, it's now Mrs. Parker. I got remarried this spring," Melanie's mom answered with a broad smile.

"Congratulations," Ellen said, "that's great. I had no idea."

She looked at Melanie, surprised that she hadn't mentioned it to Ellen at school. They'd had all those afternoons of unpacking and numbering books while Melanie fulfilled her community service hours for National Honor Society.

Melanie shrugged in response, then said, "I thought I'd told you. Sorry."

"Well, have a great summer."

"We will," Melanie's mom said, then added, "It's going to be an exciting time with Mel starting to look at colleges and me getting ready for a new baby."

"Oh my," Ellen said, "you really are gearing up for some big adjustments. How fun."

"Well, we'll let you get back to your shopping, but it was good seeing you," Melanie's mom said as they headed to the opposite end of the aisle. Ellen smiled and waved, then glanced at the contents of her cart to make sure there were no problematic or embarrassing items. Good thing I haven't gone down the liquor aisle yet, she thought.

Running into students all over this side of Madison was something Ellen wasn't entirely used to, even after six years of teaching. The grocery store was pretty benign; the community pool another experience altogether. There she would have to fight the urge to tell the girls to appreciate their flat stomachs, firm butts, and cellulite-free thighs. They take those things for granted, she thought, and they probably look at me and all the other moms here and vow to never let themselves go the way they think we have. Little do they know that body parts have minds of their own.

As she loaded up her cart with the fruit snacks, Lucky Charms, and Pop-Tarts that her sons, Daniel and James, would polish off within days, she winced at how far she had come— or regressed—from the diligence with which she had policed their diets when they were younger. She had breast-fed each of them for a full year, had even made her own baby food. Now they consumed sugared cereal with abandon. Fortunately they were just as ravenous for yogurt, fruit, and milk. But still, the guilt she often felt wasn't far from the surface, especially when she passed other moms who bought Cheerios and apples and firmly told their toddlers that no, they couldn't have Cocoa Puffs for breakfast.

Lugging the groceries into the house, Ellen heard the boys laughing and wrestling in the family room. She called to them for some help while trying to shoo away Stella, their golden retriever mix, who eagerly sniffed the bags of food. "Sorry, Mutt," she whispered, "no rawhides or anything for you in there today." She hollered again for the boys, knowing that she was competing with the stereo. "Turn it down, guys."

"Hey, Mom, have we got a deal for you!" Her younger son startled her from behind.

"James, can you hold off on the negotiations until we've unloaded all the groceries from the car?"

"Sure. But you'll love our plan. I promise."

Ellen smiled. At eleven, James was at such a great age. Still enough of a little boy not to be blasé, but grown up enough to be fun to do things with. He was funny and sarcastic and sweet, and Ellen dreaded the thought of him becoming a moody teenager in a few short years. Daniel, at thirteen, was just on the cusp—some days chatty and happy and friendly, but at other times, with no warning signs at all, he would shut her out, sigh, and roll his eyes at everything she said.

She looked at her sons hauling in the last few bags. Just for a few minutes she paused to try to drink them in without their noticing. Daniel was so ready to be independent. He was just starting to fill out. He'd always been thin and wiry, but his shoulders were losing the slope of childhood. By next summer, he'd probably be as tall as she was or taller. How strange it'll be, she thought, to stare directly into hazel eyes exactly like her own. Did he have any idea how handsome he was? She hoped not. And then James—his pudgy toddler body had been such a contrast to Daniel's angles, and now, though he'd never be skinny, he was clearly the stronger of the two. She watched him hoist the fifty-pound bag of dog food with ease; in another few years they'd be young men. How did it all happen so fast?

The clatter of a dish falling into the sink brought Ellen back to the present.

"Good move, idiot," Daniel said to James.

"If you'd put your bowl in the dishwasher I wouldn't have knocked it over," James shot back.

"Look, guys, just stop it." Ellen hated their bickering. "I'll take care of it, okay?" She stepped between them, hoping to enable a truce. "Nothing spilled. It's not a problem." Ellen started putting away the perishables. From the dirty cereal bowls on the counter, and now in the sink, and the nearly empty milk carton in the fridge, she deduced that the boys had eaten breakfast while she was gone.

"So here's our plan," James began, having already forgotten the near fight with Daniel. Nothing fazed him. No ill will lasted more than a moment. Daniel, on the other hand, still glared at them both. "We think it'll work great for you."

"Okay, buddy, lay it on."

"Well, you know how you've been bugging us to clear out our closets and get our rooms more organized?"

"Gee, I vaguely recall mentioning that to you a few hundred times this spring."

"Well, see, we agree with you."

"There's a shocker. Could you please say that again?"

"Say what again?"

"That I was right."

"Well, that's not exactly what I said. I said, 'We agree with you.'"

"Close enough."

James laughed, and then repeated very slowly and with careful enunciation, "We . . . agree . . . with . . . you."

Ellen smiled. "Okay, now you can go on."

"So here's the deal. We clean up our rooms, you pay us, then you take us down to State Street so we can buy new posters and stuff."

"Good plan. Except for the 'you pay us' part."

"C'mon, Mom," Daniel chimed in. "Please."

Since it was June and Ellen always felt flush from receiving all of her summer paychecks at once, she agreed. As much as she tried to budget her summer money carefully, her checkbook always seemed awfully thin come late August.

"Listen, if you guys want to go today, I've got some things to return to Memorial Library. I could let you shop for an hour or so then."

"Cool," the boys said in unison as they raced off to their rooms.

"Any clothes that don't fit, put in a pile for Goodwill. Don't just throw them out," she hollered after them.

Ellen had just found a table at the Union Terrace overlooking the lake. The boys were supposed to meet her here by three. Until then she intended to sip her lemonade and read a book.

"Mrs. Banks?"

Ellen barely heard the whispered greeting, and as she turned to look she thought she might have imagined it. But no, there stood Melanie.

"Hi again, Melanie. First the grocery store, now the Terrace. You must really miss me," Ellen teased.

"I really hate to bother you now that we're on summer vacation and all . . ." Her voice trailed off.

"Are you okay?"

"Uh, not really. But, oh, never mind." And with that, the tall young woman turned to walk away. Ellen reached out and touched her arm.

"Wait a minute. What's wrong?"

"I'll be okay. It's just—could I talk to you?"

"Well, sure. Pull up a chair. I've been meaning to call you about pet-sitting in August anyway."

Ellen had first met Melanie five years ago when the very serious-looking eleven-year-old girl had knocked on Ellen's front door handing out flyers offering services as a dog walker. She had charmed Ellen and fallen in love with Stella and Boo, the cat. Several times a week for the next three summers, she had come by to walk the dog. Now Melanie was too busy for regular walks, but she always took care of the animals when Ellen went out of town.

Melanie sat down and looked out over Lake Mendota. "When do you need me to pet-sit?"

"Second week of August. Like always. Will you be back from soccer camp?"

"Yeah. And we've got nothing else planned," Melanie answered, then sighed.

"You wanted to talk?" Ellen prompted.

"It's just that, well, everything is such a mess." Melanie paused and toyed with one of the rings she was wearing.

"In what way?"

"Yeah, well. It's this whole thing with my mom."

"Her getting remarried?"

"Oh, um, I guess it's that."

"Mel? Is there a problem with your stepdad?"

"No. Stan's great. I just feel . . ." Her voice trailed off again, and she looked out over the lake.

Ellen waited for her to continue. She'd learned over the years the importance of silence. And how much kids, especially teenagers, would fill those spaces with their words and thoughts if you didn't push them to. Silence might make them uncomfortable, but urging them made them even more so. Ellen waited, sipped her lemonade, and finally Melanie whispered, "I feel replaced."

"Oh, honey," Ellen soothed, "I'm sure you do, but Stan—is that his name?—and your mom, I'm sure they don't mean to make you feel that way. They're just newlyweds."

"No, it's not them. They include me in everything. I'm almost sick of that. It's, no forget it, it's just stupid."

"Not if it has you this upset."

"It's the new baby."

"Oh." Ellen stopped to think, but Melanie was suddenly ready to talk.

"I mean, at her age? It's embarrassing. And, God, what if something's wrong with it? Why can't they behave like other parents their age? She wants me to help decorate the nursery and read all the books about the baby's development. She even said she wants me in the delivery room. That's just gross." Melanie paused to take a breath, and Ellen thought she saw tears forming in her eyes.

"Well," Ellen started, "have you told her any of this?"

"Are you kidding? She's floating around all glowy talking about prenatal vitamins and serving up cottage cheese at every meal. Isn't she supposed to feel barfy at the beginning? She acts like this is the most natural thing in the world."

Ellen wanted to tell her that it pretty much was, but she knew this wouldn't be very helpful. "Is it just her excitement that's bothering you?"

"No. Yes. I don't know. I mean, I should be glad she's happy. But a baby?"

"I really think you might want to talk to her about this."

"Yeah, well, I don't think she'd hear me if I tried."

Ellen wasn't sure what to say. She suspected there was more to it than Melanie was letting on, but didn't want to force it out.

"Hey, Mom, we got some great stuff."

Ellen turned in the direction of James' interruption. His round face was flushed with the sun and with excitement, and his blue eyes shone. Daniel stood back a bit from him, curbing some of his enthusiasm with his cooler demeanor.

Her two sons, so dear to her but so different in temperament and appearance. So loved from the moment she'd first thought she might be pregnant with each of them. She'd been overwhelmed with her emotions, and she knew how preoccupied and focused she had been. Would she be that way now, she wondered, if she were going through it again like Melanie's mom?

"Mom? You ready to go?" Daniel asked.

Ellen glanced at Melanie, not wanting to end the conversation yet.

"Go ahead, Mrs. Banks. I've got to go over to the bookstore and meet my mom," Melanie said, then added with disgust, "She's getting more baby development books."

Glancing into the rearview mirror as she drove home, Ellen's eyes lingered on her sons, while she worried about Melanie. Looking at the boys' smooth, soft skin, and their faces that hadn't yet gone through all the changes of puberty, she could still feel their arms thrown around her neck when they had been scared or tired toddlers. In their thirteen- and eleven-year-old faces, she could see glimpses of the men they would too soon become, but she could also still see traces of their baby features.

She had so worried about what a new sibling would do to Daniel, but she recalled the first day she had brought baby James home. Ellen had rested with a cup of raspberry tea in the family room while James slept in his cradle. Daniel had walked into the room he would now share with the baby. The room had been carefully turned into a nursery when Ellen had first been pregnant with Daniel. She had wanted it to be happy and bright because that was the kind of world she wanted to create for her child. She and Tim, now her ex-husband, had picked out a wallpaper pattern of circus characters in primary colors. Ellen could still recall standing in the room, after the crib and other furniture had been delivered. She had twirled around in it, taking everything in—the freshly repainted wooden shelves that Tim's grandfather had made for him when he was a baby; the toy box that had been hers as a child, and was now filled with extra baby blankets and stuffed animals; the changing table and crib with their warm honey oak stain—she could smell the new wood. As the sun poured in through the window, making the bright and cozy room almost blinding, she felt that she had truly created a nest for her children where they wouldn't feel cold or hunger or fear.

That day when Ellen brought James home from the hospital, she had set down her tea and walked into the hallway to spy on Daniel and James. She had heard Daniel singing his little made-up songs to the baby. Then she peeked around the doorway and saw Daniel standing next to the cradle, staring at this new person who had invaded his world. He handed James his beloved, tattered stuffed donkey. The same donkey that had one side of it worn smooth from Daniel rubbing it as he fell asleep. James had continued to sleep, but made happy little snuffling noises, and Ellen had walked out of the doorway so as not to intrude on them.

~~~~~~~

"Hey, Mom. I still need new shoes."

Once again, James startled Ellen out of her thoughts.

"Mom? Did you hear me?"

"Yes, I did. Why do you need new shoes now? Rather than right before school starts?"

This was an annual battle between Ellen and her son. For one thing, shoe shopping with James was one of the most time-consuming, frustrating excursions of life. He always had some image of the perfect shoe—it mattered little to him that it had yet to be envisioned or created by anyone else. So they would trudge from store to store, seeking the Holy Grail of sneakers. When he finally gave up and selected a subpar substitute he could live with, they would run into one of two obstacles—it was either not available in his size, or it was prohibitively expensive. Ellen's preference was to have to suffer through this experience only two or three times a year, the most important time being right before school started. Every kid needs new shoes for the first day of school. If he got new shoes now, she'd go through the whole shoe-shopping ordeal all over again in less than three months.

"Mom. Just look at these shoes. Barely any tread left."

"I haven't noticed it slowing you down any."

"It's a safety issue. Really," James said, grinning. His earnestness could always make her smile. Especially when he used it to tease.

"He'll need new ones before we go to Dad's," Daniel chimed in, pulling the headphones to his Walkman away from his ears.

"Hah! I told you you could still hear us with those on." James pointed at his brother accusingly.

"I never said I couldn't, you idiot."

"Hey, guys, back to the argument at hand. Why new shoes

before you go to Dad's?" Her ex-husband had recently moved to Detroit. The boys would visit him the last week of July and first week of August.

"Because you know how much he hates it when our shoes look ratty," Daniel said with a sigh, then put his headphones back on and nudged up the volume.

"Maybe he could take you shoe shopping then," Ellen muttered, then said louder to James, "How 'bout a compromise: we'll go right before you go to Dad's so they'll still seem new for school."

"Okay," James agreed happily, opening a bag of fruit snacks he had stashed in his pocket. "Just be sure to leave plenty of time."

Ellen nodded and smiled as she pulled up to the house.

After dinner, Ellen sat on the screened porch finishing her wine and listening to the boys shoot baskets in the driveway. Her thoughts wandered back to Melanie. She tried to imagine what was bothering the girl so much about her mom's pregnancy.

"Hey, Mom." Daniel suddenly stood before her sweating and panting. "I think Melanie is parked in front of our house."

Ellen hurried to the front yard, peering toward the car partially obscured in the shadows. As though she could read Ellen's thoughts, Melanie was there.

"Hi," Ellen said, leaning toward the open window on the passenger side, "how are you feeling?"

"Lousy. Grumpy. Crabby."

Ellen refrained from asking about the other four dwarfs, saying instead, "I'm glad to see you again. I'm sorry I had to run off this afternoon."

Melanie's only response was to take the keys out of the ignition.

"Care to take a walk?" Ellen asked.

"I guess."

Ellen hollered to the boys that she would be back in a little bit. Then she and Melanie walked in silence down the leafy, dusk-lit streets. Without any formal decision, they headed to a nearby park. Melanie started talking as soon as they sat down at a picnic table, more to herself, it seemed, than to Ellen.

"It's like they're making a new family without me."

"But you'll be the big sister."

"Not really. The kid's never going to know me. I'll be gone in two years."

"True, but think about how excited he'll be when you come home. And you'll be surprised how much you'll love him. Or her."

"That's what everybody says. But babies are also messy and loud and . . ." She looked away.

"It's okay if you want to cry."

Melanie's shoulders started to shake. Kleenex, Ellen thought, I need some Kleenex. That's something my mom always had a wad of up her sleeve, and I never have any.

"It's stupid," Melanie whispered as she wiped her nose on her sleeve.

"What is?" Ellen asked. She wanted to get to the root of all of this.

Melanie sighed. "I don't want to share her. Not with Stan. Not with some new kid. She doesn't even see me anymore."

"Oh, I don't believe that."

"No, really, she probably wishes I was going to college this fall rather than in two years. Other than this new baby, all she talks about is me looking at colleges. It's like she wants me out of the way so she can try again for the perfect little family that she blew the first time around when my dad took off."

"Melanie, you're a smart girl. Do you really think that's how she feels?"

"Sure," Melanie mumbled in response.

"You really think she wants you out of the picture?"

"Yeah."

"Any evidence of that?"

Melanie smiled slightly through her tears. "You're all about evidence, aren't you?"

It was Ellen's turn to look confused. Melanie continued, mimicking Ellen's teacher voice, " 'Where's your proof?' you'd always nag at us, and then you'd tap the open page with your finger." They both grinned before Melanie continued, " 'C'mon, folks,' you'd say, 'the text always wins. Where's your evidence? Your quotes?' "

"Well?" Ellen prodded.

Melanie's face darkened again. "The evidence is the baby."

"I can see why you would think the baby is proof your mom wants to start all over. But you're only looking at this from your point of view. What about your mom's? Or Stan's? You know, in class we don't just talk about evidence; we also talk about how important point of view is in a story. How tricky first person can be because it so limits perspective. That's how you're looking at this. Why don't you ask your mom for her point of view? Share yours?"

Melanie scratched at some chipping paint on the picnic table, then said, "The evidence is pretty clear. They're starting a new family and I'll hardly be in it. I don't think a different point of view changes that."

"Nothing is that black and white. Nothing. It's always shades of gray. I don't think you've really got any proof. Talking to your mom about it might help you sort this out. You could try that."

"I'll think about it."

"You do that, Melanie. And remember, very little in the world is as simple as black and white."

"Easy for you to say. You had your kids close together. You didn't go and spring another family on them. That's how you get the 'happily ever after' stuff."

Yeah, Ellen thought, and my marriage was such a rousing success.

Ellen and Tim had gotten married when she was twenty-three, and he was two years older. She had degrees in English and education, and she was ready to play adult. It didn't really register with her that playing was not the same as living— or surviving. She was determined and organized, and she could cook. True, she had not honed her housekeeping skills any, but she was fun and kind and smart—and she was a good wife.

Too bad she hadn't married a good husband. Tim looked like a down-to-earth, hardworking guy. The kind of boy her father referred to as a good provider. Except others didn't see the self-doubt he couldn't shake. His inability to be happy or satisfied with what he had. His unquenchable desire for something more—a newer car, a bigger house, a more stylish suit, a pretty young assistant. Ellen couldn't believe how her life had turned into a cliché, but it slapped her in the face when Tim admitted that while Ellen had been home playing earth mother to their beloved firstborn, Daniel, he had felt neglected and left out. So what else had there been for him to do but find attention and solace in the arms and bed of his assistant, Shannon, who understood him so well? Ellen tried not to gag. She had wanted to cry and scream and plead— wasn't that what was expected in this situation? Wasn't that what all the movies and books scripted? But all she had felt was anger and a sick humor. And then she had had to run to the bathroom to throw up.

Tim came after her, worried. "Are you okay? Oh God, I'm so sorry. I made you sick." He sat there with his head in his hands.

"No, you idiot, I am not okay—I'm pregnant."

Well, that certainly wasn't how Ellen had planned to tell Tim that they were expecting another baby, but gosh, with all this exciting news about his new life, when was the right moment going to present itself? Tim stood uncomfortably in the hallway, waiting for Ellen to clean herself up.

When she walked out, he said, "Do you want me to sleep on the couch—or leave—or something?"

"Sleep on the couch? Please, Tim, this isn't *The Dick Van Dyke Show*. Do you want to leave?"

"No. I don't know. I don't know what I should do here."

"Yeah, well, I don't know what to do here, either. But I'll be damned if I'm going to tell you to leave. Don't think I'll give you permission. I'm fighting for this marriage. Right now I'm not sure why—but if you leave, it won't be with my blessing or on my orders." Ellen had spoken quietly, then gone to bed. She was amazed at the numbness she felt. She knew she had sounded hard and uncaring, but she felt as if she were in a bad B-movie. She rolled over onto her stomach. There was a baby growing there. What kind of life would this baby have? She wanted the tears to come because then this would all seem more real; she'd know that it was really happening.

And then, a year later, Ellen had sat down to pay the bills. The boys were napping, and this would be a good time for her to catch up on things. She turned on the stereo and was singing along to Bonnie Raitt when she opened Tim's American Ex-

press card bill. She usually just glanced over the list of expen-
ditures, since he used this card almost exclusively for work
and most of the items were reimbursable business expenses.
One item caught her eye. Flowers. Fifty dollars' worth. Almost
four weeks ago. She went to look at the calendar. Was the date
a family birthday? She shook her head at that. Ellen handled
all the birthdays for both sides of the family. What could it
have been? January eighteenth. Too early for Valentine's Day.
She kept pushing back the suspicion that was surging to the
front of her brain. Shannon. No. Tim wasn't seeing her anymore. He showed up at home right after work. He didn't go in
on the weekends anymore. He hardly ever went in after dinner,
and when he did, he called her. Please God, she thought, we
made it through this horrible year. Things aren't feeling safe
yet, but we're working our way back. Oh God, I'd know if he
was back with her, I'd smell it on him. Wouldn't I? That sense
of knowing had given her a sense of security; she believed—or
wanted to believe—that she wouldn't ever be that blind and
vulnerable again. January eighteenth. It seemed familiar to
her. Why?

She thought back to last year, to what was going on last
January. Well, that was when all hell had broken loose. It was
in late January that he had told her about the affair, that she
had learned that she was pregnant with James. Ellen stopped
still in front of the calendar. She reached out to the counter
with her hand and closed her eyes tight to stop the spinning
she felt. Breathe deep, she thought. Get a grip. There had to
be a valid reason. A client, she thought. Maybe a deal was
closed or they landed a new account. He just hadn't told her.
Please, that had to be it. But even as she was trying to regain
her composure, she was walking to the desk again, where she
had been sitting, and reaching for Tim's staff directory that
listed addresses, phone numbers, birthdays.

And there it was. Shannon Leclair's birthday.

Oh, fuck, Ellen thought. He sent her flowers on her birthday. Oh, fuck.

She put her head down on the desk. She held the front of the desk with both hands. Hard. She gripped it until she was sure she was leaving little dents from her fingertips. How do I do this? And then she heard James cry. As if she were watching herself from afar, she got up and walked into the boys' room. She smiled at James as he turned toward the door. She softly said, "Hey, Piglet, how'd you sleep?" She picked him up and inhaled the scent of him. Oh God, she thought, this is all a bad rerun of last year. And she carried him into the family room to nurse him awake.

After James ate, she put him on his quilt on the floor and gathered some toys for him. He smiled and laughed and drooled. Daniel walked in then, wiping the sleep from his eyes and asking for a snack. She kissed the top of his head and went to get him some graham crackers and milk. He ate them seriously, concentrating on picking up the crumbs by licking his finger, touching the crumbs on the table with it, and licking his finger again. Ellen leaned against the doorway watching them. Daniel was so much her child in his approach to things: cautious, eager to please, responsible. And then there was James, the light of her life. Already she could see that his approach was more headfirst. He'd dive in, take no prisoners, but he had a smile that could get him out of Moscow.

Be strong, guys, she prayed softly. Give me the strength. I don't know how to do what I've got to do, she thought. She turned to the kitchen. Dinner. Okay. The chicken was marinating. She would roast new potatoes. The lettuce was washed. She got out the cruet for the vinaigrette, reached for the olive oil, white wine vinegar, Dijon mustard, and garlic cloves. This I know how to do, she thought. It reminded her of when she was first out of school. It had felt so strange. She knew how to be a student. How to play the game. How to do it well. It defined her. She was good at it and she enjoyed it. It had been a relief to go back to school a year later for her master's degree. She felt the same way about mothering, about cooking. These had become instinctual actions. Descriptors. Movements that helped her to stay grounded and sane.

I don't know how to be a wife anymore, though, she mused. Did I ever?

She heard Tim's car pull into the garage; knew what his movements would be. He walked in the back door and called to them. Daniel came running and grabbed Tim around the knees. "Daddy. Daddy." Tim laughed, lifted him up, carefully checking Daniel's hands to see if they were sticky.

"El, can you get these crumbs off him before he gets them all over my tie?"

Ellen smiled wanly and reached for the kitchen towel as she replied, "Sure." She wiped Daniel's hands and kissed them. "Just making sure they're clean, munchkin." Setting the towel on the counter, she caught their reflections in the window over the sink. God, we look like we're posed for a Christmas card, she thought. Or take Daniel out of the shot, and you've got a photo right out of our wedding album. Her face, just at his shoulder, her blonder hair in contrast with his brown. How had they come to this? Who was he behind the clean-shaven face? Who lurked behind his blue eyes and dimples? And what about me, she thought. Her dad used to call her a Breck girl—straight hair tucked behind her ears, hazel-brown eyes, and an easy laugh. Who am I becoming? How much longer can I play the part of suburban housewife? Will I still fit the playgroup mom role tomorrow?

Tim thanked her and walked in to say hi to James. Oh

God, Ellen thought, this is such a nice little family scene, and it is all going to get shot to hell. She set the table, listening to Tim talk to the boys as he changed out of his suit and tie. She knew he was putting on his sweats and would come in and tell her dinner smelled good. She knew he would ask her if she wanted some wine. She knew he didn't have any idea what he had walked into, and she also knew that she had to do this even though she didn't think she could.

They made it through dinner, and if Tim thought Ellen was acting strangely, he didn't show it. They talked to the boys, they talked about them, they talked over them. They just didn't talk to each other.

After the boys had been bathed and snuggled and tucked in, Ellen made herself a cup of tea and, gripping the mug tightly, asked Tim if they could talk. He lowered the paper he was reading and nodded yes.

"I was going through the bills today—" She took a sip of tea before continuing. "—and there was a charge for flowers on your Amex card." Ellen didn't want to have to frame it into a question. She didn't want to be accusatory. She wanted Tim to explain it all away. He didn't.

"Oh." He quietly folded the paper and put it on the floor next to his chair. He raised the recliner to its upright position. He leaned forward with his elbows on his knees. "They aren't really reimbursable. I mean they're not a business exp—"

"I gathered that," Ellen interrupted quietly, but with a force that masked the tremor in her throat. "They were for Shannon, weren't they?"

"Yes. I'm sorry."

"Sorry for sending them?" She glared at him. "Or sorry I found out?"

"Both, I guess. Ellie, uh, I am trying. And I haven't seen her out of work. I can't help how I feel."

She stood up. "I don't understand what you want from me. I know I can't go through this again."

"I know. I don't think I can, either."

Ellen sighed as she slowly sat down again on the arm of the sofa.

"You have to leave. You have to leave this weekend. I don't know who or what to trust anymore." She swallowed hard and wished she had something to do with her hands. She ran them through her hair, and then held her palms over her face. She put them on her knees and wished she didn't feel like she was walking underwater as she looked at Tim and talked to him. "I can't even trust my own instincts anymore. I thought, I really did, that things were getting better. I don't know, maybe I just wanted to believe it so badly, I decided it was my instincts talking to me."

She looked out the window into the blackness of the night and wondered again what someone looking in that window would see. She realized that she wasn't even talking to Tim anymore; she was really trying to tell herself something important.

They decided they needed time apart. At least Tim said this would give him a chance to reevaluate the choices he'd made. Ellen bristled at his use of the word *choices*. It seemed so safe, so minimizing compared with the grenades she felt he had lobbed into their lives with his infidelities.

They had never lived together after that day. Over the past ten years, they had established an almost friendly relationship. Once she had gotten over the hurt and betrayal—and once Shannon had dumped Tim almost as soon as he'd become available—Ellen had found that her life was happier without him in it.

See, Melanie, Ellen wanted to explain, things don't always happen when you want them to happen. And yes, I had my babies close together, but there was nothing fairy-tale about it.

Chapter
Two

The relaxation of summer gradually began to drift into Ellen's daily life. The first week or so after school let out she invariably woke up at the crack of dawn, but by the end of June or the first of July she could usually sleep in until almost seven thirty. She treasured the slowed-down pace: reading books for fun and not just to teach, enjoying a leisurely second or third cup of coffee before the boys woke up, finishing *The New York Times* crossword puzzle on the porch.

Summer was also the time for reconnecting with the boys. So much of the school year felt like a forced march of sports practices, homework assignments, and project deadlines. Ellen always craved and reveled in the simplicity and ease of summer. Not once, she knew, would she have to say, through clenched teeth, to one of her sons, *This is not my project. I've already passed fifth*—or whatever grade they were in—*grade. You have to take responsibility here.* During the summer they had more meandering conversations. She laughed more. They got each other's jokes.

Plus, summer compensated for Wisconsin's harsh winters. Ellen believed the lushness and warmth of summer was hard-earned. Certainly people who lived in milder climates couldn't fully appreciate a late afternoon at a Wisconsin lake. The days were mostly clear, mild, and sunny, and the evenings, other than being filled with the annoying drone of mosquitoes, were cool and peaceful. Ellen spent every moment she could in her garden or on her porch.

Melanie had left a short message on Ellen's answering machine the day after their long talk. She'd said simply, "Thanks for talking to me yesterday. I'm going to soccer camp for two weeks. I'll talk to you when I get back."

She thought again of Melanie's comment about leaving for college after two more summers. How many more summers would she have with the boys around full time, she wondered. Take it slow, she told herself. Revel even in their noise and clutter.

"So what day will you guys be getting to the lake house?" Anna asked as she and Ellen fought their way to a jewelry stall at the Art Fair on the Square. Every year, the weekend after the Fourth of July, artists from all over the country descended on the Capitol Square. Most of their wares were too pricey for Ellen, but she and Anna always tried to make a few purchases while battling the heat and the crowds.

"Well, the boys'll be in Detroit before then with Tim, but I'm still planning on Saturday the seventh."

"That'll work out great. And you'll be able to stay the whole week, right?"

"Yeah, we wouldn't miss it."

"I can't believe you have to drive to Tim's to get the boys. It was one thing to split the driving when he lived in Milwaukee, but Detroit?"

"I know." Ellen sighed, looking at the price of some silver earrings. "He doesn't seem to attach any more value or importance to my time than he ever did."

"What a dope."

"Yup." Ellen pointed to a booth on the other side of the street. "I remember them from two years ago. They had some great prints, just what I'm looking for in the bathroom."

"Meet me at the woven fabrics booth down there when you're done."

Ellen was flipping through the second box of prints—mostly color photographs taken in the south of France—when she heard her name. She turned to see some of her students.

"Hey, guys. How's it going?"

They mostly talked about the fair being boring, which Ellen expected, but as they were saying goodbye, one of the girls turned to another and said quietly, "Did you tell her about Melanie?"

"Shh. No," the second girl said, shaking her head and walking away.

"Wait," Ellen said. "What about Melanie?"

"Uh, she can probably explain it better to you than me," the first girl said. "Something with her soccer camp." The girl looked at the ground as she spoke.

She began to walk away without adding anything else, and the second girl muttered to her, "God, you don't have to blab it to everybody."

Ellen wanted to ask for more details, but figured it was just high school gossip. She saw Anna waving to her so she headed that way.

"What do you think of this throw for my living room?"

Anna asked, holding out a beautiful woven cloth in shades of sage, cream, and pale blue.

"Great. It'll go great," Ellen answered distractedly. Anna eyed her for a moment to try to determine what was wrong, but before she could ask, Ellen blurted out, "I ran into some students. They started to tell me something about Melanie but then they clammed up."

Anna looked puzzled. She'd gotten to know Melanie as a great babysitter for her youngest daughter. They made their way to the shade of the Capitol grounds and sat on the grass under a tree close to the building so they were far removed from the crowded sidewalks and street. "Something bad?" Anna asked.

"I don't know. She came to me a few weeks ago. She was all upset about her mom getting remarried and having a new baby," Ellen began. "She was feeling replaced." Ellen paused and gathered her thoughts. Anna waited wordlessly for her to continue. "I told her she ought to talk to her mom. I really mostly thought she was being pretty bratty. Typically self-centered and sixteen."

"That sounds about right."

"I know, but her friend just now made it sound like something had happened. Not something good."

"Like what?"

"I don't know. I'll call her house and see what I can find out."

"I sorta got kicked out of camp," Melanie said.

Ellen had called under the pretext of verifying the dates for pet-sitting. She knew that teenagers exaggerated and hadn't wanted to be seen as a snoop. Melanie's mom had simply told her that Melanie was home, had been in a minor accident, and would love some company.

"Kicked out?" Ellen asked, wondering what she'd done. She wanted to ask about the stitches on her upper lip and the big white bandage wrapped around her head like a turban, but didn't want to upset her mother, who was sitting at the foot of the bed and looking even more ashen and fatigued than Melanie did.

"I sort of screwed up." Melanie paused and took a sip of juice, then looked down in shyness.

"I'm sorry," Ellen said, then looked at Melanie's mom. This was awkward. It wasn't like a school conference or parent night where the roles of Ellen and the parents were clearly established. This was personal and private; this was a family matter. Ellen stood clumsily, then moved over and sat on the edge of the bed as she searched for something to say. "I'm glad you're okay, though." Ellen groped for words as she took in more stitches peeking out from the neck of Melanie's T-shirt.

"She's lucky not to be hurt worse," Melanie's mom said, then added, "and she'll be fine with some more rest."

"What happened? Your mom mentioned a car wreck when I called."

"Yeah," Melanie said, looking down, then up at her mother. "But it wasn't around here."

"Her camp was up near Stevens Point," her mom explained.

"And one night I took off."

"You what?" Ellen asked.

"It was stupid, but these two other girls and I snuck out." She paused then and looked at her mom. "Could I have some more juice?"

Melanie's mother nodded and excused herself. Melanie waited until she heard her mom opening the fridge before continuing. "We were going to hitchhike to some bars. My mom doesn't know that. We got picked up by some drunk guys."

"Oh, Melanie, what were you thinking?"

"I wasn't. Anyway, these guys started driving really fast, and we got scared. Then one of them started asking if we had boyfriends. We didn't know what to do."

Ellen thought again how teenagers think of themselves as immortal. They don't get it, she thought.

"So what happened?"

"He missed a curve and went off the road. We ended up upside down in a ditch."

"My God. Was anyone killed?"

"No. Amazingly."

"I'm so sorry. But I'm so glad you're okay."

"Me, too. I'm pretty much grounded for the rest of my life, though."

"Yeah, well, if you were my kid I'd be doing the same thing. You need to rest up anyway."

Ellen and Melanie chatted a few more minutes, but Ellen knew she should be leaving. She stood up and began searching for her keys in her purse, but then she paused, looked at Melanie, and asked, "So, do you think your mom and Stan are glad you're still around?"

Melanie looked surprised at this question and said, "Well, yeah. Why wouldn't they be?"

"You thought they wanted to get rid of you."

"Yeah, I did, but I never thought, I mean, I knew they didn't really," Melanie stammered. "Jeez, Mrs. Banks, they didn't want me dead."

"Of course not. I didn't think you meant that. I just wondered if this helped you see things any more fully."

"I think so. I mean, Stan was totally broken up when they first saw me. My mom was crying and everything, but she was also mad already. Stan was like, 'I just got you, I can't lose you.' Stuff like that."

"Good. Okay, I better get out of here and let you get some rest. No more running off, okay?"

"I know. Thanks. And I'll still be able to pet-sit for you next month."

"Are you sure?"

"Yeah."

"Okay. I'm just gonna go tell your mom goodbye." Ellen patted Melanie's shoulder and headed to the kitchen.

"Thanks for letting me stop by for a visit," Ellen said.

"Oh sure. And I just want to thank you. I know that Melanie came to talk to you earlier this summer. About the baby and all."

Ellen reached out to touch Mrs. Parker's arm and was surprised to have her turn in for an embrace. Ellen patted her back and said softly, "This must have been so scary for you. I can't imagine."

Melanie's mom nodded and slowly pulled herself out of Ellen's hug. "Given all these hormones surging through me I'm even more emotional. But I think Melanie is feeling better about things now. She had quite a scare. We all did. I just had no idea how alone she felt. How pushed aside."

"Don't beat yourself up about that."

"I know. I was just so happy. I couldn't imagine she wasn't as well. I always wanted another baby. I wanted that for both of us."

"Well, sure," Ellen said.

Mrs. Parker swallowed hard several times in response, then finally said, "I feel so guilty now."

"For what?" Ellen said, leaning against the counter.

"Is this fair to her? Is she really going to be okay? Or am I just being selfish?"

Ah, Ellen thought, so I'm not the only mom in the world who plays that game of second-guessing. *Did I do the right thing? How much have I scarred my kids this month?* "You know, Mrs. Parker, I'm no expert or anything, but I think your guilt, well, I think you need to let that go. You can't undo what happened to Melanie, but you also can't neglect what you and your new husband want. It's your life, too."

Melanie's mother nodded thoughtfully and dabbed at her eyes with a tissue. "Well, thanks, I better get this juice to her. Thanks again."

Ellen smiled in response and said, "I'll let myself out. Take care. And good luck with both your babies." Then she headed down the hall to the front door. And I thought parenting was exhausting when they were toddlers, she said to herself. It only gets more complicated and they keep moving all the boundary lines. As she stepped out of the cool house into the July warmth, she let out a deep breath and whispered, "Crisis over for the summer. At least I'm not dealing with both ends of the parenting spectrum. A new baby and a teenager? Good God. Now I just have to find a pair of shoes for James."

Chapter
Three

"Whoo hoo," Ellen said quietly so as not to wake up Daniel and James, who were sleeping in the backseat, "we're back in Wisconsin." When the boys were younger, they had always cheered with her when they had crossed over the state line after visiting her parents in Missouri. Ellen still loved the rustic dark brown sign in the shape of the state, welcoming them to America's Dairyland. Had the boys been awake today, Ellen knew her cheer and greeting would have been answered with groans and rolled eyes. Her sons were definitely at the age where they thought just about anything she said or did was proof positive that their mother was a dork.

"Whoo hoo," she said again.

She smiled to herself and sighed quietly. She had picked the boys up from their father's that morning. Now they were forty minutes from Lake Augusta in southern Wisconsin and Anna's lake house. She and the boys had been coming here for ten years. It was a tradition for all of them, a last gasp of summer before school began. This was a week to fall asleep listening to the water lap at the dock, watch the sun burn away the early-morning mist, and laugh deeply as the kids played and she and Anna solved all the problems of the world late at night on the dock, drinking wine and watching for falling stars.

Ellen had been coming to Lake Augusta and the surrounding town of Bainbridge ever since she and Anna had met twenty years ago as nervous college freshmen. Madison was just a thirty-minute drive from the lake, but the lake seemed remote and removed from their hectic lives at home. Ten years ago when the demise of Ellen's marriage had become a certainty, she had sought refuge with Anna and Anna's husband, Sam, for a week. They had helped her see that life would someday make sense again, and an August tradition had been born.

As she accelerated the car to pass a truck, Daniel woke up. "Where are we?" he mumbled.

"Forty minutes more, babe. You managed to sleep through half of Illinois."

Daniel stretched, fiddled with his CD player, and nodded at her before looking out the window. She could hear the bass beat of the music he was listening to, but chose not to make an issue of it this time. Daniel was her serious son. Even as a child he had been pensive—she remembered how carefully he would approach a task, whether it was building with Duplo blocks or pulling on his socks and Velcroing his shoes. All the details would be considered and then taken care of. This served him well now in school; his math teachers consistently praised his habit of not skipping steps and always showing his work. She'd been pleased to see his sense of humor as well. His comments surprised people; if a child could be droll, Daniel was—and so different from his younger brother, James, who now slumped against the seat next to him.

~~~~~~~~

James jolted awake as Ellen exited the highway and stopped at a red light. He always woke up this way—suddenly and startled. He looked out the windows, face puffy with sleep, but soon relaxed as he recognized how close they were to the lake house.

"I'm thirsty."

Ellen laughed softly and passed him back some water. James was not one to dwell on pleasantries. "You can hop in the lake in twenty minutes, kiddo. We're nearly there."

"Mom?"

"Hmm?" Ellen glanced in the rearview mirror.

"I don't feel so good," mumbled James.

"Oh, honey, I'm sorry. We'll be there real soon."

"Uh, Mom?"

"What? Just remember this the next time you want two hot dogs—"

"I'm gonna puke."

Ellen swerved to the shoulder, hoping no car had been too close on her tail. Daniel, more alert than she would have given him credit for being, adroitly slid open the door and tried to move out of James' way. He'd been caught in the path of his brother's car sickness before.

James leapt out of the car even before Ellen had turned off the ignition. As she watched in her side mirror for a safe time to open her door and get out, she heard Daniel's play-by-play of James' vomiting.

"Oh man, James," he said, "not there."

Before Ellen could ask for clarification, Daniel said to her just as she got out, "Looks like you'll have to go shoe shopping all over again."

~~~~~~~~

Three days before Tim was to arrive to take the boys back to Detroit, Ellen had fortified herself with coffee and taken James to the mall to buy new shoes. He was excited and enthusiastic at the outset; she knew the pleasant mood would not last. It lingered through the first two stores, began to waver in the third, and completely disappeared in the fourth. He had walked in, approached the wall with shoes mounted on it from floor to ceiling, and announced after a cursory look, "Nope. Nothing here."

"James. You couldn't possibly have looked at every shoe. We just walked in."

"Fine. I'll look some more."

Ellen slumped on one of the benches. A clerk in his late teens or early twenties, clad in a referee uniform, hurried over and asked, "Anything I can help you with, ma'am?"

"Oh, I doubt it. My son is looking for shoes, but he's pretty picky."

The clerk smiled and said, in a friendly, optimistic voice, "I'll be able to help him find something he'll like."

"Good luck," Ellen muttered.

She watched the clerk advance toward James and ask, "Hey there, sport, looking for shoes?"

James nodded glumly. He hated, as Ellen did, fake friendly and cheery clerks. Shoe shopping was serious for James, a mission, not something to be taken lightly.

"What activities do you need these for, sport?"

Ellen was amused, despite her fatigue, by this interchange. Good, she thought, let somebody else, anybody else who is not me, try to pry open the mystery of what sort of shoe James is looking for.

"I didn't hear your answer," the clerk prodded again. "What special things will you need these shoes for?"

James finally leveled his gaze at the clerk and answered, "Nothing special. Just living."

The clerk was taken aback and looked to Ellen for help. She finally said, "James, what do you think? Anything you want to try on?"

He shook his head in response, and they headed out into the mall.

"James," Ellen said, "there are no more stores for us to look in. Can you maybe scale back your expectations?"

"I guess. But I hate it when store people suggest shoes to me. I feel like I have to try them on even if I don't like them."

"Well, you don't. Just try to be polite, though."

"I know."

"Did you see anything anywhere that you want to look at another time?"

"Maybe in that last store. But I don't want that stupid guy to call me 'sport' again."

Ellen laughed and said, "Honey, he probably will; just try to ignore it."

They had returned to the store, and James did find two pairs of shoes to try on. Ellen vetoed one pair because of the cost. "James," she said, "I refuse to spend one hundred and twenty dollars on shoes."

"But, Mom, they're the only ones I like."

"No."

He slumped in his chair and glared at her. Ellen held firm.

"Fine," he snapped at her, "I'll take these." And to make clear which ones he'd selected and how angry he still was at her, he kicked the box.

"Great," she said with forced patience, "want to wear them home?"

"No."

Rounding the front of the car she saw the not even three-week-old shoes drenched in vomit.

"You can't possibly save those, Mom," Daniel offered helpfully.

"I know." Ellen reached in her purse for some tissue. "Here, sweetie," she said to James, "wipe your mouth."

"I'm sorry, Mom."

"I know, babe. Don't worry. Let's get these shoes off." Ellen dug some paper towels out from under the front seat and carefully pulled the shoes off James' feet. Daniel mentioned he'd seen a garbage can back down the road, so she headed that way to dispose of them. When she got back to the car, James was swishing some water around in his mouth and spitting it out.

"Feel better, kiddo?" she asked as she leaned toward him to feel his forehead with her cheek.

"Yeah. A lot better. Sorry."

"No problem. Want to get back in the car now?"

He answered by clambering over Daniel's legs and putting on his seat belt. As Ellen pulled the car back onto the road to the lake, Daniel said, "At least those weren't the ones you really liked, James."

"Mom?" James asked as Ellen neared the lake house.

"What?"

"I feel lots better now."

"Good."

"So, like, can I go in the lake as soon as we get there?"

Ellen looked at him in the rearview mirror. He certainly looks healthy, she thought. "I guess, but take it easy, okay?"

"I promise," he said with a smile. "And Mom," he added as she pulled into the driveway, "can I still get new shoes for school?"

Her answer was drowned out by the shouts and waves that greeted them from the driveway. Before the van had come to a complete stop, the boys were out the door giving high fives to Sam and the girls, and quietly accepting Anna's hugs with awkward one-armed hugs of their own. Ellen felt the relaxation drape over her. She knew that by the end of the week the knot she so frequently felt between her shoulder blades would have melted away.

By the noises emanating from the house, it was clear the boys were wasting no time in getting their swimsuits on. In just moments, Ellen knew, she'd hear five splashes as each kid cannonballed off the dock and into Lake Augusta's cool embrace.

"Hey, babe, glad you got here in one piece." Anna smiled as she hugged Ellen.

"It's nice to be out of the car. What a great day." Ellen looked up at the deep blue sky and around at all the lush trees and shrubs. The flower boxes at the windows overflowed with red and white impatiens, and the wooden screen door gleamed with a fresh coat of shellac. She could already feel herself breathing more deeply.

As they walked into the galley kitchen, she saw that Anna had gotten out the acrylic wineglasses and the Mexican dip and chips that, over the years, had accompanied their traditional first-day-at-the-lake all-day lunch. The wide windows overlooking the yard and lake let in the breeze, but even so the mixed scent of cedar closets, damp towels, and open bottles of suntan lotion assured her she was back in Bainbridge.

"Let me get in my suit and I'll help you carry this out," Ellen called as she hurried to her room.

~~~~~~

Now, sitting on the dock, watching five blond heads—Ellen's boys and Anna's three daughters—bob up and down in the water, Ellen and Anna dug into the Mexican dip and toasted one another with their wineglasses.

"To another great week," they said in unison.

"You know," Ellen said, "this is so perfect. I can't believe I get to come here for free. Think of the people who spend a thousand dollars for a week like this."

Anna chuckled and replied, "Good thing you offered to let me copy your notes in that Chaucer class."

Ellen smiled, remembering how they had first gotten to be friends. Could it really be twenty years ago that they had met? She looked at Anna's face, which was so dear to her. Anna's blue eyes were warm, yet held a strength and sure sense of self. Ellen could never lie to Anna, and she had always felt like part of that was Anna's eyes.

"So, anything exciting to report?" Anna asked.

"From my life?"

"You did just have two weeks without kids. Kick up your heels any? Pick up any men while nosing around the bookstore?"

"Let me try to remember everything," Ellen said with a laugh. "I know you don't want me to forget any juicy details."

Anna scooped up some dip on a cracker and waited for Ellen to continue.

"Hmm. Well, the gas man came to read my meter."

"I take it that's not a euphemism."

"Correct." Ellen took a swallow of wine. "There was this bag boy who offered to carry my groceries to the car."

"But you declined."

"That's about it for exciting encounters with the opposite sex. Unless you count gritting my teeth while Tim gave me all sorts of parenting pointers about the boys."

"He didn't."

"Of course he did. He always does. I just nod like I'm listening and remember what a drudge of a husband he was."

"Jerk."

"Yeah, but a jerk who has recently been dumped by his latest young girlfriend."

"Really?"

"I couldn't get any scoop from the boys, but she is out of the picture and apparently he is not happy about it."

"Serves him right," Anna muttered.

Ellen nodded, then smiled as Sam approached carrying a bottle of wine to refill their glasses. "How cool that your lake house comes with its own cabana boy," she said.

"At your service, ladies," he said with a grin. He placed the bottle between Anna and Ellen, then pulled off his shirt and warned, "Control yourselves." They all laughed. Sam had the same slim figure he'd had in college. His only signs of the middle age that was creeping up on all of them were the deepening lines around his eyes and the hint of gray at his temples. Ellen had often told Anna that Sam would be one of those men who was even better-looking at fifty and sixty than at thirty. He wouldn't ever get soft and flabby; he'd simply gain character as he aged.

"I just got off the phone with Sean," he said, pulling up a deck chair and sitting down. "He's coming out for the afternoon. Lisa's visiting her sister with the kids."

Sean and Lisa were Madison friends they camped with and went to football games with. They had lots of money, and Lisa had the best figure of the whole group, but Anna and Ellen had decided that despite being beautiful people who took trips to trendy destinations all the time, Sean and Lisa were also two of the kindest, most generous people they knew, so they liked them anyway. Besides, Sean was a doctor who humored their occasional hypochondriacal tendencies. On one camping trip he had patiently done, as Sam referred to them, "mole checks" of the women's backs to rule out any cancerous spots. Ellen still grinned at the memory, especially the thought of their friend Ed walking down to the beach, roaring with laughter as he approached.

"You look like baboons in the zoo," he had said, "picking off the nits and eating them."

"Hey, Mom!"

Both women looked out to the lake, ready to respond. It was Sarah, Anna's fourteen-year-old daughter. The other four kids were whispering and planning behind her.

"Can we walk over to the public beach?"

Anna and Ellen looked at each other and shrugged.

"Sure," Anna said. "Just wear shoes and keep an eye on Caroline."

Caroline was the baby. Even at six, she was still thought of that way by all of them. But the boys had always felt very protective of her. With Sarah and twelve-year-old Emily, they fought like siblings, but they never bickered with Caroline. Ellen smiled as she saw Daniel help Caroline with her shoes and then hold her hand as she navigated the rocks on the way to the worn path that led to the beach a mile down the lakeshore. James held back shrubs for her, and they were on their way.

By the time Sean arrived, the kids were due back from the beach and Anna and Ellen had returned from a quick run to the grocery store. Ellen paused in making a marinade for salmon steaks to greet Sean with a big hug. They planned to grill the salmon to go with vegetable kebabs, oven-roasted potatoes, and sliced French bread. When the boys walked in to grab some sodas and say a quick hello to Sean, Ellen noticed their sunburned cheeks and shoulders.

"Guys. Don't forget the sunscreen, okay?"

They looked at her and sighed, prepared to argue, but she stopped them cold by adding, "Unless you want me to take charge of slathering it all over you." Grumbling but resigned, they walked out.

"You know, Ellen, I can't get over how different the boys look from each other," Sean said.

And he was right. Although both were blond, Daniel had a dark, almost olive complexion and a slight build. Because of his slenderness, he appeared taller than he actually was. James, with the white-blond hair and blue eyes of a Viking, was solid—he weighed fifteen pounds more than his older brother and was half an inch taller.

"Are you sure they're related?" Sean joked.

"Well, I distinctly remember giving birth to them both. I think it's a reflection of their father's multiple personalities."

That night, after Sean had left and the kids were whispering in their sleeping bags in the living room, Ellen relaxed in her bed. She loved the night noises: the water, the occasional voices of fishermen in their rowboats, the breeze in the branches. She loved to fall asleep knowing that tomorrow would be a full day of talking, laughing, and letting the sun work on melting away that knot between her shoulder blades.

The sun streaming in through the windows woke Ellen early. She padded into the kitchen to start the coffee. The sleek Krups coffeemaker seemed out of place below the knotty-pine cupboards that lined the walls. While she waited for it to finish brewing, she leaned against the doorjamb and gazed at the bundle of blankets and pillows on the floor of the living room. Right in the middle was a puddle of blond heads, with their bodies sticking out like the spokes of a wheel. She had to look closely to differentiate the five children, as their faces were nearly obscured by the blankets and their hair. What a bunch of sweeties, she thought.

Ellen went back to her room to pull on an old faded sweatshirt and beat-up khaki shorts. Then, grabbing a mug of steaming coffee from the kitchen, she walked out into the early morning. The wet grass was cold on her bare feet; even the dock felt chilly and damp. She walked out to the end of the dock and sat on the edge, dipping her feet and ankles into the still, dark lake water. She watched as the ripples her movement had created radiated toward the lake's center and then disappeared. The cold water sent shivers through her, but the coffee warmed her and she turned her face to the sun, closing her eyes and bathing in the light. This was her favorite part of the day here. All the hours ahead stretched before her— unhurried, unscheduled, and unplanned. The lake was nearly empty, populated only by fishermen and an occasional gull. By afternoon, the noise of Jet Skis and ski boats would cut through the shouts of children, but now the only sounds were the oars cutting into the water and birds calling to one another. She stood and walked to one of the lounge chairs, sat down on it, and leaned back. She loved the way the sun cleared the mist rising from the lake, revealing the vibrant blue of the sky. Sipping her coffee, she was startled by a hand on her shoulder. She turned to find James. His face was still puffy with sleep, but he grinned, tickled that he had successfully snuck up on her.

"Morning, munchkin."

James mumbled a greeting and then edged his way onto

her lap. She was thankful that he still needed to snuggle. He deftly fit himself onto her and rested his head on her chest. In so many ways, James was leapfrogging into adolescence, but at this moment he was still that little boy who wanted to snuggle his way into wakefulness. They didn't talk, just watched the lake come alive.

Later the late-afternoon sun edged toward dusk as Sam, Anna, and Ellen alternated between dozing on the dock and watching the kids in the lake. Ellen thought they looked like blond seals, dipping and diving, their hair plastered to their heads. The lake buzzed with activity, and it always took Ellen a day or two to get used to how far out the children could go and still be able to touch the bottom. Anna reached for her book and adjusted her sunglasses as Ellen's hand groped under her chair for more sunscreen. Sam stood up, stretched, and jumped into the lake. He swam out to the kids and then back to the dock several times. He climbed out and shook his head to spray Anna and Ellen with water; they laughed. He started to take drink orders, but their responses were drowned out by a Jet Ski roaring past them. All three looked at each other and shook their heads, then glanced out to the kids.

"Those damn things keep getting too close to the swimmers," Sam muttered.

"Maybe we need to put up some buoys," Anna suggested. Then, repeating their drink orders, she added, "We just want more wine."

Sam had just started walking toward the house when he turned suddenly back to face the lake. Something in his expression alarmed Ellen.

"What?" she asked. But there was no answer—he just took

several running steps and dove shallowly into the lake. Anna and Ellen sat up sharply to watch him. Looking out to the children, Ellen felt her entire body contract with fear. The Jet Skier was slowly circling back. And there were only four blond heads surfacing.

Chapter
Four

Ellen and Anna struggled to stand up. Neither could look at the other—their faces were glued to the scene unfolding before them. It seemed very far away to Ellen, almost as if it were happening on a stage or in a dream. She heard herself whispering over and over, "Please, God, no." She felt Anna grab her hand and squeeze. The scene became clearer. Of the four heads above the surface, only one had a buzz cut. She heard Anna say something. Ellen turned toward her and realized Anna was on the phone.

"We need an ambulance. Fire number six-two-three-nine."

Ellen looked to the water again and saw Sam rushing through the water to the dock carrying a very still, limp body. She couldn't move. Anna helped him lift the child out of the water and onto the dock. Screaming sirens began to intrude on the twilight's quiet, and Ellen heard a deep, low, almost guttural moan—and then discovered it was coming from her. Sam's movements seemed to be in slow motion. She watched him check the airway and listen to hear if the heart was beating. Isn't that what paramedics do, she thought. Why aren't they here yet? I should tell Anna to call for help, she thought, having already forgotten the phone call Anna had just made.

The paramedics rushed to the dock, and Ellen pushed forward. James. It was James. Water dribbled from his mouth. Ellen reached forward to touch his cheek. Was he breathing? She looked at his chest. His smooth, round belly. Yes. He was breathing. She leaned into him, but strong arms firmly yet gently pulled her aside.

"Ma'am. Let us work."

Such kind eyes, Ellen thought. The young, tanned paramedic went to work. Ellen looked up. It was so quiet. The other four children still stood out in the water, just where they had been. Their faces were frozen in fear: eyes wide, mouths making O's. She couldn't meet Daniel's questioning gaze.

A Jet Ski floated empty near them. Ellen was gradually aware of the silence, broken only by the crackle of the ambulance's radio. People lined the shore and neighboring docks, but there was no noise. Even the policemen who had arrived with the paramedics stood back.

James was lifted onto the stretcher, and Ellen followed. They were now all running. When she climbed into the back of the ambulance, Anna grabbed her arm.

"What?"

"Here." Anna handed her a towel and some clothes. "Dry off. Put these on. We'll meet you at the hospital."

Ellen dropped the clothes on the floor next to the seat she was in. Anna met her gaze and quickly reached in to squeeze Ellen's hand and kiss her forehead before the doors swooped closed. Ellen thought she heard Anna yell to Sam to call Sean.

Ellen watched silently as the paramedics worked on James. Why isn't he waking up? she thought. The bruise and cut on his head must hurt. Why doesn't he cry? She wasn't aware she shivered uncontrollably until one of the paramedics looked at her and handed her a blanket from a nearby shelf. She was still wearing her damp swimsuit. For a fleeting moment she feared they wouldn't let her in the hospital without shoes. But then the ambulance slammed to a halt and the doors flew open and she was swept in through the confusion. The doctors and nurses ran down the hall with James' stretcher. Ellen felt lost and out of touch. Why don't they slip, she wondered. Is that why they all wear tennis shoes? She reached up with her hand to touch her face and discovered her mouth was hanging open. How long has it been like that, she wondered numbly. God. How stupid do I look? She caught her reflection in the mirror. Barefoot. Wrapped up in an orange blanket. Hair slicked back from swimming. I look like a refugee. I'm freezing. With her hand, she forced her mouth shut. Do I just stand here?

"Ma'am?"

Ellen turned. She looked into the soft, green eyes of a nurse.

"We need some information," the nurse said, guiding her to a nearby chair.

"I don't have any shoes."

"That's okay. We'll even get you some clothes. My name is Laurie. Can you help me here, and then we'll go check on your son?"

Ellen looked at the nurse. She looked calm. Competent.

"He's okay, right?" Ellen asked.

"They're working on him." Laurie spoke directly and slowly to Ellen, not breaking their gaze. She's talking to me like I'm a child, Ellen thought, and started to get angry. The nurse seemed to sense this and reached out for Ellen's arm. "Listen to me. We need some information. They want to transport him to University Hospital in Madison. Can you help me here?"

Ellen knew she had to hold on. And she appreciated the concern in the nurse's expression. She'd caught the use of the present tense in Laurie's words. James was still okay.

"What do you need?"

"Name and age?"

"James Banks. He'll be twelve this fall."

"What happened?"

"Um," Ellen paused. What had happened? The kids had been swimming and playing. Then the Jet Skier. Then Sam diving in after them. As she told this to the nurse, she saw it like jerky film shots. It reminded her of filmstrips shown in elementary school where the movement seemed disjointed from the sound.

A bustle at the door made Ellen and Laurie look up.

Anna and Sam were ushered in by a doctor and a nurse. Anna reached for her, but Ellen sat numbly like a child, her arms holding the blanket around her. She tried to find words. Sam came to her and wrapped his arms around her from behind as Anna knelt on the floor at her side and took her hands. The nurse who had brought them in quickly found some chairs and then backed out the door. The doctor stood by the door and waited. Then he coughed and started to speak.

"Your son has sustained a severe skull fracture."

Ellen felt herself begin to tremble and Sam held her even tighter. Ellen saw Anna mouthing the words to a prayer. The doctor paused, and Ellen realized he was groping for words. And maybe for time. Ellen stared at him, wanting to meet his eyes.

"And . . . ," she prompted. He coughed again.

"He is not regaining consciousness like we'd like to see. The Med Flight helicopter will be here any minute. We're transporting him to University Hospital. They'll get all the information you gave the nurse." He paused again, then added, "We've done all we can here. I'm very sorry."

Ellen put her head down and stared at the floor. Speckled linoleum. She'd always thought this kind of floor looked like vomit. Handy, she thought, for a room in this place. I wish I could throw up. Something to prove I'm still functioning. She hadn't cried. Had barely spoken or moved since she'd arrived. Laurie was speaking softly to Sam and Anna, asking about transportation to the hospital and other details.

"Honey?" Anna looked at her. "Let's get your clothes on." She started unwrapping the blanket that Ellen had been clutching. Ellen let it fall to the floor and then felt completely vulnerable. Standing in this little room in her damp, cold swimsuit with the smell of sunscreen and her own sweat sharp in the air, she had never felt so helpless before. Sam walked out to give them privacy as Anna slipped the straps down Ellen's arms. "Do you have the clothes I gave you?"

Ellen shook her head, guessing they were still on the floor of the ambulance.

"That's okay, I've got jeans and a T-shirt here. Even underwear."

As Anna handed clothes to her, Ellen obediently put them on. Finally, she looked at Anna and asked, "Where are the other kids?" The last she had seen of them they had been standing in the lake where James had gone under. In her mind, they were still out in the water like statues, marking the spot.

"Sam's folks came over."

"Are they still in the water?"

For a minute, Anna was confused, but then she said, "No. They're in the house."

~~~~~~~

When they walked out to find Sam, Ellen turned to Anna and said, "I need to see James. Before the helicopter ride."

"Okay. Let's find the doctor."

Laurie, the nurse, appeared then and led Ellen to the trauma room. Ellen wondered how Laurie had known what she had wanted but couldn't summon the energy to ask.

Before the wide, swinging doors behind which James was being treated, Laurie paused and took both of Ellen's hands in her own.

"Try not to be too shocked with what you'll see. All the equipment is helping your son. He needs a ventilator for breathing and he's also got some IV tubes. He won't respond to you. Not yet."

Ellen took a deep breath, closed her eyes, and went in. It felt as if she were in a movie or TV show. This can't be real, she thought. I'm just going through motions. She could see herself walking in and looking and then, when she saw James' pale skin and his bruises, it became real and she felt her legs start to shake. Laurie grabbed her elbow.

"You okay?"

Ellen nodded and propelled herself forward.

When she reached James, she knelt by his face. She touched his cheek. So soft. She touched his white-blond eyebrows. And then clasped his hand. She silently begged him to grab hers back.

"We've got to move him. Med Flight is here," a doctor ordered.

She leaned up close to his ear. Maybe he could still hear her. She whispered, "I love you, James. All the numbers. All the numbers."

And then he was wheeled out. Ellen backed into the hard,

cold tile wall as James was moved. No, she wanted to scream. Not yet. We're not ready. She slipped to the floor, felt the hard tile against her head as she rocked it back and forth. Good, she thought, I can feel that. It hurts. I'm not numb.

"All the numbers," she called out to an empty, but visibly used trauma room.

When the boys had been younger, almost still babies, she had been tucking them into bed one night and Daniel had asked how much she loved him. He'd wanted something concrete to measure it by.

"Do you love me more than the house?" he had asked. She'd nodded yes.

James had chimed in with, "Do you love me bigger than one hundred?"

She'd smiled and said, "Yes." Both had been learning their numbers.

"More than all your dollars?"

"Yes."

"More than a million?"

"Yes."

On and on, until they'd run out of amounts they knew. She'd kissed their soft, sweaty foreheads then and said, "I love you all the numbers." This had been shortened to just the last three words, and it had become their code. It was something the boys would even let her say in front of the car pool.

Now, after calling out the words to the empty room, Ellen pulled herself up and walked out the doors. Laurie was there waiting for her. In less than an hour, this woman Ellen had never seen before, had never had reason to meet, was the one person who seemed able to help Ellen hang on to her sanity. Laurie smiled and Ellen tried to really look at her. Up until now, all that had registered was Laurie's green eyes and her low, calm voice. Now Ellen saw the slight crinkles around her eyes and her solid figure. She had shoulder-length brown hair that fell in waves around her tanned, round face. She had a bouncy step, yet her perkiness seemed grounded or tempered. Laurie saw she was being examined and held her hands out to her side as if to say, *Well?*

"Were you a cheerleader?" Ellen blurted out.

If Laurie was surprised by the question, she didn't show it. Instead she laughed and said, "Yup. Is it that obvious?"

Ellen shook her head and said more to herself than to Laurie, "I can always tell. It's the voice and the walk." Then more loudly she said, "Where are Sam and Anna?"

They were pulling the van to the front of the hospital for the thirty-minute ride to Madison. James was probably nearly there by now. Laurie hugged her at the door, and Ellen watched her wave until they were out of the parking lot. They rode in silence until Sam coughed, and she looked up at him.

"What?"

"Before we left the house, we got in touch with Tim. He's flying over as soon as he can. He'll try to be here first thing in the morning at the latest."

Ellen looked out to see the headlights coming at them.

"When did it get dark?" was her only response.

Nearing Madison from the east, the brightly lit Capitol building beckoned to them. Ellen stared at it, remembering how she and Tim had walked up State Street to the Capitol grounds on summer evenings when they were first dating. We were so young then, she thought. Only nine or ten years older than James is now. Things were so easy then, so simple. We loved each other. We thought we had a life mapped out. How did all these intervening years get in the way and take over?

"Ellen?" Anna's voice brought Ellen back to the present. "The police were at the lake house before we left."

"Oh, God. Why?" Ellen's mind raced. Was I at fault? Did I let James go out too far?

"They might be charging the boy on the Jet Ski. For hitting James," Sam told her.

"Charge him with what?"

"Well, uh, reckless use of a vehicle or something. It kind of depends . . ." Sam's voice trailed off.

"Depends on what?" Ellen questioned, and then his meaning struck her. Depends on if James lives, she thought.

"They'll want to question you. And the kids."

"When?" And all she could think about was Daniel facing the police. What must be going through his mind, she worried. "How was Daniel when you left?"

"He was, well, very subdued. Scared. Pale." Anna said. "He wants to talk to you. And James." With the last two words, Anna's voice broke. Ellen reached for her hand from the backseat. And then they were at the hospital.

University Hospital had always seemed like a maze to Ellen. Wings went off at odd angles; the few times she had ever been there she had always gotten lost. Sean, who worked there, always said it was quite logical, but she still doubted him. Now, headed to the red emergency entrance, she saw Sean waiting outside the doors for them. He greeted her wordlessly with a big hug, and then began walking them through the labyrinth to the trauma and intensive care area.

Sean led them to a small, private room. It had four chairs and one small, worn yellow sofa. There were no windows. Two tables held neat stacks of magazines. It felt like the inside of an airplane—neutral colors, recycled air; a place for waiting and then, upon exiting, for having arrived somewhere new.

They sat down, and Sean punched in some numbers on a beige phone Ellen had not noticed before. "Will? The mother is here."

Then they waited. Soon an intense, dark-haired doctor of about fifty walked in. He had wavy hair, tanned skin, and an aura of confidence about him. His etched features reminded her of a Roman statue. He sat across from her and said, "Mrs. Banks."

"Yes?"

"I'm Dr. Stalnovick. We're working on your son. We need to place a pressure monitor between his skull and dura. We need your consent for surgery." With that, he held out a clipboard with waiver forms for her to sign.

In her daze, Ellen almost wanted to ask, work on your bedside manner much? This guy took the idea of brusque to a new level. But then she looked at his hands, which seemed deft and strong. His fingers were long. And then she thought, he's going to be working on James' head. He can be a total cretin, for all I care, as long as his hands and his brain can do what they need to do. Ellen glanced at Sean, who nodded his okay. She signed the forms, and the surgeon hurried out.

"Sean? Speak to me in Mom-English, okay? How is James?"

All four of them pulled the chairs together facing each other, and then Ellen reached out to touch Sean's arm and added, "Thanks for coming."

He smiled, patted her arm, and began talking to them.

"We think, based on his injuries, that James was hit in the back of the top of his head by the Jet Ski. He was probably in a prone position, stomach down, below the surface of the water, and the ski hit him from above, perhaps on the downswing of one of its bounces. If he'd been more upright, we would probably see a neck injury as well. So he's lucky there."

Sean paused and kneaded the area between his eyes. "But the skull fracture is severe. There has been massive trauma to the brain. We don't know how that will affect permanent brain function."

He's drifting into doctor-talk and medical euphemisms, Ellen thought. It must be really bad.

". . . to reduce swelling of the brain." Sean paused and looked around at them to make sure they comprehended all he'd said.

"I'm sorry, Sean. I zoned out for a minute. What's going to reduce the swelling?"

"Holes. Drilled in his skull."

Wow, thought Ellen. I could have used some euphemisms for that. Then she asked, "When will we know anything?"

"Brain swelling peaks at forty-eight hours. These are the critical hours. We'll know a lot more then."

The waiting began. Ellen felt as if she were watching her life as a bad made-for-TV movie. The drab room, the chairs upholstered in fake leather, the rancid coffee. After an hour, they even stopped trying to make small talk. Flipping through old issues of *Woman's Day, People,* and *U.S. News,* Anna or Sam would comment on an article, but no one could concentrate on an entire issue. The still air was broken briefly by a pizza deliveryman. Ellen hadn't thought about eating, but now she realized she hadn't eaten since a late breakfast twelve hours ago and some chips and Mexican dip on the dock before the accident.

"Who ordered this?" Anna asked the deliveryman. He pulled out a slip of paper and shook his head.

"Doesn't say on the form. Just tells where to take it."

They looked at each other questioningly and then dug in.

Ellen doubted she would feel any urge to eat, but then found herself not only enjoying the pizza, but wanting a soda, too. Sam must have wanted one as well, because he stood up and reached in his pocket for some change.

"Sean, can you show me where a soda machine is?" Sam paused, as if waiting for the drink orders. "Anna, you want diet, no caffeine, right? El, high octane all the way?" She smiled and nodded. That's how they classified Coke Classic. And in her mind, nothing went better with pizza.

After the men left, Ellen and Anna looked at each other. For the first time since the dock they had some time, just the two of them, to talk. Ellen was terrified that Anna would know what had been going through Ellen's mind those few seconds before James had been brought to the surface. But it was there, in the air around them, and Ellen knew she had to speak it.

"Anna. On the dock . . . You know I love you. And your girls. But . . ." She looked away. How could she say this? To Anna? The term *best friend* seemed so junior-high-ish. But that's what they were. Or closer. Neither of them had a sister. They filled that hole for the other. They traded clothes and books. Anna had taught her how to fold a fitted sheet. Ellen had shown Anna how to make piecrust from scratch. They finished each other's sentences. No one but Anna would she allow in the dressing room with her. No one but Anna would tell her, *You can't wear that skirt length. Your calves are too chunky.* Ellen wanted Anna's shapelier legs. Anna wanted Ellen's slimmer hips. They agreed that they needed to combine their cup sizes for the right figure. Ellen started again, "I just . . ."

"I know," Anna said quietly, and set her pizza down on a paper towel.

"Maybe. But I have to say it. For those few seconds, before

we knew who it was, I, uh, I was begging God to please let the boys be okay." She put her face in her hands. And then she sat up straight and looked at Anna. "I wanted the girls to be fine, too. Can you understand? I didn't want you to lose anyone. But, even more, I didn't want me to."

"Ellie, it's okay."

"No. Maybe this is my punishment for being selfish."

"This isn't a punishment. El, what do you think I was thinking? It's called being a mother."

Ellen shook her head slightly. This mother thing, she thought. It just hurts too much. It's too scary.

The doors burst open and Sam and Sean returned with sodas and napkins.

"Hey," Sam said, "we found out who sent the mystery pizza. It's from Laurie, that nurse at the Bainbridge hospital."

The doctor came in a bit later. The monitor had been successfully placed. They hadn't had to drill the holes in his skull for a window, since the fracture itself was relieving the pressure. Time would tell.

"Can I see him?" Ellen asked.

"Yes," Dr. Stalnovick replied. "A nurse will be here in a few minutes. She'll get you prepared."

"Will? Could I take care of that instead?" Sean asked.

"Sure, that'd be great."

Ellen looked at Sean. All her questions filled the air, but she didn't know where to start. She glanced at her wrist to see what time it was, then realized her watch was still back at the lake house—she never wore it out to the dock. Anna had seen her glance and said, "It's one A.M."

One A.M.? Ellen shook her head. This had happened less than eight hours ago.

"Ready, El?" Sean stood up and held the door open for her. Walking to the pediatric ICU, Sean talked to her quietly and slowly, much the way Laurie had in Bainbridge.

"Let me prepare you for what you'll see, okay?"

Ellen nodded and started steeling herself. I can't fall apart here, she thought. James will sense if I'm panicking.

"Physically, on the surface, he won't look too bad. A little puffy or swollen, but he'll look like James." They paused outside of the room. "But there will be a great deal of equipment that might frighten you at first."

"So it won't be as bad as it looks?"

"No. It *is* as bad as it looks. We're hoping it doesn't stay that way." Sean waited for her to absorb this. "He's still on the ventilator. That's one of the tubes down his throat. He'll have another tube in his nose to remove stomach secretions—"

"Is that how they'll feed him, too?" Ellen interrupted.

"No. He can't have anything in his stomach. There will be twenty or so probes on his head to measure brain activity. And cardio cables on his body for blood pressure and other measurements. Ready?"

Ellen answered him by carefully pushing open the door. The room was very dim and seemed abnormally quiet for so much machinery. James was flat on his back, but the mattress was raised slightly to elevate his head. There were foam blocks on both sides of his head. A nurse brought a chair next to the bed and motioned for Ellen to sit down.

"Can I touch him?"

"Yes. Please do. You can talk softly, sing, whatever," the nurse answered kindly.

Sean left then, and Ellen looked at James closely for the first time since the accident, tuning out the presence of the nurse, who continued to work. Ellen reached for his pudgy hand and started caressing it, and then his whole arm. Her fingers lightly petted the pale hair on his arm. She wanted to rub his head but was afraid to do so. Except for all the wires and tubes, she thought, he really just looks like he's sleeping. His body looked so sturdy—already she could see the faint outlines of the muscles and shape he would have as a man. But the stillness and straightness of his body was unnatural. He never slept like this. He always curled up on his side, knees bent, sheet wrapped tightly around him. She looked at his strong, solid legs. He looks so healthy, how can he not be okay? She leaned down and brushed his forehead with her lips. His skin felt warm and dry, and he still had the smell of the lake water and a tang of sweat on his skin. She sat back, still touching his hand, and watched him breathe.

A doctor came in behind her, and Ellen jumped.

"It's okay," the nurse said to her quietly. "He's just checking some monitors."

Ellen got up to leave, but the nurse motioned that she could stay. Ellen watched the doctor open each of James' eyelids and shine a light into it. He then wrote some notations on a chart and watched as the nurse administered some medications to the IVs. The doctor left after nodding slightly in Ellen's direction.

"What was he looking for?" Ellen asked the nurse.

"Any pupil reaction to light. Also pupil size."

"Did he see any reaction?"

"There's been no change."

"Do you think there ever will be a change?"

The nurse paused, checked some of the monitors, and finally turned to face Ellen. "I can't answer that."

"Can't? Or won't?"

"Listen, I can give you percentages and odds and gut feelings. But this is your son. As predictable as closed head traumas might seem, there's no sure way to know what'll happen.

The brain's an amazing organ. Incredibly fragile and amazingly resilient. I don't know what we'll see. He's made it this far, though."

Ellen thanked her, and the nurse put her hand on Ellen's shoulder before walking out.

Chapter
Five

Ellen must have dozed off. The doctor from the surgery was talking to a nurse in the corner of the room. When Ellen sat up and rubbed her face, they looked over at her, and Dr. Stalnovick pulled a chair up next to her.

"What time is it?"

He looked at his watch and told her it was just before six A.M.

"How is he?"

"There hasn't been a change, but it's only been twelve hours. The first forty-eight—"

"I know, I know," Ellen cut him off. "They're the ones that tell us everything." She hadn't meant to sound angry, but no one was telling her anything. James hadn't moved. The unreality of all of this was starting to fade—and the realness of where she was terrified her. "Why's he breathing so fast? Why's he so still?"

"We have his ventilator set at an abnormally high rate. That will decrease pressure in his skull." He paused, then added, "We have him on paralytic drugs." When he saw Ellen's eyes widen in alarm he quickly added, "That's to keep him from struggling against the ventilator." He saw her relax a bit. "It will also help prevent any head movement that could put pressure on his brain."

Ellen sat back and looked dazedly around the room before her eyes settled on James' still, pale figure. "Can he hear me? Can he hear what we are saying?"

"We don't know that," Dr. Stalnovick told her.

Ellen's mind raced to old medical shows. Isn't hearing the last thing to go, she thought. Do I dare ask them?

Before she could verbalize her question, the nurse turned to her and urged, "Talk to him. Sing to him. If we see any spike on the monitor, it will be a good sign."

The doctor stared at the monitors and the nurse continued to hover over James, checking instruments and constantly working on him. Ellen heard them talking about intracranial pressure spikes and watched them check the ventilator as well as frequently manipulate the ventilator bag by hand. They worked with a sense of calm urgency. Ellen knew from the serious looks on their faces that they were concerned. She would have expected these early hours to be a time of quiet watchfulness, but the medical personnel were constantly streaming in, adjusting medications and checking machinery.

Ellen pulled her chair close to the bed again.

"I love you, James. I'm here, baby." Then she started singing, softly and slightly off-key. She was on the second verse of "O Little Town of Bethlehem" when Anna walked in. Ellen looked up, slightly embarrassed. "It's his favorite. He always wanted me to sing that to him at bedtime, no matter what the season."

Ellen looked back at James, finished that verse, and started on the next one. When she was done, she touched his cheek and stood up and walked toward the door. "I know all the verses. Because of him." Before she walked out, Anna leaned over, kissed James' hand, and then followed Ellen out the door.

In the hallway, Ellen paused for a drink of water, then leaned against the wall, closed her eyes, and felt the coolness of the tile on her cheek. When she opened her eyes, Tim was striding to her, with his arms held open. Ellen rushed into them and pressed her face into his chest.

"I'm so sorry. I'm so scared," she repeated over and over until the words ran into one another and then she was sobbing. Anna and some nurses helped them into their waiting room.

Sam tried to bring Tim up to date on what had happened since the phone call the evening before. Tim hadn't been able to get a flight, so he had driven all night from Detroit.

"Can I see him?"

Ellen wiped her face and blew her nose.

"Sure. But let me prepare you." She was now the expert on trying to help others not be shocked or shaken by what they would see and hear in James' room. Sam offered to go in with Tim, and Ellen agreed to wait behind. I don't want to see his face when he first sees James, she thought. I don't think I could bear it.

When Tim and Sam returned, she saw the same numbness in Tim's face she had felt herself until this morning. She knew his brain couldn't get around what had happened. He sat quietly in a chair and looked up at her.

"When will we know more?"

"Forty-eight hours." She was now repeating the mantra. "Forty-eight hours, minus the twelve already. Tomorrow night at six."

As much as had happened between them, they were still parents together. Nobody but us knows how this feels, she thought. We're the only two who know and care about what he looked like when he was born and how his head smelled when he was a baby. We're the only ones.

The rest of the morning was a blur. Ellen spent most of the day in the room with James, talking, singing, and rubbing his legs. As dazed as she felt, she was starting to distinguish the different sounds the machinery and monitors made. At first, the cacophony was deafening. Now she knew the steady beep came from the cardiac monitor, and she even liked the swoosh of the ventilator. It was the noises that occurred irregularly that startled and frightened Ellen the most, and usually because she knew them to be associated with quick movements or reactions from the nurses. She didn't know what they all meant, but she'd seen it often enough to know that a high, piercing electronic scream would be followed by a nurse briefly disconnecting the ventilator, which caused a lower-pitched scream, to manually ventilate James.

She took breaks every few hours. Tim had gone out to the lake house to bring back Daniel. He was also going to contact the sheriff and find out how the investigation was going. They hadn't decided when Daniel would see James, but Daniel had made it clear on the phone that he very much wanted to be with them. When Ellen took a break around noon, she found that Kevin and Meg, her next-door neighbors, had arrived, bringing sub sandwiches, fruit, and a cooler of soda. Ellen hugged them, and then, in answer to their questioning looks, held her hands up helplessly and shrugged, finally saying, "We won't know anything more definite until tomorrow. Late afternoon or early evening."

They talked aimlessly and Ellen tried to eat. At one point she glanced in a mirror and was startled. My God, she thought, I could be an extra in *One Flew Over the Cuckoo's Nest*. She was trying to comb out her hair with her fingers when Anna found her.

"El, would you want to go home and take a shower?"

"Oh, I can't leave."

"You can be gone for a little bit. It might do you some good."

"Well, okay. Will you sit with him?"

"Sure. Do you know when Tim will be back?" Anna asked.

Ellen glanced at her wrist, again looking for her watch.

"Soon, I think. What time is it?"

"About two. El? What about calling your parents?"

Ellen paused. She knew she should call them. They would want to know and would want to be here. But she still hesitated. Having family come from far away made it sound so much scarier. Besides, she thought, how would she get the words out? Anna knew Ellen had been avoiding this. Last night things had moved so quickly, but now, well, now it was time.

"Ellie, I'll help you. But they need to know."

So they sat by the phone together and Ellen fumbled through her wallet looking for her calling card. Her fingers trembled as she dialed their number. The phone rang three times and Ellen was filled with mixed hope and fear that they wouldn't be home. Do I leave a message for them, she wondered. But in the middle of the fifth ring her mom answered, sounding bright and happy and calm.

"Mom?"

"Hi, Ellen. How are you? Having fun at the lake?"

"Mom," Ellen began again and stopped. For the first time since arriving at the hospital, Ellen felt her chest begin to pound, and her whole body trembled. "James had an accid—" Her voice broke and she held the phone out to Anna as she put her head in her hands, and the sobs burst out. They were the cries of a child: heaving breaths, gulping air, and flowing tears. She heard Anna talking, explaining the situation to her mother. Could see, in her mind, her mother's hand flying to her mouth, her other hand motioning for her father to pick up the extension. She knew her dad would sit in a chair, numbly listening to news of his critically injured grandson. He will crumble, she thought. He will be an absolute puddle. Mom will take charge, will get them here. She knew her dad would pull himself together once they arrived in Madison. Dad will be strong for me then, she knew.

Anna hung up the phone and came over to her. "They'll be on the next plane. They love you."

I know, I know, thought Ellen. And that's part of what had made her fall apart. Hearing her mom's voice broke down all her adult defenses. With her mom's voice she was transported to nine years old again. I can be strong in front of almost anybody, she thought, but I can't fake it in front of them.

The tears had felt good, she thought when she was finally done. They had been inside of her, like a fist, and now there was a little more room in her chest. "I'm going to go take that shower now."

Meg had offered to drive her to her house, but just as they were walking out the door, Laurie walked in.

"Hi. How are you?"

Was it just last night that Ellen had met her?

"I brought you the clothes you left in the ambulance."

"Thank you. I'd forgotten all about them. I was just getting ready to go home for a quick shower."

"Need a lift?"

Ellen looked at Meg, then back at Laurie. "Meg is taking me. She lives next door. But thanks."

"No problem. Do you mind if I look in on James?"

"That'd be really nice. See you when I get back if you're still here."

After Ellen left, Laurie turned to Anna and said, "We sort of met last night. I'm Laurie Brainerd."

"Anna Johanssen." Anna pulled out the sports page from the pile of newspapers on a nearby table and added, "I'm going to go read this to James. Did you want to look in on him?"

Laurie seemed to sense an underlying question in Anna's words.

"I suppose you're wondering why I'm here," Laurie asked.

"Well." Anna paused and brushed her bangs back with her hand before adding, "It does seem odd. Aren't you busy enough at your own hospital?"

"I don't follow all of my patients to Madison," Laurie said, laughing softly.

They walked into James' room, and instinctively Laurie checked the monitors and glanced at his chart. Anna pulled a chair up close to his bed and stroked his arm. Before she opened the paper and cleared her throat to read she turned again to Laurie and asked, "So why are you here?"

"Too often when families are transferred from our hospital for a critical case like this, they feel isolated or stranded here in Madison because they're far from home and family. When we can, we like to follow up just to make sure the family gets the support they need."

"But you knew Ellen lived here. You knew we were driving her here." Anna tried not to sound as if she was challenging Laurie's concern, but it didn't make any sense to her.

"And sometimes," Laurie continued as if Anna hadn't interrupted, "the situation hits way too close to home."

"And this one does?" Anna asked.

"I have a blond-haired, blue-eyed little boy at home. He'll look just like James in a few years. And I have a fourteen-year-old son who loves to Jet Ski."

As Ellen began walking from Meg's car to her house, she was startled to see her front door open. Melanie came out with Stella jumping up and mouthing at the leash.

"I just came by to walk her," Melanie quickly explained.

"Thanks. I'd forgotten you were taking care of her." Ellen reached down to pet Stella's head. "I—" she began, then stopped and gazed blankly down at the dog. No one spoke. Then Ellen started again, "I don't know when we'll be back."

"That's fine. I'll come till whenever."

Ellen nodded, and Melanie stood stiffly as Stella sniffed them both and pulled at her leash.

"I'm really sorry about your son," Melanie said, then asked, "Is he—are you—gonna be okay?"

Ellen shook her head, then said, "We don't know yet. I'm just here for a shower."

"I'll get going, then. Stella's been great."

Ellen watched as Melanie led the jumping dog to the street. Then she took a deep breath and walked up the porch steps.

When Ellen walked into her house, she carefully averted her eyes to not see any of James' things. I can't see them, not now, she thought.

Ellen stepped over the mail piled on the floor below the

mail slot in the wall. I love this old house, she thought to herself. The dark woodwork, the hairline cracks in the plaster walls. She remembered how, after Tim had left, she'd felt almost comforted by it. Strengthened. Fortified. These walls must've seen so much in their seventy years. She reacted to old-house smell the way some people did to new-car smell. She wanted to nestle into it. Bottle it. Would the house be able to hold her up through this? she wondered. Single-mindedly, she got herself to the bathroom, peeled off her clothes, and let the hot water pound her back, neck, and head. She felt it pouring down her arms and legs. While she washed, she could smell the hospital as if it were oozing out of her. When she shampooed her hair, she kneaded her scalp until it felt raw, as if she were trying to rub away all that had happened. Toweling off, she felt oddly removed from the ICU and James' room. Coming home had been an all-too-brief respite from James' condition. She saw the rays of sun from the skylight in the bathroom and smelled the freshly cut grass from a neighbor's yard. She was almost reluctant to go back to the artificial light and medicinal smells that were waiting for her.

Donning a white T-shirt and black knit jumper, she slipped on sandals. She brushed her teeth vigorously, and the minty toothpaste almost burned her fuzzy-feeling teeth and gums. She pulled her hair back into a clip and fluffed her bangs. She went to reach for her makeup and found the medicine cabinet partly empty. Surprised, she started to call to Meg, then stopped herself. Most of my stuff is still at the lake, she thought. She rummaged around in the linen closet for the stash of samples of moisturizer and makeup she usually tossed in there. This will have to do, she thought. At least my lipstick is in my purse.

"Okay, Meg," she said walking into the living room, "let's go back."

～～～～～

Returning to the hospital waiting room, Ellen found the vigil continuing. Sam, Sean, and Kevin talked, occasionally made phone calls, and carefully watched the women. It was as if the men were looking to them for a guide as to how stoic or emotional they could be. They were scared—a child in their circle was in critical condition. Ellen wondered if Sean had told them more than he'd told her. She also wondered vaguely about their jobs—Sam was on vacation for the week, and Sean worked here, but Kevin and Meg? They should have been at their offices. What day was it anyway? She had to think hard. Monday? They'd gotten to the lake on Saturday. This had happened their second afternoon. It was now the next day. Okay, Monday.

"Did Tim get back with Daniel yet?" she asked.

"No," Sam answered. "He called from the car. He was taking Daniel out for an early dinner. He's also called his dad. He said they'd be here by six."

Ellen went to James' room. Laurie was standing outside. "Hey, you're looking much better," she said.

"Thanks. Is Anna in with James?"

"Yeah. The doctors didn't want us both in there. It's almost my turn. We've been reading the sports section to him."

Ellen nodded, smiled in appreciation, and entered the room. It was more jarring to her now after having been home.

"Anything?" she asked Anna.

Anna shook her head, then said, "The doctor was looking for you."

Ellen found him at the nurses' station, reviewing charts. "Looking for me?"

"It's been twenty-four hours. There has been no improvement."

"Not even from the surgery?"

"No. But we weren't expecting much. That mostly keeps things from possibly worsening." He jotted down some notes, then turned his full attention to her. "Have you called in relatives? These next few days could be very difficult."

"My parents'll be here soon."

"Good. You'll need all the support you can get. James is very severely injured. You need to know that." His voice softened a bit, and then he added, "You may be faced with some very difficult decisions. Would you like to speak with the chaplain?"

Ellen's mind raced. She nodded, then found her voice. "I'd like my own minister, please. Could you call her?" She didn't even wait for his response. On a piece of paper she wrote down the name Irene Sherer, and the name of her church. Passing it to him, she said, "Thanks," then headed back to James' room. She'd forgotten to ask if Daniel would be allowed to see James, but decided not to go back to check. He'll see him, she thought, even if I have to sneak him in.

The evening was a blur of arrivals—Ellen's parents, Tim with his dad and Daniel, Irene. Ellen found James' room almost a place of refuge. It was her one place of privacy, the one place where the only questioning eyes were her own, the one place she could cry silently and freely. The waiting room was too full of stunned, frightened glances and awkward small talk. She finally told Anna and Sam to go on home for the evening. They'd been with her and away from their girls for twenty-four hours. When they came to hug her, though, and to tell her they'd be back in the morning, Ellen found she didn't want to let go of them. Meg had offered to stay the night, and Sean said he'd be back in the morning, but to feel free to page him if she needed.

The hardest arrival for Ellen had been Daniel. He'd looked so small and shaken. This was his little brother—and he couldn't remember a time without him. Ellen had tried to prepare him for James' appearance, but she'd still felt his whole body tremble when he had first walked into the room with her. He had touched James' arm, whispered in his ear, and then she'd walked him out into the hall. He'd turned to hug her fiercely, and she knew he was trying not to cry. He'd looked up at her then and said, "Just hold me till I quit shivering."

She'd done so, with her cheek pressed to the top of his head, the two of them embracing so tightly an observer wouldn't have known which one of them was holding up the other.

Ellen found it hard to meet her parents' eyes. They looked so pale and confused. She knew it frustrated her father to be unable to orchestrate this. He'd spent his life organizing and arranging and protecting. And now he was unable to use any of those skills and abilities. He'd had his own insurance company. No policies covered this, though, did they? You can't really insure against a family crisis, she thought, at least not in any way that matters.

About midnight, her parents offered to take Daniel home to get some sleep. She handed them her house keys, and the rest of them dozed intermittently until morning.

When Ellen awoke, she felt very tense. She knew that this was the last leg of the forty-eight hours, and by tonight they'd have more of an idea of James' true condition.

Late Tuesday afternoon, while Ellen sat with James and told him who was waiting to visit, one of the nurses came in and motioned for her to come out into the corridor. When Ellen left the room, Dr. Stalnovick walked into it with two others.

"They need to do some tests for response," the nurse explained, "now that it's been forty-eight hours."

Ellen nodded and began to make her way down to the waiting room, but the nurse added, "You might want to wait here. The tests don't take long and they'll want to give you the results."

Ellen leaned against the wall outside James' room, and though she tried to hear what the doctors were saying inside, she couldn't make out anything more than a low murmuring. Closing her eyes, she became aware of how much more muted the sounds were outside James' room. If she'd thought about it, she would have recognized many of the same noises and alarms she'd become accustomed to, but her world was now so closed and narrow that she paid no attention to beeps or alarms not attached to James.

What a strange workplace, she thought. She was so used to the chatter of a high school. This quiet, punctuated by mechanical noises, would make me nuts. It's soothing, but in a mind-numbing rather than a relaxing way. It's like a drug, she thought, to keep us wacko moms from screaming.

"Mrs. Banks?"

Ellen startled, opened her eyes, and swallowed quickly. It was the nurse.

"They're taking James for another CAT scan. Then they'll want to see you."

Ellen was ushered into a room down the hall, and before Dr. Stalnovick and the other doctors came in, another nurse led in Tim and her minister, Irene. Ellen felt the fear start to well up in her. Okay, she thought, our forty-eight hours are up. And by bringing in Tim and Irene, the news isn't going to be good.

They waited for the nurse to come back. Ellen tried to close her eyes and relax. She tried to force her mind to picture

James as healthy and frisky again. Maybe, she thought, I can will him off that hospital bed. She could see it so clearly—his grin, so quick and pure and impish, and his smooth, round cheeks. She knew if he suddenly woke up he'd think the bed was cool—he'd love the idea of rails and of being able to raise and lower the mattress. He'd immediately want to show it off to Daniel. Just as she was imagining him leaping off the end of the bed, Dr. Stalnovick jolted her from her dream.

"Mr. and Mrs. Banks," Dr. Stalnovick said and paused, popped his knuckles, then folded his hands. "The CAT scan results aren't encouraging. They support the findings from some of the other response tests we did to check for brain activity and response to stimuli." He paused again, and Irene reached out to put her hand on Ellen's shoulder. The door opened and Sean came in with a man and a woman in green hospital scrubs. Ellen's mind raced. Oh God, she thought, more surgery?

"What kinds of tests?" Tim asked. He stared intently at the doctor.

"Well, in one we put cold water in his ear. We're looking for a reaction to the cold. In another, we press on his sternum with our knuckles. We see if there's any reaction to the pain."

"And?" Tim challenged. Ellen knew he was fighting for calm.

"There was no response."

"Then try more tests. Try different tests," Tim snapped. He wasn't going to accept two simple tests.

"There's one more test we're going to perform. We'd like you to be present for it."

"What's this one?" Ellen asked.

"It's a blood flow study. We inject a substance so we can do a fluoroscopy. It shows if any blood is circulating in James' brain."

Ellen and Tim watched silently while the doctors and nurses prepared for the procedure. They watched on a small screen, and Ellen refused to believe they were looking at a picture of their son's brain. It just looks blurry and gray, she thought. It reminded her of the sonogram her obstetrician had done when she was pregnant with James. He had tried to point out the head and other parts of the body, but as much as she had wanted to see a baby on that screen, all she'd seen were blobs.

Ellen tried now to see the details of this image. Please, she silently prayed, let me see some movement. Something that will back me and all of us away from this horror.

But there was no movement, no sign of anything flowing on the monitor.

The room was hushed as each person there watched and hoped.

Ellen reached up to grasp Irene's hand. She looked at Sean. "Tell us," she pleaded. "The truth. Sean?"

When Sean looked at her, his eyes filled with tears. "Ellie. Tim. There's no change. No blood flow. No brain activity. Not even on the most basic level."

"How can that be? He's breathing. I can feel his heart beat." Ellen looked from face to face. Finally she looked at Irene. And in Irene's eyes she saw profound sadness. "No. No. Come on. Call God direct, okay? He's eleven. His body is perfect," Ellen pleaded.

"Mrs. Banks?" Dr. Stalnovick waited for her to look at him. "Much of his body is perfect. But not his brain. And the only reason he is breathing is because of the ventilator. Look—" He held out a printout from one of the machines. "See this flat line? There are no spikes. No variations. He's brain-dead."

And at this, Ellen began rocking back and forth in her chair, moaning and calling out, "No, God. Oh, no." Her words echoed down the quiet halls. Blindly, she reached out for Tim and they rocked together while everyone else in the room waited. When Ellen finally looked up, she saw tears streaming down all their faces.

"Ellie?" Sean knelt in front of her. "There's something else we need to talk about. This is Dr. Mora"—he nodded to the short, black-haired woman in scrubs—"and this is Dr. Kennicott." The tall, sandy-blond man smiled kindly at her.

"We'd like to ask you to consider organ donation," the tall doctor said to her. While he paused to let the words sink in, Ellen thought, that's it. My brain is going to explode. I always wondered what happened when you were faced with the unimaginable. This is it. My brain's going to explode and then I won't feel anything ever again. A scene flashed into her head of the woman in line when she had gotten her driver's license renewed. She had grumbled that it wouldn't matter if she donated her organs because she'd be dead. Could that be the way they were talking about James now? She realized she was slowly shaking her head back and forth. Make them all go away, she thought. I'll go sit with James and lock the door behind us. I'll never let them in.

"Go away," she growled at them, surprising even herself that her thoughts had been spoken. "Go away!" she screamed at all of them.

Everyone started filing out, but Tim and Irene stayed with her. She brushed their hands off her. "Don't touch me," she warned as she began to stalk around the small room. They sat quietly, but flinched when she began throwing magazines, and they seemed truly frightened when Ellen let out a screaming string of obscenities, cursing all doctors, all tests, and even God. Anna heard her down the hall and came running in the door.

"Get out, get out!" Ellen kept screaming. Irene and Tim

did leave, but Anna sat in a chair and waited Ellen out. Finally, exhausted, Ellen lay down on the plastic sofa, held her face in her hands, and sobbed. Anna came to her then and ran her fingers through Ellen's hair, brushing it back and massaging her head and neck. Twice a nurse checked up on them, but both times Anna waved her away.

Ellen's sobs weakened and finally faded completely, and then she struggled to sit up. Wiping her face, she looked at Anna and said, "Don't let them give me any shots."

"Okay."

"I don't want them to tranquilize me. Promise."

"I promise."

"I want to hold him. I want to sit in a rocking chair and hold him in my arms. And sing to him. And smell his hair."

"I'll go tell them."

When Ellen walked into James' room a few minutes later, Dr. Stalnovick and the organ donation doctors were there, talking to Tim and Anna, and they looked at her expectantly.

"How much time do we have?" She surprised even herself with the calmness of her voice.

"You've decided to donate?" Dr. Mora asked.

"Yes. How much time?"

"We could be ready in two hours."

Anna embraced her then, and Ellen spoke now, only to Anna. "Can you tell everyone in the waiting room? They will want to say goodbye. And call Laurie." Anna nodded and left. "I'm going to hold him. Unplug whatever you can. Find me a rocking chair. A big one. With a cushion." I'm giving the damn orders now, she thought. I hate all of you.

A chair was brought in and all the machines except for the ventilator were removed. Several nurses and Sean handed

James to her and she fit him to her body with his head under her cheek and his legs across her lap. Hold my neck, she pleaded silently, but James' arms fell limply at his side. Sean placed them in the boy's lap. Tim came in then and pulled a chair up to her. Daniel crawled onto Tim's lap and looked at Ellen. The tears flowed.

"Can you understand?" Ellen asked him. Daniel nodded, then buried his face in Tim's shirt. Then her parents came in. She couldn't meet their gaze. This is too horrible, she thought. As she watched them kiss James and then help each other out the door, she thought they had aged twenty years. Keep rocking and humming, she told herself. If you break your rhythm you'll go crazy.

Anna and Sam were last. Ellen shut her eyes tight when she saw them at the door. She knew they'd brought their two older daughters, Sarah and Emily, with them. When Sam had told her he was going home to get them, Ellen had gasped.

"No," she had said, "I don't want them to remember James like this."

But Sam's counterargument had been convincing.

"Ellie, the last they saw of him was on the dock with the paramedics wheeling him away. So they already have that as a final memory. They want to tell him goodbye. They need to."

Sam's face had looked so sad when he said this that she knew he was right. James and Daniel were the closest things to brothers the girls would ever have. Even so, Ellen was determined not to watch this final farewell.

But though her eyes were closed, she saw it all, with too much clarity, in her mind.

She knew that Sam and Anna would usher the girls in. That Sarah and Emily would be hesitant and somewhat shy about looking at James at first. She knew that Sarah, the oldest, would hold everything inside, at least until she got back to the corridor where she would fall into her mother's arms and sob. Emily, James' twin in so many ways, would be angry, and her face would be blotched with fear and tears. While she would gingerly approach James' side, once there she would never want to leave.

Although Ellen could close her eyes, she couldn't plug her ears. She heard the sharp intake of their breath when they first spied James in Ellen's arms. Don't look, Ellen commanded herself. And she didn't. At least not until she heard Sarah whisper, "Goodbye, James."

Ellen looked at Sarah then and saw the effort in her face not to cry.

"He loved you so much," Ellen whispered to her as Sarah nodded. Then, with just a hint of relaxation, Sarah's tears began to fall.

Emily was staring at James, then up at her father, then back to James.

It's not real to her yet, Ellen thought. It's not real for any of us yet.

"Emily? Do you want to touch him?" Sam asked while Anna helped Sarah out the door.

Emily shook her head, but then reached out to pat his arm. Her sobs began before she had even fully turned away.

Anna and Sam looked back at her once in the doorway and then softly pulled the door closed.

Ellen wondered, what will we ever say to one another? What possible conversation can I ever have with anyone?

"Mom?"

Ellen turned slowly to look at Daniel, still nestled in Tim's lap.

"What, baby?"

"Is he dead?"

"No. Not yet."

She looked at Tim and saw his jaw firmly clenched. His drained face and hollow eyes mirrored her own.

"How much longer?" Daniel asked, looking only at James' slack face.

"I don't know. Not much."

Ellen amazed herself at her ability to speak a coherent sentence.

"I don't want to be in here anymore, Mom."

Ellen simply nodded as Tim helped Daniel up, and she tried not to listen when Daniel whispered a final goodbye to his little brother.

Then Tim took Daniel out and Ellen was alone with James. She couldn't look at the clock, didn't want to know how much time was left. She touched his entire body, willing her fingers to remember not only the feel of his skin, but the shape and dimensions of his arms and round belly and sturdy legs. His legs were just getting the coarse, blond hair that was different from the baby down he'd had. She rubbed his head—his buzz cut had always felt so soothing when she rubbed it. She smelled his skin and his breath. Watched his heart valiantly beat under his skin. Too soon. Too soon. She sang all the verses of "O Little Town of Bethlehem." And then she closed her eyes and kissed him. Too soon.

Chapter
Six

Once they took James to the operating room, Ellen sat in the rocker, keeping the same slow, steady beat, waiting until the procedure was complete. She knew the technical term was *harvesting;* had even heard that word used by the doctors in the hallway. And the term gnawed at her. It sounded so healthy, so hopeful. Harvesttime, especially in an agricultural state, was a time of celebration and festivals. It seemed as though every small town in Wisconsin had some sort of fair to commemorate the harvest. The term felt wrong to her now, almost an obscenity.

After the procedure, Doctors Mora and Kennicott came in to thank her and tell her James' heart, liver, and kidneys were on their way to critically ill children. Ellen had hoped she might derive some comfort from that. She didn't. I don't care about any other sick child, she thought. Why should those parents be spared my grief? She gazed at the doctors without expression. What the hell do you want me to say to you? she wondered. You just carved open my son. I never want to see either of you again. She rose up then and walked out of the room, the rocker gradually becoming still. I'm going home now, she thought. I don't know what I'll do when I get there, but I never want to see these halls again.

Ellen walked right past the waiting room where her family and friends had spent the last two days. Laurie and Sean saw her walk by and hurried out to her.

"I'm going home."

"This way, El." Sean gently guided her away from the main entrance. Ellen wondered why he was taking her the back way, but she didn't have the energy to question him.

Once they got to the parking lot, Ellen realized she had no idea where her car was, or even if it was here. The last time she'd driven it had been to the lake house. At the thought of the lake, her mind started to veer over into pictures of the accident. No, she demanded of herself. No. She wanted to erase all images of the lake from her memory. I'll never go there again. I can't.

Sean guided her to his car, and Laurie helped her in and buckled her seat belt. With a quick hug and a promise to call her tomorrow, Laurie closed the door and Sean backed out of the parking space. As they pulled out of the lot, Ellen saw the bright lights at the main entrance.

"What're all the lights for?"

"Oh, it's a bunch of newspeople. Cameras and reporters and stuff. That's why I brought you out the back way. I didn't want them to bother you."

"Thanks." Ellen leaned back into the seat and sighed. Then she turned back to Sean and asked, "What happened?"

"Huh?"

"Something big must've happened for the media to be here."

"El, they're here about you. And James."

Ellen whipped her head around to look at them. Oh my God, she thought. This has been on the news?

"Why?"

"Ellen, you've got a child who's killed by a Jet Skier. A mother who chooses to donate his organs. In the slow news days of summer, in this day and age, that's a leading story."

How long have they been there? she thought. What do they think I'd say to them?

Turning to Sean, she touched his arm and said, "Thanks for keeping them away from me."

"They'll still be calling you at home. You don't have to talk to them."

"Will they be at my house?"

"No. Sam and your dad made sure of that. No one'll bother you tonight. Anna's there."

"Where's Daniel? And my folks?"

"Daniel's at your house, too. Tim took him there and stayed until he fell asleep. Your parents are at a hotel."

They drove in silence down University Avenue and past the Ag School Stock Pavilion, and she wondered how she'd ever keep living here. She could see James everywhere. As a little boy, laughing when they'd brought him down to see the livestock, giggling and pulling away as the cows sniffed his hand. Devouring the sticky morning buns when they'd come for brunch. Licking the ice cream from Babcock Hall. When Ellen had come to Madison for college, it had been the first place she'd ever chosen to live. She'd decided, on her first afternoon, sitting on the terrace watching the sailboats and the ducks, that this was her perfect fit. She'd later come to realize how right her first impression had been. The small-town neighborhood shops and tree-lined streets of the near west side blended into the wide avenues that surrounded the Capitol and downtown campus. The practicality of a state made up of a patchwork of farms and rolling hills enlivened with the unpredictability and passion of forty thousand college students. Over the past twenty years it had become home. She might have grown up moving all over the country every few years, but this town, with its frigid winters, its occasional humid spells in summer, the autumn smells of burning leaves and grilling bratwursts, and the glorious springs, was her adopted home. It had seemed to her the best place in the world to live, the safest, the cleanest. And now it was where she'd had to let her son die, and where she'd soon have to plan his funeral.

Ellen walked slowly into the house and tried to brace herself. She wondered if the house would feel different. If even the rooms would sense James' loss. Anna was waiting in the living room, and all Ellen could do was shake her head from side to side while they sat together on the sofa.

"Daniel's sleeping," Anna said. "Can I get you anything?"

"Red wine. Is he okay?"

Anna walked into the kitchen to get some wine, and Ellen followed her. She forced herself to look on the floor by the back door where the boys' shoes were jumbled in a pile. Seeing them, she didn't flinch.

"He woke up once and called out. I sat with him and rubbed his back. He didn't talk to me but I could hear him whispering and sighing."

"That's how he says his prayers."

They sat quietly and sipped the wine. Ellen looked around the room—it all felt so charged, she thought.

"El?" Anna asked. "I'll be here until morning. You should try to sleep."

"No." Ellen stared out the window into the darkness as she spoke. She strained to see the outlines of the wooden fort the boys had built last summer. "I can't sleep."

"Maybe the wine'll help," Anna offered.

"No. It's not that I can't. I'm exhausted. But I'm afraid to sleep."

"Afraid?"

"I can't bear the moment when I'll first wake up and I won't remember this is true. And then it will be. I'll have to feel it all over again. I don't think I could survive it. Again."

Anna knew better than to try to talk Ellen into sleeping. But she also knew that tomorrow Ellen would have to make funeral plans, decide whether or not to talk to the press, and face her first full day without James.

"Would you like to try to just rest in here? On the sofa? I'll stay with you if you'd like."

Ellen agreed to that and went to gather her pillow and quilt. I'll just rest some, she thought. I won't really fall asleep.

But when Anna dimmed the light, Ellen relaxed back into the pillow, with the quilt covering her up to her chin. She felt herself falling into the blackness of sleep, and even though she wanted to pull herself out of it, she didn't have the strength to fight her way back to wakefulness.

Anna dozed, too, on the love seat, and when the sun poured through the windows, she woke up quickly, hoping to be the first awake so she would be there when Ellen woke up. Too late, she discovered. The sofa was empty and the quilt had been kicked to the floor. Anna jumped up and in the kitchen found the coffeepot nearly full. Looking into the backyard, she saw Ellen standing in the back by the raspberry bushes, holding a steaming mug of coffee up to warm her face.

"I'm sorry. I meant to wake up first," Anna called to her as she walked out. Ellen turned and tried to smile.

"It's okay. I wanted to let you sleep. You must've been exhausted, too."

"Was it hard to wake up?"

"No. I kept dreaming it all night. So waking up was the same as dreaming. I know he's gone, even in my sleep."

Ellen felt dried out. She was surprised she didn't cry all the time, but she didn't. She couldn't even feel the tears right behind her eyes or the hardness that had been in her throat for days. They weren't anywhere. Aimlessly, she picked at the berry bushes while she sipped her coffee. She could see James out here, as a toddler, picking and eating the berries right off the bush. She knew she even had a picture of it in her photo album somewhere on the shelves under the stairs. His fat little face, speckled with berry stains, laughing and so proud of himself for finding this treat. I should find that picture, she started to think, and then stopped the thought. Good God, I will never be able to look at those pictures again.

Turning to Anna, she said, "Guess I have to think about a funeral now."

"We'll help, you know. And Tim. And your parents."

"I know." As Ellen spoke she rubbed her forehead. "But do you want to know what I was trying to figure out when you first came out here?"

"What?"

"This'll sound so stupid. But what do I wear?"

"Huh?"

"No, really, I don't have funeral clothes. I have a cocktail dress or really casual stuff."

"It doesn't have to be black. Any dark color will do."

"But it's summer. I don't have summer 'business' clothes."

"We'll find you something."

As if she hadn't heard Anna, she continued, "Now, if I was a Kennedy, I'd have clothes."

"What?"

"C'mon. You've seen them. The Kennedys have great funeral clothes," Ellen said, and then, staring at the bushes, the raspberries all began to blur and she felt the tears come. Funeral clothes, she thought, and shook her head. Funeral clothes. And she let the tears pour down.

When Ellen and Tim walked into her house after meeting with the funeral director, she was startled but pleased to hear Daniel laughing from the kitchen. Then she heard the familiar low chuckle of her big brother, and she ran to him with relief.

"Oh, Jack," she said as he embraced her, "thanks for being here."

His voice was gruff with emotion as he answered, "Oh, Melon, I am so sorry."

"I know. Thanks. Where's Liz?"

"At the hotel with Mom. They'll be here soon."

Ellen knew her brother and his wife had been on a sailing vacation; she'd wondered if they'd be able to be notified in time for James' funeral, and then she'd worried about cutting short their trip.

"Sorry about your trip," she said, her voice partly muffled by his shirt.

"Oh God, don't even think about it."

"Did you bring the kids?"

"No. Liz's mom came to stay with them."

She pulled away then and asked if he wanted something to drink. Only gradually did she become aware that Tim must still be standing in the living room.

"Tim," she called, "c'mon back if you want."

"Hi, Jack," he said as he held out his hand to greet his former brother-in-law.

"I'm really sorry, Tim," her brother said quietly.

As Ellen emptied ice trays it occurred to her that this was the first time since the divorce that Jack and Tim had seen each other or even spoken. How strange, she thought. She knew at any other time Jack would have wanted to lay into Tim and try to take him out for hurting his little sister, but given the circumstances he could only express condolences.

"Ellen," Tim said, "I think I'm going to leave now. Are you sure you want to take care of getting things back to the funeral home before the visitation tomorrow?"

Ellen nodded, her back to him, as she filled the glasses with iced tea.

"Because I can do it if—"

"No," she said just a bit too loudly. "I've got to buy something else anyway."

Tim looked at her for a long moment before he answered, "Ellen. You don't have to buy those."

"Yes, I do."

Jack looked at them both, trying to decipher the meaning behind their words. "Anything I can help with?" he asked.

"No," Ellen said, "just something I have to take care of. Tim, thanks for going with me today. We'll see you at the visitation."

Ellen and her brother waited until Tim had left before walking out to the screened porch with their tea.

"Melon," he said, using the nickname he'd bestowed on her before she was even born, "what do you need me to do?"

Ellen took a deep breath and looked out at the backyard before answering.

"Well, first, don't tell me I'm crazy, and, second, don't tell Mom what I need to go shopping for."

"Okay," he said, "but can you fill me in a little?"

"Sure. I need to go buy James some new shoes. Before the funeral."

"Don't you mean Daniel?"

"No. He's got shoes."

Jack took a long drink of iced tea and pondered how best to respond. Ellen looked at him and waited for his arguments. When none came quickly, she said, "I don't mean you have to come shopping. I'll get Liz or Anna to go with me; I just don't want Mom to know because she'll think I've lost it."

"Ellen," Jack said slowly, "why are you buying shoes for James?"

"Because I have to."

With that, Ellen got up and walked back into the house, leaving Jack on the porch. As she neared James' room, she realized she was holding her breath, and she caught herself too late to keep from knocking on his closed bedroom door.

Daniel poked his head out of his room when he heard the knock and said, "Mom? Are you okay?"

Flustered, Ellen nodded and reached for the doorknob.

"I closed his door when I got up this morning," Daniel explained. "Was that okay?"

Ellen reached for him then and pulled him close. He held on reluctantly, then clung tightly. "Of course it's okay, babe. I was just, oh, preoccupied I guess. He never did close his door, though, did he?"

Oh God, Ellen thought, are we already reminiscing about him? Can he be that much in the past already?

"Do you want me to get his clothes?" Daniel asked. "I overheard you and Dad talking. I know you need to pick some out."

Ellen shook her head, but then she saw a shadow of disappointment in his eyes and asked, "Want to help me?"

"Sure."

Quietly, they edged toward James' dresser.

"What do we need?" Daniel asked as he opened the top drawer.

"Are you sure you want to help with this, honey?"

He nodded yes, but she could see doubt cloud his eyes.

"Well, if you change your mind, it's okay with me."

"So, we just have to get his clothes, right? Like, good clothes, I'm guessing."

"I was thinking khakis and a golf shirt; maybe that red-striped one he liked."

"Okay," Daniel agreed. "Does he need boxers? Or socks?"

"I don't know. Let's take some just in case."

They gathered up the clothing and then Daniel stopped mid-movement as if he'd just thought of something. "I'll be right back," he said and hurried out to his room. Within seconds he had returned, holding out a light gray Abercrombie & Fitch T-shirt of his own. "James always tried to sneak this on under a shirt," he explained. "He kept asking me to trade it to him. I never would. I think he should wear it under the golf shirt."

Ellen gulped, then nodded as she took the shirt from Daniel's hands. He held it a moment longer, then released it. She wanted to pull him close, but he had already turned to leave.

Ellen backed the car out of the driveway, the bag of James' clothes on the floor between her and her sister-in-law.

"I need to stop at the mall real quick."

"I know," Liz said. "Jack told me."

They drove quietly, and it wasn't until Ellen pulled into a parking space that she asked, "Do you think I'm nuts?"

"No," Liz said. "I think you need to do whatever you have to do."

"Thanks."

As they wended their way through the parked cars to the mall entrance, Ellen said, "You know, I'm amazed that I can function. That I can carry on a conversation. That I can breathe."

"I don't know how you are doing any of those things."

"I just always thought when something like this happened that you'd become a total vegetable. Weep and wail. Be inconsolable."

"It's okay that you're not."

"Is it? I mean, that's how I feel inside. So how come that's not how I am on the outside?"

"Maybe you're numb. Maybe you know you have things you have to do now."

"I don't know."

"You know, El, I worry about you after this."

"What more can possibly happen? There is no 'after.' There's just a big hole in my life."

"No, I mean after the funeral. After we all go home."

Ellen nodded her agreement. That's when I get to be a zombie, she thought. That's when I get to sit and stare and become catatonic. All she said, though, was "Here's the store."

She headed straight to the wall of shoes, searching for the pair James had wanted, the pair she'd deemed too expensive. A clerk hurried over.

"See anything you like?"

"Three weeks ago I was in here with my son," she began, and then the memories flooded over her. She blindly reached out for a chair. Liz grabbed her from behind and helped her to a nearby bench.

"Do you need me to call someone?" the clerk whispered to Liz, as he looked about nervously.

"No. Just give us a few minutes," Liz said. The clerk hurried to the other side of the store.

"Ellen? Do you see the shoes?"

She nodded limply and pointed, then said, "Those white leather ones with the navy stripe. The Nikes."

Liz reached for the sample shoe. "This one?"

"Size eight."

"Wait here, El. I'll get them."

Don't fall apart here, Ellen told herself. Hold it in. You've still got the whole length of the mall to maneuver through. She saw Liz at the cash register, then watched her sign the charge receipt and grab the bag the clerk held out. Stand up, Ellen thought, and walk toward the door.

Liz met her halfway, hugged her, and said, "Don't ever think that you're not feeling this loss enough. Don't ever worry about people misunderstanding what you do."

"Are you sure you want to do all that, Ellen?" her father asked. "It doesn't make any sense."

"It makes sense to me."

"It's not that we have a preference which you do—burial or cremation—it's just, why do both?"

"Look, Dad, it's what Tim and I decided."

Ellen couldn't bear the thought of burial; couldn't imagine sealing James up and having him entombed in perpetual darkness and dirt. Cremation, to her, seemed more light-filled and, while just as permanent, at least less heavy. She knew trying to explain this to anyone was pointless, and she resented any implication that she should need to try.

At the same time, although she didn't want a burial, she wanted a visitation with an open casket. She needed to see James one more time, and she believed Daniel needed it, too. At the funeral, however, the casket would be closed.

"Ellen," her mother began, "think of the cost. Why pay for embalming and a casket when you are going to cremate anyway?"

Good thing they don't know about the new shoes, she thought, then said, "Look. The decision has been made. So there's no need to discuss it."

"Tim mentioned he wanted to bury the ashes," Jack said.

"Yes. That's what he wants to do."

"Is that something you want us here for?" her mother asked.

"Really doesn't matter to me," Ellen answered, feeling more and more as if this conversation was turning into an intervention.

"We just want to do whatever'll be most helpful to you," her mom said.

"Thanks. Great. The most helpful thing will be to end this conversation now."

"But, El, you might want us at the cemetery," Liz suggested.

"Why? I won't be there."

All four of them looked at one another and then at Ellen as if trying to decide who among them should ask the next question. Ellen spoke before any of them had a chance to do so.

"Listen. I can't stand the idea of burial, whether it's a casket or an urn full of ashes. This is James we're talking about, not some vague entity. I don't care about the cost. It's the last time I'll get to spend money on him." She stopped for a moment to catch her breath. "Tim and I are dividing up his ashes," she said, ignoring the raised-eyebrow glance her mother gave to Liz. "Tim is going to bury his half. I won't be present for that. That's for Tim and his dad. That's what they need."

"Honey?" her dad asked.

"My half," she began, "my half'll be tucked away in the back of my closet or someplace like that until I know how to part with them." Ellen ignored the tears that had begun streaming down her face and added, "I couldn't care less about the expense or the lack of reason in any of this. Nothing adds up right anyway. There's no way to tally an accurate or fair amount." She wiped her cheeks with the back of her hand and then whispered, "Oh, yeah, you might as well know, I also bought new shoes for James today."

Ellen's father backed out of the driveway with Ellen sitting stiffly in the front seat. She stared at the house as it seemed to recede, but she knew she was the one moving slowly away. She heard Daniel giving his grandpa directions to the funeral home. She knew from there a limousine would take them to the church.

I really don't think I can do this, she thought. The big maple tree in her yard blocked her view of the front door—she was now turned in the front seat looking back at her house. She didn't want to let go of it with her eyes. These streets of old trees and established houses had always seemed so friendly to her. So benign.

Her mother reached up and patted her back. Ellen flinched. Don't touch me, she wanted to yell. Leave me alone. Her mother's touch, while well-meaning, felt like such an intrusion into her grief. Her nerve endings were too raw. But Ellen also knew that she was doing the same thing to Daniel. This desire to touch, to hold, to comfort, it's what mothers do, she thought. Maybe it's an attempt to return your child to infancy or at least young childhood—where everything can be fixed by a kiss or a cuddle. She pictured a long chain of mothers, through the ages, reaching out to their children with a touch, and the children pulling away, almost like those accordion paper dolls little girls make. It's pointless, she thought. We want to hold and comfort, but we can't do that when it really counts. All we do is irritate.

~~~~~~~

They were now at the funeral home and she saw Daniel's eyes fix on the sleek, black limousine parked across the driveway from them. The width of that driveway from her car seemed unnavigable. She stared at it and couldn't even fathom cross-ing that gulf of blackness. Her father helped Daniel out of the car and then came around to open the doors for her mother and for Ellen. Out of the corner of her eye she saw her father stumble slightly as he reached for her door. It occurred to her that this must be the hardest thing he had ever done— escort his daughter to her son's funeral—but she couldn't think about his grief, couldn't take that on. Her car door opened, and she sat dumbly, thinking, I need to turn and put my feet down on the pavement. I need to push myself off the seat and out of the car. I can brace myself on the door frame. Then I need to straighten up, put one foot in front of the other, and propel myself over to the limo. I've gotten out of cars millions of times before, never ever thinking about it. Her father leaned in and offered his hand. She looked at him and shook her head.

"Come on, Ellen. Let me help you out."

"Not just yet, Dad."

He waited, and she heard other cars pull up. She looked across to the limo and saw Daniel talking to his grandmother. I've got to get to him, she thought, and pulled herself out of the car.

Settling in to the deep, soft seats of the limo, she looked out the smoked-glass window. She saw Daniel eyeing the TV set and stereo behind the driver's seat. She knew he wanted to try them out.

"Go ahead," she said to him softly.

"Really?"

She nodded absently and turned her gaze back out the

window. She heard the audio switch as he flipped through channels, saw her mother frown briefly at her father, and knew that watching TV in a funeral limousine would not be deemed acceptable by any etiquette maven.

When they arrived at the church, Ellen reminded herself that she knew how to get out of a car. She didn't want to repeat her performance from the funeral home. Irene, her minister, was waiting for her out front. They were escorted to a small room off the main hall—they would then walk into the sanctuary together right before the service began.

When Irene came to the room for them a few minutes later, Ellen reached out for Daniel's hand, and they began walking into the sanctuary. One foot in front of the other, she told herself, but as she glimpsed the small casket on the stand at the altar, surrounded by flowers and pictures, Ellen reminded herself of something even more basic. Inhale. Exhale. Inhale. Exhale.

Weeks later, Ellen would try to remember those first days after James' death and the funeral preparations. All that she could recall were fragments or bits of images.

Anna had found her a simple, short-sleeved navy coat dress. Ellen doubted she'd ever wear it again.

Three other images stuck out like magazine covers in her mind. One was of James' classmates at his visitation. Their stunned and drawn faces had echoed around the funeral home. She'd wanted to apologize to them for making them face the adult world much too soon. While the boys, with their awkward hugs, tried to hold back tears, and the girls, with grief and tears so raw and fresh, made their way around the funeral home, Ellen felt the love they'd had for James. Many of them, prompted by their parents she was sure, promised to come and visit her, and while a part of her hoped to see them, another part of her brain was screaming, no, don't, because then I'll catch glimpses of how James would've been growing up with you.

The second image was of the press, waiting outside the church after the funeral service. She'd chosen not to speak to them, although Tim had made a brief comment that had been aired over and over. She'd often been bothered with how the news media approached and intruded upon a family after a tragedy. Now, being on the receiving end, she was surprised at the lack of anger and invasion she felt. It wasn't that she viewed them benignly; rather she thought how pathetic they were—waiting around for a chance to thrust a microphone in her face and scream an inane question her way. What she was truly tempted to do was turn toward one of those oversized fuzzy microphones, held out by some blond woman with perfect hair and piled-on makeup, and give the honest answer: *I feel dead. I want to curl up and die. I want him back. I don't care about God's will. I didn't have enough time.*

The final image, and the one that still caused her to feel blood rushing behind her eyes and taste bile in her mouth, was the memory of all the people who in expressing condolences also suggested how donating James' organs must give her great comfort. Bullshit, she wanted to scream. There was no comfort in that. Nearly everyone who had passed her and given her a hug had commented on how generous she'd been and how at least James' heart, liver, and kidneys were still working. Some even went so far as to add that this kept a small part of him alive. She knew they were earnestly trying to give her comfort, but she wanted not only to curse at them but to claw their eyes out as well. I don't give a damn about his heart still beating, she thought, unless it is still attached to his brain. Screw it, she thought. Why should I have spared someone else my agony?

She knew it was selfish to think this, but she couldn't feel any other way. And she also knew that these thoughts were the real reason she avoided the press. She couldn't pretend to be like the calm, grieving, noble parents she had seen on the news following some other horrible accident and donation. I can't fake it, she thought, and I can't bear to let the world see how truly selfish and hateful I feel.

Chapter
Seven

When school started, three weeks after James' death, Ellen felt a sense of relief. For once she loved the bells ringing, which were now proof to her of time passing. Previously, the bells marking the beginning of a class period too often seemed like the starter's gun of a race—and of a race she was always doomed to lose. There was never enough time to finish the class discussion she was leading, never enough time to work with students individually, never enough time to eat lunch. But now the bells were tangible proof that time moved onward, and that same movement of time propelled her forward, like a boat on a wave, away from the nightmare of August.

Once the first week was over—days of awkward hugs from teachers and overheard whispered conversations between students—Ellen's "celebrity" status faded and she was able to get on with the teaching of English. She found comfort in the routines of the school year: assigning seats and lockers, being strict and no-nonsense for the first few weeks, bitching with her colleagues about administrators who seemed to have no real-world connection to a classroom. Even her lessons, especially at the start of the year, had a perpetual sameness to them. Only now she found that her attempts to bring literature to life for her students too often struck a nerve in her she'd never before had reason to know was there.

With her ninth-graders, she always started with a unit detailing the elements of fiction: how all the pieces—plot, conflict, character, et cetera—are necessary to make a story whole. In previous years, she'd developed almost a spiel about this, showing an old TV show to find the elements there and discussing the summer's blockbuster movie to chart out the action. That had always been the most delicate part: drawing the diagram for rising action (as the tension and the excitement build), peaking at the climax, and finally, the falling action. Over the years she had cultivated a very sober demeanor to discuss this as well as the ability to ignore the embarrassed and knowing looks of the kids as they glanced around the room, whispering that it sounded just like sex. It had been inevitable that when she defined *climax* (the moment of highest excitement when the tension has built up and needs to be released), a few boys would put their heads down and pretend to have coughing fits. She knew that they didn't think she understood the innuendo, and she wanted to keep it that way. This year, however, she skated right through this lecture, but when she got to the idea of conflict, and how necessary it is to plot, she stumbled. Years ago, she had begun using the example of heart monitors to show conflict. They would talk about what a normal one looks like—regular, evenly spaced spikes.

Then she'd ask, "How interesting is that?"

Not very, they'd all agree.

"But," she'd ask, as she drew big, dramatic spikes at erratic intervals, "how interesting is this?"

"That's an exciting one," a student would invariably answer.

"Right. And that's what you need to make a story exciting."

And then, for fun, she'd show a totally flat line. "What kind of story is this?" she'd ask.

"Dead."

And they'd go on from there. Throughout the year, when they would discuss literature, someone would always bring up the "heart line" of a story.

This year, however, she knew all too well the drama of a flat line.

She also found that many of the stories and poems she taught would now be difficult for her since so many of them involved grief, and loss, and death. She hoped that someday her sorrow would have built up enough scar tissue that it would be numb to such reminders, but right now, oozing and open as it was, she found that not only were there certain works she simply could not teach, but her perspective on others had shifted as well. Now, in *Romeo and Juliet,* the lives cut short and the grief of the parents fascinated and horrified her, rather than the rashness of their decisions and the fierceness of their love. In previous years, her students had asked—sometimes teasingly and other times angrily—"Why does everything we read have to be sad?" and "Why do you always teach stuff where people die?"

As she'd told Anna, "I used to so blithely explain that literature deals with the beauty and tragedy of life, and sadness and death are inextricable parts of that. I'd also say that tranquility, at least in literature, is boring."

"Don't you think that's still true, though?" Anna had challenged.

"It is. It's just so hard to teach now. But it's not like I have many options. I can't change the whole curriculum."

"Yeah. You already have to be pretty careful about no sex and no swearing in books."

"True. If I take out death I'll be teaching the Bobbsey Twins."

Still, though, there were many class periods when Ellen had to concentrate most on not thinking or feeling, but on simply reading from the lecture and discussion notes she'd written before she personally knew what tragedy felt like.

On the last Saturday in September, Ellen looked out the kitchen window while she sipped her coffee and announced to the quiet, empty room, "Today we rake leaves." As much as she loved gardening, Ellen's abhorrence for all other yard work had grown steadily stronger in Tim's absence. She used to joke that the only time she still got mad at his leaving was when she was cutting the grass. But sunny fall weekend days could be scarce, and raking wet, rotting leaves was far worse than dry, crisp ones.

Rooting through the jumble of tools in the dark, narrow garage, Ellen finally found caked, muddy yard gloves and a rake. "This damn garage," she muttered after bumping into the side mirror of her car. "How was this ever thought of as even one-car-sized?" She hurried to get out before spying any spiders. Moments like these made her reconsider her disdain of those new subdivisions on the far west side of town. What would she give for a house with a full-sized garage, coat closets, and new plumbing? As she headed into the front yard, though, the sun glanced off the stained windows on either side of her chimney. I'm not gonna sell out just for clean new spaces, she thought.

As she began raking, she felt the pull and stretch of her back and shoulder muscles as she gathered the leaves into piles, and she almost found herself enjoying the work. Physical strain feels good, she thought. Then she heard Kevin from next door walking over through the leaves.

"Hey, El, good to see you out working," he greeted her with a smile.

"Well, thanks," she answered. "I figured you'd be calling the authorities on me if I didn't get out here pretty soon."

Kevin laughed and started to help her with the leaves. His yard was always perfectly maintained, and while he always seemed amused by her comments that with a few extra banjos they could film the sequel to *Deliverance* in her backyard, she feared there was an undercurrent of disapproval in his good humor.

They raked together companionably until their work was interrupted by Meg, Kevin's wife, walking over with an offering of muffins.

"Thanks, Meg. These look great," Ellen said with a smile.

"Just out of the oven," Meg responded. "Why isn't Daniel out here working?"

"Oh, I'm just letting him sleep a little more. He's got soccer in a bit."

"El? You doing okay this morning?" Meg spoke with concern and worry.

Ellen raked as if she hadn't heard, wishing she didn't have to look up. It was James' birthday today. Or it would have been. What was the correct term once the birthday person was dead? Ellen kept focusing on the leaves, raking and reraking the same spot. Meg stood by quietly, waiting and watching.

"El?" she prompted.

Ellen sensed Kevin backing slowly away to a more distant corner of the yard, and she had to smile slightly. Men never wanted to be around a woman in tears, she thought.

Finally, Ellen stopped raking and looked at Meg. Meg's

eyes were moist. She and Kevin had been the ones Ellen had called in the middle of the night when she had gone into labor with James. They had hurried over to stay with Daniel.

"I'm not okay. But I'm not a mess, either. At least not yet."

Ellen resumed her work. Mindless activity, she thought. But at least I can see progress. A clean swath of grass. A pile of leaves. I'm productive in some simple, yet measurable way. Meg picked up the rake Kevin had been using and started piling the leaves at the curb.

"I can't hear his voice anymore. At least not often," Ellen blurted out. "I see him. I feel him. His grin is as sharp as can be. But I'm losing his voice."

Meg didn't answer, which relieved Ellen. What could anyone say to that, anyway?

They continued pulling the leaves into place until the front yard was raked and framed by a neat pile along the curb. The sun felt hot on their backs, and they sat on the front steps surveying their work.

Ellen looked out at the vivid greens and reds and oranges of her yard. Suddenly she turned to Meg and said, "I envy him."

Meg looked startled and said softly, "Oh, El."

"It's true. He's done. He's not in pain. He's not missing anybody. He's just wherever he is. And wherever that is, he knows about it. It is home to him now. I envy that. His peace."

They looked at the piles. A few years ago, the boys would have been leaping around in them, messing up her tidy heaps.

"I yelled too much," Ellen murmured. "Why was I always so impatient, so . . ." Her voice drifted off.

"Oh, Ellen. You were a mom. You're a great mom. That's part of what we do. Yell at 'em. And love 'em."

They watched the late-morning activity pick up in the neighborhood. Several other families were working in their yards, and the rustling crackle of raking leaves was an undercurrent to the day. Minivans full of soccer and football players made their way out of driveways and down the streets, crunching the gravel and leaves as they passed.

"I hate almost everybody these days. Not you or anything. But pretty much every family I don't know."

"Hate them? For what?" Meg probed.

"For having normal, regular humdrum lives. I can't hate your family. Or Anna's. Or, you know, our other friends. But strangers, well, I hate 'em. They're easy to hate. Why me, I wonder. I know, I know, I should ask, *Why not me?* But since it *was* me, I feel like asking, *Why not them?*"

Ellen saw the worry in Meg's eyes and stopped her monologue. Don't lose it, she warned herself. Don't let too much out. It's okay to let people see my grief, she thought. But I don't want them to also see my loss of reason.

"Thanks for helping me rake, Meg. And for the muffins."

"Sure. Hey, you want me to stay around longer?"

"No. Really. And thanks for listening. Sorry I ran on there." Ellen pasted a brave smile on her face. "I need to get Daniel up and moving for his game. Thanks again."

By the end of the first month of school, Ellen had begun to feel that, at least at work, she was no longer holding her breath. She and Daniel were slowly coming to grips with the hole in their family. Setting the table for only two did not always bring her to tears, and she was gratified that in their grief, she and Daniel had not crawled into isolated corners, but had become a very tight unit.

As she told Anna, "It's like we've spun a cocoon around ourselves."

But a cocoon, while snug and warm, is also very dark.

〜〜〜〜〜

The darkness increased and the warmth faded with a phone message she received one rainy afternoon in early October.

"Mrs. Banks? This is Sheriff Downey from the Washington County Sheriff's Department. I, uh, need to inform you that the county prosecutor has determined that no charges will be filed against the Jet Skier, Benjamin Buchanan, who was involved in the Jet Ski accident injuring your son. If you have any questions—"

Ellen hit the replay button before he could finish. No, she thought. This is nuts. Listening to it again, she slammed her hand against the wall when he said "injuring." You stupid, stupid people, she raged silently, *injuring* isn't the right word. Try *killed*. She hit replay again, thinking she must have misheard him. Surely he meant that charges will be filed, she thought. When she'd talked to the police, they had sounded so clear about it, only questioning what the charge would be. Reckless homicide? Vehicular manslaughter? Her child was dead, someone's careless actions had led to his death. No charges? Impossible. When the message played again, she wrote down the phone number, then punched in the buttons on the phone.

"Washington County Sheriff's Office."

"Sheriff Downey, please." Ellen willed her voice to stop shaking.

"Just one minute."

"Downey here," he barked into the phone.

"Sheriff? This is Ellen Banks." She paused for a minute and fought for control. "I received your message." They were both silent. Then Ellen continued, "I don't understand. Why aren't charges being filed?"

"Ma'am, it's out of our hands. We made our recommendation to the county prosecutor. The final call is up to him."

Ellen rubbed her temples for a moment, as if trying to force these words to register in her brain.

"Excuse me. Didn't you recommend that charges be filed?"

The sheriff cleared his throat and coughed before answering. "We're, uh, not really at liberty to say."

"Wait a minute." Ellen paused and knew her voice had taken on the calm, controlled, but scary tone that years ago some students had dubbed her "Clint Eastwood voice." "Wait. This is my son who is dead. How can you not be 'at liberty to say'?"

"Mrs. Banks, since no charges are being filed, the matter is closed." His words were meant to be final and end the conversation, but they only enraged her.

"Closed?" she questioned. "There is no fucking way this is closed. I want to know—did you recommend charges or not?"

"Ma'am. The matter's closed." And he quietly hung up.

Ellen stalked around the kitchen with the phone still in her hand, and it wasn't until the annoying recording came on reminding her that her phone was off the hook that she hit the hang-up button. She slammed the receiver down on the table so hard that the battery clattered out.

"Closed?" she muttered.

And she knew something Sheriff Downey and the prosecutor didn't know. She knew that she had a mother's rage and anguish on her side, which made her strong. She'd held her child as he died. They had no idea what she was capable of and how hard she would fight.

Willing herself to breathe slowly and calmly, she looked at the clock and saw that she needed to pick up Daniel from soccer practice in fifteen minutes. Time enough, she figured, to call Anna.

After fighting to fit the battery back into the phone compartment, she raged into the phone, and barely heard Anna say, "Wait. I have an idea." Only when Anna repeated herself did Ellen pause and take a needed deep breath.

"What?"

"Well, Sam's cousin, Jim, is married to a lawyer. She'll at least have an idea of what might've happened. Let me call them."

"Please. Anna, this can't end here."

"I know. Don't worry. We'll find something out. Hey, what're you and Danny boy doing for dinner?"

"Uh, leftovers, I think."

"Come over. I've got a big pot of spaghetti sauce simmering on the stove. Maybe we'll even get some legal scoop tonight."

"Okay. Say about six?"

"Great."

Ellen dashed to the car to retrieve Daniel, dreading having to tell him about this latest development. It's hard enough for me to process, she thought, but I'm already cynical. He's just a kid—and he's been taught that actions have consequences. But when he hopped in the car after practice, he glanced at her face and knew immediately that something was wrong.

"Mom? What happened?" His eyes burned with worry. Christ, she thought, he's had a speed lesson into adulthood these past few months.

"Danny, I talked to the sheriff today. They aren't sure they are going to press charges against the Jet Skier."

"Well, when will they decide?"

Ah, she thought, there's the problem. They did decide, and I tried to soften the news, but you immediately found the weak spot.

"Honey, a decision has been made, and—" She looked at him as she paused. "—and at this time they're not pressing charges. But I'm going to talk to some attorneys and see what we can do."

Daniel looked out the window then; Ellen glanced sideways at him, and she saw him swallow hard several times, his eyes filling with tears. He made no effort to wipe them away when they spilled over his lower lids and down his cheeks. They drove in silence, and then as she turned off the car's ignition in their driveway, Daniel, still looking straight ahead, asked, "Mom? Will this ever be over?"

"Oh, baby," she said, pulling him to her, "someday. Someday."

Anna and Sam did have news for her that night. When they'd talked to Jody, the lawyer wife of Sam's cousin, she said she'd make some calls. She was a trial lawyer, but strictly covered civil suits, not criminal cases. However, one of her best friends from law school, Bob Hansen, worked in the Madison district attorney's office, and she'd give him a call. She promised to get back to them that evening.

When the phone rang while they cleaned up the kitchen, they expected it to be Jody; instead it was Bob Hansen. Sam quickly handed the phone to Ellen.

"Hello, this is Ellen Banks."

"Hi, Mrs. Banks. My name's Bob Hansen. Jody Waterford's a friend of mine, and she called me about your situation."

"Thanks for calling so quickly, Mr. Hansen."

"Sure. Now, what's your concern?"

"Well, I don't know how much background Jody gave you, but I don't understand how and why the attorneys in Washington County chose not to press charges. When I'd last spoken to the sheriff, he'd said it was a done deal with the only question what the specific charge would be."

"The sheriff didn't tell you why they'd reached the conclusion they did?"

"No. He told me he wasn't 'at liberty to say.'"

"Well, that's just wrong. I'll find out for you."

"Thanks so much."

"What number can I reach you at tomorrow?"

"Well, after three thirty, I'm at 555-3498. And Mr. Hansen?"

"Hmm?"

"I don't just want to know why. I want to know if there is any way I can change the decision."

"Once I know why the decision was made, I'll know how to proceed. I'll call you tomorrow." Hanging up, she felt hopeful. And when she repeated the conversation and watched the strain in Daniel's face ease, she remembered the force that was giving her power.

The next afternoon, the phone was ringing when Ellen unlocked the door. She ran to it, nearly tripping over her dog, Stella, and stepping on the cat who was eager to greet her.

"Hello?" she panted into the phone.

"Mrs. Banks? Bob Hansen here."

"Hi. Thanks for calling back."

"Listen, I have some information, but I'd like to review it with you in person."

"Sure, should I come to your office?"

"Well, at this point, it would be better to meet elsewhere. Could I stop by your home this evening?"

Ellen agreed and gave him directions to her house, then she looked around frantically. This place is a dump, she thought. She'd never been even close to a meticulous housekeeper, and when she was busy or overwhelmed, it became even worse.

Anna had dubbed her the Queen of Clutter; looking around now, Ellen saw once again how aptly the name fit. She went into overdrive as soon as she hung up. He was coming at seven thirty. That gave her a few hours, but dinner needed to be squeezed in, too. She was glad she'd put the ingredients for stew in the Crock-Pot this morning before leaving for school. Okay, she thought, focus on the living areas first. Magazines were tossed out or put into neat, and hopefully attractive, piles. Mail was sorted into junk and bills—she tossed the junk and placed the bills on her desk. The stacks of folded clothes were carried from the dining room table into the bedrooms, dishes put in the dishwasher, and counters and tabletop wiped clean. Glancing at her watch, she figured she had time to vacuum, but not to dust. Once these major jobs were done, she spot-cleaned. Daniel came in at five thirty and shook his head and smiled when he saw her bustling about. Without asking, he knew from experience that his mom cleaned that frantically only when someone was coming over for the first time.

"Getting started on homework, Mom," he called to her as he walked into his immaculate room. He had all the tidiness she lacked. At six thirty she called him to dinner and explained what had happened so far.

"Have you told Dad about this?" Daniel asked as he poured himself some milk.

"Not really," Ellen said, then added, "but I will. Once I know what's really happening."

Ellen didn't want to have to tell Daniel that Tim had already made it clear he had no interest in helping her pursue the case. She'd been stunned when he told her this when she had called to rant about Sheriff Downey.

"We can't let this just stop, Tim," she had pleaded.

"Why, Ellen? What's the point?"

"My God, Tim, that kid killed James. Don't you think he needs to be punished?"

"Look, you do what you need to do. You always have. But count me out. A trial isn't going to change anything for me."

Ellen dreaded having to tell Daniel this. She knew he'd want an explanation, demand a reason. Just like all the times he and James had asked why Mommy and Daddy didn't live together anymore. Her refrain of "Daddy and Mommy weren't making each other happy" had eventually worked, but until it had she had been tempted to add that Daddy thought he'd be happier sleeping with other mommies but Mommy wouldn't buy that.

She wondered what partial truth would suffice now.

A few minutes before seven thirty, the doorbell rang.

"You must be Mr. Hansen," Ellen said while making room for him to come inside.

"Please, call me Bob, Mrs. Banks."

"Okay, Bob, but call me Ellen."

They smiled and Ellen thought, wow, nice, smart, and good-looking. They sat in the living room, and he began right away.

"Here's what I've learned so far. Sheriff Downey did recommend pressing charges to Adam Rifkin, the prosecuting attorney for Bainbridge. Rifkin, though, makes the final decision, and he has decided not to press charges."

"But why? If the sheriff—"

"Lots of reasons. In cases like yours, it isn't clear-cut that criminal charges should be filed. It depends—"

"On what?" Ellen cut in. Bob smiled at her and waited for her to sit back before continuing.

"On whether the prosecutor thinks it's a case he can win. On whether he is friends with the accused. On whether he thinks a public purpose would be served. On whether he thinks criminal intent was involved. See, a careless act is not inherently criminal—even if it does result in an injury or death." He could see this troubled Ellen and went on to explain, "One of the questions has to do with negligence and recklessness. The attorney has to examine what sorts of precedents exist in previous court rulings to classify a careless or negligent act as criminal."

"But this kid killed my son," Ellen pleaded with him.

"I know. And I think it was criminal. I think it should be prosecuted."

"Is there anything I can do?"

"Yes. I can't guarantee it will work, but you can petition the circuit court to overrule this decision and order a criminal trial."

"How do I go about doing that?" she asked as she grabbed a legal pad and a pen.

"You file a request. I'll send you the paperwork tomorrow. Once you've made your plea, the judge will make his ruling. That could take up to six weeks."

"How long before I can address the judge?"

"That could take up to two months. As soon as the request is filed, we have to get it on a judge's docket. And there are certain judges more amenable to this than others."

Ellen put her head in her hands and sighed. "So it's the luck of the draw?"

Bob reached out and patted her arm then. "I wish I could pull some strings, but I can't. There are two judges we want. But even if we don't luck into either one of them, we've still got a good chance. And if the worst happens, we can file an affidavit for a new judge. But it's not time to worry yet. Now, for the paperwork, I'll need the police reports. Do you have those handy?"

Later, Ellen walked him to the door, and he promised to put the paperwork in the mail to her the next day. He would follow up, and she should feel free to call him with any questions or new developments.

"Bob, I don't know how to thank you. I really appreciate your help."

"Hey," he said with a smile, "I didn't go to law school just to be the butt of jokes, you know."

"So you fight for truth, justice, and the American way, too?" she teased.

"Something like that."

Chapter
Eight

"I mailed in the papers today. Bob made sure everything was in order. This could be decided before Christmas!" Ellen said over the phone to Anna.

"That's great. Oh, I'm so glad you got connected to this lawyer."

"It's such a relief to be able to take action. I don't know what I'd have done if I'd been cut off here."

"Is there anything for you to do now?" Anna asked.

"Well, Bob told me he'd help me work on my statement or argument to the judge. I can't believe he's willing to do this."

"Jody said he was a really good guy."

"Cute, too."

"Really? Is he married?"

"Anna, please. I don't know."

"What, you don't even look for rings anymore? You used to be able to spot them a mile away."

"Believe me, when we were joking the other night, it felt really fun. I like to banter. But it seemed too wrong."

"El, you're allowed to flirt, you know."

"I know. And I even laugh sometimes—and some of those times I don't feel disloyal to James. But to meet a potential love interest out of James' death? That's just ghoulish."

"I know. But it sounds so good to hear a sparkle in your voice. I'm glad for you that you can direct your energy forward to a possible trial—and if in doing that you have to spend time with a handsome, single guy, well, that makes it even better."

"You're right. But I don't want anyone thinking I'm forgetting James. Or that I don't still ache for him."

"No one thinks that. Relax. And get some sleep. It's late."

After hanging up, Ellen closed down the house. Her evening routine: get the coffee ready for morning, check the thermostat, let the dog back in, fill the water bowl for the pets, lock the door, check on Daniel who was asleep, and, finally, walk into James' darkened room, sit on his bed, and say her prayers. This was the one time of day she would allow herself to fully feel the ache of missing him. She'd smooth his pillow, tighten his covers, and prop up the stuffed animals the cat had invariably knocked over. Some nights she would almost go into a trance remembering him and would be startled out of her reverie by Stella sniffing her or the furnace kicking on. At these moments, she would feel anew the pain of his loss and be struck by the unreality of it all. If only she could go back to that day, she would catch herself thinking, and call them in, or warn them about not going out too far. How could all this have happened?

The next evening at dinner, when she told Daniel about her efforts to ensure that a trial would take place, he interrupted her and asked, "What're we doing for Christmas?"

"I don't know, babe. I've got a few ideas," Ellen lied. Actually, she'd found herself unable to think about the holidays—Thanksgiving or Christmas—at all. When the ads came on TV, she would walk out of the room or change the channel. And when her mind started to wander into holiday territory, she forced her thoughts to detour neatly around it. Since the divorce, she and Tim had alternated taking the boys on the holidays, and it gnawed at her that Tim had had the boys for what turned out to be James' last Christmas. The years she'd had the boys she always stayed home. Her rule was that any extended family was welcome to come be with them, but she was adamant that the boys wake up in their own beds and that Santa come to their house. Her traditions went beyond just Christmas morning, too. On Christmas Eve they always had lasagna, went to the candlelight service at church, had friends over afterward, and then, after everyone had left, they turned off all the inside lights except for the sparkling, clear white lights on the tree and set out cookies and Coke for Santa and carrots and water for his reindeer. Then by the light of the tree and the flickering firelight, they would read *'Twas the Night Before Christmas* and *The Polar Express* and look at their photo albums of previous Christmases. They all three cherished these traditions so much that even after the boys knew the truth about Santa, they would still set out treats for him, and in the years the boys were with Tim they'd go through these steps the night before they left for his home. But, Ellen thought, *as well as we are functioning without James, I don't think I can bear the rituals this year without him.*

"Ideas? But, Mom, I meant who might come visit us," Daniel said.

"Maybe we should go visit your cousins. What would you think of that?"

"I like how we do it here," Daniel whispered, looking down at his plate.

"Well, then, we'll have Christmas here. Just like always," Ellen said, trying to keep too much emotion from her voice.

"Sorry, Mom. It's just . . ." Daniel groped for words.

"I know, honey. It's just that too much has changed already, hasn't it?"

Daniel nodded when Ellen said this. Oh my, she thought, I haven't really looked at this from your pain. Poor kid. You can't recall a time without your boisterous, pesky brother. I can, although I don't want to. But you, you've lost the sharer of your whole life. She reached across the table and covered his hand with hers.

"Honey pie, we'll make a Christmas just for us."

Knowing that she needed to keep the normal routines for Daniel helped Ellen to feel more normal herself. That and the regular updates from Bob about the case were what propelled her out of bed in the morning. Bob was feeling very optimistic. The request for the trial had been placed on Judge Solari's docket, and Bob assured her that Solari would be sympathetic to her argument. The hearing was scheduled for December fifteenth. Bob had agreed to accompany her to the hearing, but it would be up to her to try to convince the judge that the accident merited charges being filed and a trial date being set. Bob had warned her that she needed to keep gratuitous emotion out of her argument.

"Just persuasively state the facts" was how he kept putting it.

Ellen wrote and rewrote, practicing in the mirror and on the phone to Anna and Meg. She even found herself addressing the steering wheel of the car when she was at stoplights. Be succinct, she reminded herself. Don't bore or irritate the judge. Point out how the community will benefit. I hope Solari remembers what it's like to have your eleven-year-old hug you good night. And how new so much of the world can seem to them. And how sweet and soft their faces look when they first get up in the morning.

As much as Ellen was preparing herself for the Christmas she knew Daniel needed and deserved, she was relieved she would not have to create a Thanksgiving for him as well. He would be with Tim and Tim's dad in Milwaukee. She had planned to spend the day alone—give herself the entire day to wallow in her sadness and missing of James. She'd put on such a good front the past few months. She'd held together for Daniel, and because it wouldn't honor James' memory to have her become a blubbering lump. But still, she planned to give in to the grief on Thanksgiving—pick at the scab of it, so to speak, to maybe strengthen the resulting scar tissue. Anna wouldn't hear of it.

"Don't be an idiot," Anna had pointedly told her. "You're coming over here."

"Anna, I don't feel thankful. I also don't want to drag you down."

"Honey, look, take the morning to grieve. Then take a shower and come over."

"Oh, I don't know. How about if I just come over in the evening, maybe just for pie?"

"Hey, if you're not here to help me cook the turkey, we'll never get to the pie. Besides, I count on you to make the gravy."

"Okay," Ellen said, weakening. "But don't expect me to partake in Sam's annual what-I'm-thankful-for recitation."

"We'll see."

The night before Thanksgiving, Ellen found herself making apple and pecan pies and singing along to the radio. She'd told Anna she'd be over about one and had promised to call at ten to remind her to put the turkey in the oven. "Baste it," she'd kept reminding Anna, "every thirty minutes. Cover it with cheesecloth and baste away."

Thanksgiving morning she watched the Macy's parade as she made cranberry-raspberry sauce and a sweet potato casserole. This might be okay, she thought. It was a glorious fall day—sharp colors, bright blue sky, enough of a chill in the air to feel crisp and to justify wearing her new sweater. Carrying the food to the car, she caught the whiff of logs burning in a fireplace, which mingled with the scent of apple and pecan in her pies. Doing good so far, she complimented herself.

When she got to Anna's, Sam helped her cart in her load of food, and she and Anna sipped wine as they peeled potatoes. Anna's brother and parents would be joining them later.

Finally, with the turkey carved and the food spread out on the buffet table, they filled their plates and went into the dining room. Sam reminded them, "Be ready to share what you've been most thankful for this year."

Ellen smiled bravely. She'd always thought of this as such a lovely tradition. Sam always started, and then they worked their way around the table. But this year, she thought, I can't imagine what I'll say. She tried to catch Anna's glance to let her know she wasn't up to the task, but then worried that not only would she be obvious in her omission, but the omission itself would put a pall on the afternoon for the others. I'll think of something, she told herself, and then tried to position herself near the end of the speaking order. Maybe I'll get an idea from somebody else; steal one of their thankfulnesses. Ellen tried to concentrate on what people were saying, but found instead that all she could think about were her shaking hands and the lump in her throat. Suddenly, she realized everyone was looking at her—it was her turn and she hadn't a clue what to say.

"I'm thankful for," and she paused. Anna reached over and grabbed one of her hands. "I'm thankful for my friends," she began again, "and for Daniel's bright, sweet face every morning." Ellen quickly put her head down, and there was a pause before Anna's brother said he was thankful for his job promotion.

The first few bites of turkey stuck in Ellen's throat, and she thought, oh no, I'm going to break down right here. "Excuse me," she muttered as she pushed back her chair, "I need to check the oven."

Blindly pushing her way through the swinging door, she grabbed the counter and held on as if it were a life raft. The tears streamed down her face and she hiccupped her sobs. Anna was there then, leading her to the sofa in the family room.

"I'm sorry. I'm sorry. I don't want to ruin the meal," Ellen said.

"Hush. Go ahead and cry," Anna soothed.

Taking deep breaths, Ellen regained control and said, "I miss him so much it hurts. And it's the little things, you know?"

Anna nodded and kept listening.

"His voice on the phone. I know it sounds silly, but I loved his voice on the phone. It always sounded so, oh, hopeful and expectant. Vulnerable and trusting. I'll never hear it again. And the way he'd smile when he saw me in the car pool line. It was so pure and clear and honest." Ellen stretched and wiped at her eyes. "I should go home."

"No. Stay here with us."

"Let me sit here, then, just for a minute. I need to get composed. But you go back to your family. Please."

"Okay."

After Anna went to rejoin the meal, Ellen thought about James so hard it was as if he were in the room with her. She remembered the relish with which he ate and the jauntiness of his stride. And then, as if James were encouraging her, she walked back to the table, picked up her napkin, and sat down. Everyone else was trying to eat without watching her too closely. She ate some stuffing, and in the quiet she said, "Sorry about running off. Is it okay if I add something?" They all murmured assent, but she saw Anna's parents exchange nervous glances as if to say, *What now?*

"I'm thankful—" She paused and regained composure. "—that God trusted me with James for almost twelve years."

Three weeks later, Ellen strode into Judge Solari's courtroom, trying hard to dispel her nervousness. Bob Hansen was right beside her and directed her to a chair at a table up front. She had her statement typed out, but she knew that she wouldn't need her notes. She had practiced so many times she felt that the words would flow out of her even if she was sleeping.

"All rise. The Honorable Judge Albert Solari presiding. Court is in session."

Ellen peered at the short man buried beneath the folds of his black robe and hidden behind thick glasses. His head was bald save for the thick, tufted eyebrows that jutted out at sharp angles. He's the one Bob wanted? Ellen wondered questioningly.

"Mrs. Banks."

His voice, when he spoke her name, belied his gnome-like appearance. It was rich and low and filled with warmth. I bet he's a wonderful grandpa, she thought. Hope so. She stood and approached the podium in the small, artificially lit room.

"Your Honor. I'm here today to argue that criminal charges be filed against a young man whose actions on a Jet Ski led to the death of my eleven-year-old son. From the copies of the police reports, which I included with my written request, it's clear that the police who were on the scene agree with me. Benjamin Buchanan, who was seventeen at the time of the event, drove his Jet Ski in an area where children were playing and, in so doing, hit my son, James Banks, in the back of the head. Two days later, James was dead." She paused and took a breath. She once again felt as if she were watching herself from afar. "His actions were more than simply careless. They were reckless and negligent. I ask that this egregious behavior, which is a threat to the lake community as a whole, be prosecuted to the fullest extent of the law."

"Mrs. Banks, I understand your concern. But the county prosecutor decided against going forward with the case." Judge Solari spoke calmly, but with warmth.

"I know that, Your Honor, which is why I'm here. I'm asking you to overturn that decision and declare that the trial should proceed."

"Thank you for your time. My ruling will be announced within the next sixty days."

In the hallway, Ellen protested to Bob, "Sixty days? Why so long? Is that a bad sign? Do you think he was sympathetic?"

"Hey," Bob rebuked her, "get a grip. You did great. They always say sixty days. You were clear and precise. You were earnest. That's always good. We'll know when we know."

"So what do I do now?"

Bob glanced at his wristwatch before responding, "You let me buy you lunch."

They walked to a café down the street from the courthouse just off the Capitol Square. It felt so strange for Ellen to be having lunch in a restaurant. In school, lunch was thirty rushed minutes of trying to eat while chatting with teachers and the occasional student who would stop by with a question, checking her mailbox, and hurrying on to her afternoon classes. Sometimes she would even have time to dash into the restroom. She had always thought that no one appreciated lunch in a restaurant more than teachers. Even though the café was packed with lawyers and state workers, Bob maneuvered them to a booth in back, and Ellen began to relax as she peered at the menu.

"What looks good to you?" Bob asked.

"Anything that doesn't get reheated in a microwave," Ellen said with a laugh, thinking about her colleagues back in the faculty room. She felt slightly guilty about taking the whole day off from school, but when she'd arranged for the substitute, she hadn't known how long the hearing would last, and her principal had urged her to take the whole day anyway.

Ellen finally decided on the pasta special and Bob ordered a Caesar salad. This is nice, she thought. It's fun to talk to an intelligent, attractive man. His horn-rimmed glasses made him look as smart as she had found him to be, and she liked his closely cropped dark hair. At brief moments like this, she could almost block out what had transpired in her life. How she had come to know this man. But then it would all come flooding back to her. Oh, James, she thought, what teachers would you have had this year? He'd been so excited about sixth grade—a new school, lockers, a bus ride. And now, well, now he'd be a perpetual fifth-grader, never getting older, never moving on. Like Keats' Grecian Urn, she thought, making note of another work that would be hard to teach. He'll never be a sulky teenager, never wreck her car, never have a first job.

"But you feel good about what went on today?" Ellen finally asked. "With Judge Solari and everything?"

"Like I already told you, we'll know when we know. But he could have initially rejected it from the papers you filed. That he didn't shows he thought there might be merit to your claim. So at least you made it over that hurdle."

They chatted well past the crunch of the lunch hour and were still lingering over coffee when Ellen looked at her watch and exclaimed, "Oh my gosh! It's past three. I was supposed to pick Daniel up from school." She snatched up her things, thanked Bob for the lunch, and hurried out. But not before Bob invited her to dinner on Friday night.

Daniel was waiting for her in front of school. She was only ten minutes late.

"How was school, babe? Sorry I'm late."

"Pretty good. I've just got a little history homework. So, I was wondering—" He paused to gauge her mood. "Can we get a tree today?"

"Good idea," Ellen tried to respond lightly before she switched lanes to head out to the tree lot. She so wanted Daniel to experience a good Christmas. Even though she didn't feel the spirit, she was determined he not lose yet another piece of his childhood. Wandering around the tree lot, she let Daniel lead the way. She shrugged and nodded at every tree he held out for her approval.

"Fine, great," she'd respond when his eyebrows arched up at her in question. After she paid for their selection, Daniel directed the man carrying the tree for them to the car and they tied it on the top.

"Don't drive too fast and avoid railroad crossings if you can," the man reminded them, and he waved and hollered "Merry Christmas!" when they drove away.

The whole way home, Ellen kept checking the rearview mirror, fully expecting to see the tree topple off the car, while

Daniel chattered about getting it set up. He offered to string the lights since she'd always struggled with that, and he told her he'd take care of the tree when they got home, she needn't worry.

He's so brave, she thought. He's holding on to the traditions so hard. She smiled at him then, and said, "You got it, kid. I'll make supper, and then we'll put on the ornaments." She didn't want to think about opening up the ornament box stored in a corner of the attic. All the Styrofoam stars with glitter glued on. The felt cutouts. The cookie-dough bells and angels. Ellen had painstakingly written names and dates on the backs of every ornament the boys had ever made. Every year they'd been able to choose one or two new ones that she would also write names and dates on. She'd told them that these would be theirs when they first had trees in their own homes. What would be the price of opening that box?

As Daniel fumbled with the tree stand, Ellen went through the mail. Bills, a few Christmas cards, nothing that really caught her eye until she saw the return address of the Great Lakes Regional Transplant Center in bold green type. Her hands shook. What now, she wondered. In the first few days after James' death, she had fended off reporters who wanted to talk to her not only about the accident but also about the generosity of the decision to donate James' organs. I just can't talk to them, she'd told herself and others at the time. I don't feel warm and fuzzy about it. I feel cold and angry and empty. She knew that at some point the families of those who had benefited from his organs might write to her, through the center, but she had not wanted to imagine those letters and those families. She didn't want to know their stories. She had even told Laurie once, when Laurie had called to check up on her, "I can't fake it. I don't feel better about anything. I feel like they want to parade me around as noble and giving. I'm not. I'm mad and I'm angry and I'm jealous that their children are still alive."

"I know," Laurie had murmured softly. "They don't really expect that of you, you know. They just want to express their gratitude. That's all."

"I still can't. I don't care if I appear selfish. But they don't want me as a spokesperson, I can promise you that." Ellen had felt her eyes flash with anger when she said this. "And you want to know why? The horrible truth? I couldn't honestly tell anyone to make the same choice I'd made. It didn't make me feel any better."

"But what about the lives James touched, even in death?"

"Don't turn into one of them," Ellen had pleaded. "I don't care. I lost a child. I'm not gracious enough to be glad other families didn't have that same grief. I'm just not that good of a person."

Ellen viciously ripped open the envelope from the transplant center, and several smaller envelopes scattered out. She tore open the first one and saw it was a Christmas card and thank-you note from the family whose child had received James' liver. Her eyes filled and she ran to the bathroom. She held a washcloth under the cold-water faucet until it was soaked, then she leaned her head over the sink and held the cloth up to her face. She sobbed into it and soon the cloth was warm with her tears. She let it drop, then she picked up the remaining cards and methodically ripped them into little pieces, the ink running across the paper from her wet hands. She stuffed all the scraps into the wastebasket and tamped them down with her fist. She stripped off all her clothes and wrapped herself in her warm, red velour robe hanging on the back of the door, stumbled to her room, and crawled into bed, pulling the down comforter up to her chin. She sobbed into the pillow and finally slept.

Hours later, she was awakened by soft, muffled music. She had no idea how long she'd slept and had to shake her head to get her bearings. Nighttime, she thought. Oh God, I forgot dinner. She padded through the dimness, into the hall and toward the music coming from the back of the house. It wasn't completely dark, but she couldn't identify where the light originated from. Not a lamp, she knew, but what? As she peered through the kitchen and into the family room, she gasped. The Christmas tree. Oh my God, she remembered. It stood, majestically, in the corner. The lights had been painstakingly applied so no cords were visible. The ornaments covered the branches, twinkling in the warm glow of the lights. Even the tree skirt, draped around its base, was perfectly placed. And on the floor, his face hidden in shadows, lay Daniel, sound asleep under his comforter, with the dog and cat under his arm, lulled to sleep by the Christmas carols emanating from the stereo. You dear, dear child, she thought. She went to him and softly kissed his cheek; he stirred and reached up with gangly arms to hug her.

"Like it?" he mumbled.

"Oh, honey, it's perfect." Music played in the background, and she thought of the words from the Christmas story: "Unto us a Son is given." And she felt the complete truth of that passage: given, yes, but ultimately taken away, too.

When she started to help him up to go to his bed, he struggled against her and said, "I want to sleep here."

So, quietly, Ellen went and collected her own pillow and quilt and stretched out on the floor next to him. She put her arms around him and held him close as she drifted off to sleep.

~~~~~~~

The next day she told Anna what had happened.

"I feel so guilty, you know? I think I'm doing so well and then *wham*, I crawl off and leave him to put up the tree."

"Look, you don't have to always be so hard on yourself."

They sipped tea in the late afternoon, lost in their thoughts.

"If it wasn't for Daniel . . ." Ellen's voice faded off.

"Hmm?"

"He's the one who keeps pulling me back. He keeps me from getting too close to that edge."

"El? Does he know that?"

"Huh? I don't know. I'd guess not, but, well, I've never thought of that."

"I mean, that's a lot to put on a kid. Maybe you should talk to Irene, or a counselor or something."

"Well, I talk to Irene often. But I'm not one for group grieving."

"I didn't mean a group. It's just that you're so, I don't know. You're so spent."

"Well, grief is tiring. And anger, that's even worse. Anger is exhausting."

"Can you let any of it go? Seems to me that holding in all that rage is what's the most dangerous. And damaging."

Ellen slowly shook her head. "It's not even James' death that I rage about. It's dumb stuff. Nonproductive stuff."

"Like what?"

"I'm mad about the divorce all over again. I mean, Tim can still have more kids. I can't. And I know—" Ellen held up her hand to ward off Anna's unspoken argument. "—I know another baby is not going to replace James. But I don't even have that option. I'm still mad at Tim for that. He called the other night to talk to Daniel, and I was suddenly so mad I could barely speak to him. He thinks it's because he wants no part of the trial."

"Is that part of it?" Anna asked.

"I almost wish it was because that would make more sense. But it's the holidays I missed with the boys and can never get back. Stupid stuff, I know."

"Not stupid, hon, but like you said, there's nowhere to go with the anger."

"At least if Judge Solari rules in my favor, I can focus anger there. I can direct my fury at Benjamin Buchanan—and at making sure he's called up to pay for his recklessness."

Chapter
Nine

Ellen felt so strange getting ready to go out to dinner with Bob. She liked him. He was funny and handsome and smart. Anna had done some investigating through Jody and found out that Bob had gotten married right after law school. His wife was a doctor. They'd divorced four or five years later. No kids. Apparently, according to Jody, the issue of kids had been one of the major factors in their divorce—Bob wanted them, his wife didn't.

Ellen's dating history since her divorce had been amusing and laughable—at least to her friends. And with time, even Ellen laughed about it.

As Anna pointed out, Ellen always seemed to choose men who were unable to commit, and she also tended to be attracted to men who needed to heal in some way. Even Tim fit the prototype perfectly. Even though Ellen saw this pattern herself, she kept falling into it. Anna's mantra to Ellen had become, "Find one who's already fixed."

The most humorous part of Ellen's dating life, however, was in her role as pre-fiancée to the world. Every man she'd dated—even if the date consisted only of one dinner—wound up marrying the next woman he went out with. Anna and Ellen had once charted it all out; they'd wondered if perhaps there was some way to market Ellen's knack of helping men find the right woman. Who, coincidentally, was never Ellen. She had joked that her advertising slogan could be, *Want to get married, but not just yet? Take me to dinner, then you'll meet the woman of your dreams.*

Fortunately for Ellen, her life was full of family and friends and work. But sometimes her bed seemed too big for just one person. And sometimes she wished for a welcome-home hug and kiss from an adult.

The doorbell rang, and Ellen glanced at the clock in a panic. Oh God, she thought, that can't be Bob already. Daniel ran to answer the bell as Ellen rushed to close the bathroom door. Can I hide out in here? A quick look in the mirror reminded her of all the preparations she still had to do. Frantically she grabbed the styling mousse; when she heard Anna's laughing response to some comment of Daniel's she knew she didn't have to go into hyperdrive.

"You scared me to death," Ellen said, opening the door to talk to Anna.

"Oh, a little nervous about our big date, are we?" Anna teased.

"No," Ellen answered too quickly.

"I just stopped by to see if you needed anything."

"And to snoop a little bit?"

"Maybe. Here, let me help you dry your hair." Anna reached for the styling brush and the blow dryer.

"You don't have to do this, you know."

"I know. But it's kind of fun. I mean, I get to date vicariously through you."

"Most dating sucks."

"Okay, most of it might. But not all of it. Not all the time."
Anna was quiet as she finished styling Ellen's hair. Then she
added, "Maybe this guy could be your Atticus Finch."

Ellen didn't respond right away. Partly because she was
startled to have Anna give voice to what Ellen had been
thinking. Anna used to tease that part of Ellen's problem with
finding the right guy was that she was looking for a fictional
hero. And not just any fictional hero—Atticus. With his sense
of honor, his belief in justice, and his quiet wisdom and love
for his children, Atticus Finch had been her dream man ever
since Ellen was a teenager, even before she'd known to picture him as a young Gregory Peck.

Finally, Ellen murmured in response, "Well, he is an attorney. And he seems like a really nice guy."

"Have fun, sweetie. Now I'll scoot out of here and let you
finish."

Daniel wandered in again as Anna was leaving. He would be
spending the night at his friend Joey's house, and he was curious about Ellen's plans. Ellen had made it a point over the
years not to make a big deal out of her dates. She never introduced men to the boys until she felt confident they'd be
dating for a while, and she usually tried to play down the importance of any dates she did have. She had stressed to Daniel
that this dinner with Bob was not a big deal. She'd convinced
him quite handily. She had less success convincing herself.

Bob was taking her to a small French restaurant right on
the Capitol Square. It was one of the nicest places in Madison.
Small and intimate, with exquisitely prepared food, it had
been featured in *Bon Appétit*. Ellen wondered how Bob had
managed to get a reservation on a Friday night with such short
notice.

So the question now was, what to wear? Ellen settled on a stretchy black velvet dress with long sleeves, a scoop neck, and a long, easy skirt. It was as comfortable as sweats, but looked classy. When Ellen checked herself in the mirror, she wished she had more cleavage. Then, turning to check her appearance from another angle, she amended her thought. Wish I had any cleavage.

The doorbell rang, and, hurrying to get it, she called to Daniel, "Don't forget to lock the door when you go to Joey's."

During the drive downtown, Ellen glanced at Bob. He looks nice, she thought. We even sort of match. He was wearing a black-and-cream tweed sport coat, black slacks, and a light blue oxford cloth shirt. Nice tie, too, she mused. And he's a perfect height for me—half a head taller so nobody's neck gets scrunched. Ellen chatted about her day, he laughed where appropriate, and she caught herself relaxing.

Dinner was wonderful. They ordered wine and took their time with their salads and entrées. Bob reminded her somewhat of Sam in his ease with ordering and his sense of how to make a dinner out relaxed and special. Ellen always enjoyed going out to eat with Anna and Sam. They never made her feel like a fifth wheel, and Sam knew just how to order. He took over, not in a domineering or showy way, but with graciousness and warmth. She felt that now with Bob. And, she thought, even Anna would have to agree that he seems "fixed."

While they lingered over coffee and crème brûlée, with the candlelight flickering on the table and the Capitol dome lit majestically outside, Ellen found herself looking at Bob's hands. She always found hands sexy if she was attracted to a man. She couldn't quite define how they should look, but she knew it when she saw it. And now, looking at Bob's fingers encircling his coffee cup, she thought, I like him. I'd like to do this again. When he spoke, she glanced up to reply, and, looking at his mouth, she thought, oh my, I sure could kiss him, too. Afraid she was blushing, or that he'd read her thoughts, she quickly glanced down and brought her napkin up to pat her mouth.

When Bob pulled into her driveway, she heard the dog bark. After thanking him for a lovely evening, she took a deep breath and asked, "Would you like to come in?"

"Sure. I'd love to."

They walked to the door, and Ellen's mind raced. What was I thinking? Is the bathroom clean? What does the kitchen look like? Do I really want to kiss him?

Her thoughts were interrupted by Stella's panting and sniffing.

Ellen shooed the dog aside, led Bob in, and then asked, "What can I get you? Wine? Beer? I also have coffee and soda."

"Coffee would be great, if it's decaf."

Ellen hurried to the kitchen, and while she brewed the coffee, she heard Bob talking to the dog and knew he'd made a friend when she heard Stella's tail thumping hard on the floor. Walking into the living room with the mugs of coffee, she hollered to the dog to leave Bob alone and asked him about cream and sugar.

"I take mine black, thanks. And don't worry about the dog; I love them. Grew up with them."

Bob continued to pet Stella.

"How old is she?"

"Seven. When we got her she couldn't even navigate the stairs. I swear, she wasn't bigger than her head." Ellen laughed, remembering the sweet, squirming golden retriever puppy. "She weighs about seventy-five pounds now."

"Stella. Interesting name." Bob looked at her questioningly while he sipped his coffee.

"Ah, English teacher humor. I get a kick out of standing at the back door bellowing 'Stella' in my best Marlon Brando impersonation."

Bob laughed. I like his laugh, Ellen thought. Nice and deep. And the way his eyes crinkle when he smiles. I like that, too.

They talked about movies and music. Then how each thought the Wisconsin football team would do next year—they had just missed the Rose Bowl again this year. Finally Bob glanced at his watch, yawned, and stood up.

"I better get out of here. I have to go into the office for a few hours tomorrow."

"On Saturday?"

"I have a trial starting Monday."

"Well, thanks again for such a nice evening."

They were at the door now, and Ellen's heart was racing.

Bob looked at her and said, "I had a great time, too."

Oh no, she thought, he's going to shake my hand. Then this was all just business. Or worse, just kiss me on the cheek. That's a sign he'll never call again. The old I-like-you-as-a-friend gesture.

But then, he leaned forward and kissed her lips and it was warm and nice and soft. And there was no mistaking his intent or interest.

Watching Bob back out of the driveway, she could still smell his cologne. What a great guy, she thought. She let Stella out, readied the coffee for morning, and knew that tonight she would sleep well.

~~~~~~

When the morning light first broke through her window, she'd been awake for hours. She had not slept well. Her sleep had been marred by strange bits and pieces of dreams. In one, she was running and could never catch up to where she needed to be. In another she was trying to find the right door to open, but every door just led to another hallway full of more choices.

Drinking coffee and waiting for the paper boy, she absent-mindedly scratched Stella's ears. The dog eased her head onto Ellen's lap, and her tail softly ploinked on the hardwood floor. Why am I such a mess, Ellen thought. I had this lovely night. A really great guy kissed me. So why am I having dreams about failure and panic?

She stared vacantly out the kitchen window, not really seeing anything, and then she thought she heard a cough. When the noise finally roused her from the chair, she headed to the hallway saying softly to herself, "Hope one of the boys isn't sick."

At the instant the words came out of her mouth, she knew. Knew there was only one boy who could be sick. Knew the noise was the cat getting rid of a hairball. Knew what had caused her fitful sleep. She steadied herself by placing one hand on the kitchen wall. "I'm sorry, James," she whispered. "I haven't forgotten."

The ringing of the phone startled her.

"Hello?"

"El? How was dinner?"

It was Anna. Ellen looked at the clock. How many hours had she been sitting at the table? The sun was shining brightly, the coffeepot nearly empty.

"Dinner was nice."

"Oh. That bad, huh?"

"What do you mean? I said it was nice."

"I know. You said it was nice the way I'd say a purple cro-
cheted vest from my aunt Myrtle is nice. What happened?"

"We had a great dinner. We came back here and had some
coffee. He laughed at my jokes. He kissed me good night."

"I don't get it."

"I can't see him again. Outside of legal stuff, that is."

"Why?" Anna asked softly.

"I can't." Ellen was pensive, then added, "Oh God. Maybe
he won't help with the legal stuff anymore."

"What did he do? Why can't you see him?"

"I just can't. That's all."

"El? Talk to me."

"He made me forget about James. For a couple of hours."

"Oh, Ellie. I'm sorry."

"I know."

"But is that maybe okay? I mean, to get a little reprieve
from your pain?"

"No. Not yet."

Sunday evening as Ellen tried to plow through a stack of student essays, Bob called.

"Hi, Ellen. How has the rest of your weekend been?"

Ellen took a deep breath. How do I answer him? Do I tell
him I've been a wreck? That as much as I enjoyed our date I
can't see him again?

"Oh," she said lightly, "pretty low-key."

"I really had fun Friday night," Bob offered.

Oh damn, she thought. He's got such a nice voice. And
she thought again of how his hand at the small of her back
had fit so well.

"Me, too. Thanks again."

"I'd like to see you again."

Ellen responded only with silence, but Bob forged ahead.

"I was wondering if you had any plans for New Year's Eve?"

Stalling for time, Ellen feigned a cough, cleared her throat, and then said, "Well, I'm not sure what Daniel's plans are so I really can't commit to anything yet."

That was a lie. Ellen knew that Daniel would be spending New Year's in Milwaukee with Tim and Tim's father. That was their trade-off since she'd have Daniel for Christmas.

Bob seemed to pick up on her ambivalence and gracefully ended the conversation by saying, "Well, I'll check back with you. Thanks again for such a nice evening on Friday."

Ellen's hands shook as she hung up. Maybe it's just the holidays getting to me, she thought. Every day brings me closer to Christmas, and I'm so scared of it. For myself. For Daniel. But, she thought, leaning her head back onto the sofa, what do I feel for Bob? All weekend, when she wasn't anguishing over having met him due to James' death, she'd catch herself remembering how his mouth felt on hers. And how clean and musky his skin had smelled. And just thinking about that made the muscles in her stomach tighten.

"Mom, I know you don't want to hear this, but—"

"Now, Ellen. Don't be so quick to be negative. Your father and I have given this a great deal of thought . . ."

Ellen put the receiver down on the table and massaged the back of her neck. She could hear her mother's muffled voice. She knew that her mother was listing all the reasons that Ellen and Daniel should come to their house for Christmas this year. Ellen sighed, took a few deep breaths, and brought the phone back to her ear. Sure enough, her mother's spiel was just starting to wind down.

"... I mean, it makes perfect sense."

"Mom. You haven't listened to anything I've said to you. Besides, we already have our tree up."

"Oh, honey. You don't have to be so stubborn. So stoic. Let us help you—why make things harder on yourself?"

Ellen glanced wistfully at the clock. It was only ten in the morning. If her mother was going to broach this subject, in this way, doing it when Ellen had half a pot of coffee in her system wasn't the best timing.

"Ellen? Are you still there?"

"Yes, Mom. I'm here. And I appreciate what you and Dad are trying to do. But you can't fix this. I know you want to. But you can't."

"You're just making it worse for yourselves."

Ellen hated that know-it-all, pursed-lip tone her mother had perfected over the years.

"Worse?" Ellen tried to stem her rising anger. "Worse? How?"

"Well, you're isolating yourselves. You wouldn't come for Thanksgiving—"

Best decision I could've made, Ellen thought.

"You didn't want us there for James' birthday—"

"Well, it wasn't as if we were celebrating, Mom. You didn't miss a party and cake."

"See, El, this is just what your dad and I have worried about. You're getting snippy. Even mean sometimes. We don't want to see you go there."

"Go where, Mother? You act like I'm slipping over to the dark side."

"Don't go there." Her mother's voice shook.

When did she start talking like a nineteen-year-old, Ellen wondered.

"Look, Mom, I already 'went there,' okay? Now I'm trying to claw my way out."

They were both quiet for a few seconds, as if they were each trying to figure out the next maneuver or strategy. Ellen decided to try to pacify.

"Mom, listen, come for a visit in January. It's not that we don't want to see you. But, well, Daniel and I need to get through this together. Just the two of us. Trust me."

"Well, I know what you're trying to do. And I respect that, but—"

"Please. Does there have to be a 'but'?"

Her mother ignored her and forged ahead with what she hoped would be the knockout punch.

"But it didn't work after Tim's affair, did it?"

"Oh God, you're really digging, aren't you?"

"Well, it's something to think about."

"Yes, it is," Ellen muttered.

"We'll talk again soon, honey." Her mother's perky good-bye irritated Ellen more than anything else she'd said. After hanging up, Ellen's mind wandered back to that Christmas her mother had just referred to.

That Christmas morning, Ellen and Tim had been the first ones up. As Ellen made coffee and started rolling out the dough for the coffee cake, Tim went to get the paper. When he returned, she had said quietly, "This is probably our last year for the boys to sleep in."

He looked at her questioningly.

"By next year," she continued, "Daniel will have the scoop on Santa."

Ellen had found herself eager for the morning to begin. She loved the chaos and rush of Christmas morning. The weeks preceding were so hectic and pressured, and she had felt torn between getting the boys everything she saw that they would like and keeping some sense of propriety and control over her spending. She struggled over what to get Tim. They seemed to be finding their way past the affair, and she hoped her trust was not misdirected. She wanted to get him something special to mark her faith in him, but in the end she had not found the perfect gift, so she bought what she knew he wanted: a sweater, a book on the Green Bay Packers, and some new ties. She wondered what he had gotten for her. Had he questioned and considered and agonized over his purchases as she had?

She was anxious for the boys to wake up. She knew that Daniel, at a little over two years old, would be enchanted by the wrappings and gifts. He had been so delighted by the lights. They had let him help with the tree this year and it had been so much fun. He had first approached the tree as if it were Velcro—he thought he could simply fling the ornaments at it and they would stick. Fortunately, they'd given him the nonbreakable ones. His laugh, and baby James' smile as the ornaments tumbled to the floor, had been worth all the fallen needles embedded in the carpet.

It was going to be just their immediate family for most of that day. Ellen's parents had offered to come that year, but Ellen had turned them down. She knew her parents wanted to be there for her, but Ellen did not want to be under the microscope of their eyes as they watched every move and word Tim made, searching out evidence of more fissures in his character. Ellen had believed that she and Tim needed another year of scar tissue to form before they could take the full holiday scrutiny of her father.

Later that night, with the wrappings and turkey bones already in a garbage bag out at the curb, Ellen had sat in the living room giving James his bedtime nursing. Tim had finally gotten Daniel to bed an hour ago and then had gone to bed himself. So Ellen sat with her baby, the only light in the room coming from the electric candles they had placed in each of the windows. She tried to decipher any hidden message in Tim's gifts for her—a coffee grinder, earrings, and a gift certificate for a massage and a facial. They were all things she wanted, but she couldn't shake the sense that they were all impersonal. She sat and looked out into the cold night. The snow was blue in the moonlight, and even where the plows had kicked up slush, the snow still looked clean without the glare of the sun. James was taking his time at her breast, almost as if he was thankful for this uninterrupted time with his mom. Ellen looked into the candlelight and its reflection in the window. She noticed the little area where the warmth of the light had melted the frost on the window. Christmas always made her emotional, and now that she had sons of her own, it also seemed more human to her. It was really the story of a mother and her baby boy. And she knew that that mother had had hopes and dreams for her son. As Ellen had looked at James, she thought, okay, let me have a Christmas miracle here. Let these little shoots of belief and trust and love that are starting to come to life again for my marriage and for Tim, let those shoots grow out of the cold snow and winter that we've been through in our marriage. Please.

Ellen had not gotten that Christmas miracle. It had been less than two months later that she'd come across Tim's American Express bill. And when she had called her parents eventually to tell them that Tim had moved out, her mother's silence had been all the reproach she needed.

Ellen shook her head at the memory. Maybe her mother was right, she thought. But no, she told herself. That bill would've had the same charges on it whether or not her parents had visited that year. She sat at the table a few minutes more. She couldn't shake the sense of her family being chipped away. We're down to half of what we once were. We'll have to hold on even tighter now.

Chapter
Ten

School had been out for three days for winter break, and Ellen and Daniel had been busy. Ever since Ellen had abandoned Daniel to put the tree up by himself, she had forced herself to approach the impending holiday with a different attitude. Yes, it might be an incredibly horrible, painful holiday for her, but Daniel deserved a Christmas. His need for tradition, always strong, had become almost a craving since James had died. Ellen committed herself to creating a Christmas for him.

They had spent the past few days finishing up last-minute gift shopping, baking cookies, and grocery shopping.

Tonight, before the Christmas Eve candlelight service, Anna and Sam and the girls were coming for dinner. After the service, Irene and her family would stop by. Tomorrow, Christmas Day, Ellen and Daniel would have Christmas morning to themselves, but then her neighbors Kevin and Meg would come over for dinner with their children.

Ellen kept her fingers crossed that it would all fall into place without her falling to pieces.

"Mom? Mom? It's morning."

Daniel was shaking her shoulder. Ellen groped for the lamp on her bedside table. She squinted to see the time on her clock-radio. Six seventeen A.M.

"Merry Christmas, Dan-O," she mumbled. Then Stella leapt onto the bed, sniffling and licking. Daniel laughed. Okay, she thought, it's here. I made it through last night. In less than eighteen hours I can be back asleep. It's showtime.

Last night hadn't been as hard as she had feared. Ellen realized that if enough people crowded around her table, and enough voices clamored to be heard, it was harder to hear the missing voice, harder to see the absent face. Ellen hadn't even had to fake being jolly too much. But the loss finally descended upon her at church. When she and Daniel had walked into the cavernous sanctuary, lit with candles and brimming with greens, Irene had spied them and hurried over. With a quick hug and greeting, she asked for a favor.

"The family who was supposed to light the advent candles just called. The dad fell today and broke his arm. They're still at the hospital. Could you two fill in?"

"Oh, Irene, I don't know," Ellen stalled.

She looked at Daniel, who asked, "Would I have to say anything?"

Irene smiled and said, "Well, one person lights the candles and one person reads."

"I'll light them," Daniel offered. "The tall white one in the middle is last, right?"

"You got it. Ellen? What do you think?"

"I guess." She glanced around at the rapidly filling pews.

She looked at Daniel, who was watching her intently. Standing up straighter, she met Irene's gaze and added, "Sure. We'll be fine. You want us seated up near the front, right?"

Irene thanked her, pointed out that what Ellen would need to read was printed in the bulletin, and hurried off to collect her sermon. When the choir began leading them all in Christmas carols, Ellen looked over the words for the candle lighting. Why did I agree to this? she worried. I'll never be able to get through this. I don't want to break down in front of everyone. They're all happy. They're rejoicing about the birth of the Son.

Ellen missed everything in the service leading up to the candle-lighting ceremony. And when Irene, from the front of the altar, invited them up, Ellen felt as though she were in one of the dreams she'd had after Bob had kissed her. She knew her legs and feet were moving, but it seemed to take forever to walk up to the altar where the candles stood. Daniel took the candle lighter from Irene and paused, waiting for Ellen to begin the reading. Her eyes saw the words, and somehow the connections went from her eyes to her brain and then to her tongue. Her voice worked. Thank goodness for neurons, or whatever it is, she thought. Eyes and brain and muscles took over. I couldn't have willed myself to do this. It must be automatic or a higher power or both. The entire time as she said the words and Daniel lit the candles, she was telling herself, don't think, don't ponder what the words mean. Just say them. Like an opera singer who verbalizes syllables. If you think about the words, she told herself, you'll crack. It's just phonics. And then she was done.

She didn't break down until the end of the service, when everyone had a candle, which was then lit from the sconces at the end of each pew. And they sang "Silent Night." Then the tears rolled down Ellen's cheeks.

~~~~~~~

Now it was Christmas morning. Daniel tugged at her to hurry, and she pulled on her robe and slippers.

"Just let me wash my face," she pleaded. "Go turn on the coffee, but no going in by the tree."

After splashing water on her face, Ellen hurried after Daniel.

"Close your eyes."

When he'd done as he was told, she tiptoed into the family room to turn on the tree lights. Even though it was just the two of them, presents spilled from under the tree. She picked up Daniel's stocking and carried it to where he was waiting in the kitchen.

"Merry Christmas, munchkin," she said, handing it to him.

He opened his eyes, giggled, and then said, "Oh, wait."

He ran back to his room and soon reappeared carrying a stocking brimming with tiny wrapped packages for her.

"Merry Christmas to you, too," he said proudly.

Walking into the family room, Daniel gasped in surprise when he saw his big gift—a new stereo.

"Thanks, Mom!"

"You're welcome, honey. It's from Dad, too. Be sure to thank him when you call him later."

"Oh, wow." The expression on Daniel's face—happy and excited and surprised—was one she hadn't seen in months. "Can I put a CD in right now? I'll play one even you like."

"Sure. But can you find five of yours that I like?"

He looked perplexed at first, but upon realizing that he could load five CDs at a time, he jumped with excitement, and said, "Oh man. This is so cool. I'll even play some of yours if you want."

Ellen laughed and went to pour herself coffee as Daniel

selected music. She preheated the oven for the sweet rolls and pulled the egg casserole out of the refrigerator. She glanced at the clock. Nearly seven A.M. So far, so good.

After loading up the music, Daniel waited for her before starting to open presents.

What a sad little scene this is, she thought. One very excited boy and one woman trying to maintain her sanity and equilibrium, counting the minutes until she can go back to bed.

They took turns opening their presents, but even then they were done much too quickly. Daniel spoke what Ellen had been thinking. "It always used to take longer."

"Well," Ellen said, evading the real issue, "that's because you used to get lots of little things. Now you have more expensive gifts so there aren't as many."

"Maybe, but—" Daniel looked directly at her. "—it's mostly because of James."

"Mm-hmm." As Ellen nodded she felt her throat constrict and her eyes fill. She tried to blink the tears away, and when that failed she tilted her head back and up as if to inspect the angel at the top of the tree.

"Mom? It's okay to say that, isn't it? I mean it is true."

"Sure it is, honey. It's always okay to talk about James."

"I really miss him today, Mom." Daniel spoke so softly Ellen barely heard him.

"Oh, honey," she said, going over to him, "me, too. Always."

"Maybe you were right. Maybe we should've gone somewhere else for Christmas this year."

Ellen didn't answer right away. Holding Daniel to her, she looked out the window. It had started snowing again. Big, fluffy flakes. A Currier and Ives kind of snowfall.

"Daniel? Let's go for a walk before breakfast, okay?"

"Okay." Daniel spoke without enthusiasm.

"Get your clothes on while I put the stuff in the oven. We can take Stella if you want."

Daniel shuffled off to his room. I never thought this would happen, she thought. Me trying to buoy up Daniel.

They wordlessly walked in the snow, Stella leaping about ahead of them. This was Ellen's favorite kind of snow—fluffy and silent and soft. Not at all gritty or icy. The sky was heavy and gray with the promise of an all-day snowfall. It would cover the brownish clumps and slush that the snowplows had kicked up and that now framed the streets. Soon there would once again be clean white humps delineating the lawns from the roads. Right now even the asphalt was covered with a new white blanket marred only by their footprints.

"Daniel?"

"Hmm?"

"I think we made the right decision to stay home for Christmas."

"I don't know, Mom."

"It would've been a hard day no matter where we were. And we'd have had to face Christmas in this house without James one of these years anyway."

"I guess."

"And honey?"

"What?"

"It's okay to cry, you know. I did last night at church. And I did this morning."

"I just really miss him."

"Me too, babe."

They kept walking and then Daniel let out a chuckle.

"Look at our stupid dog," he said, pointing up ahead.

There was Stella, hind end sticking out of a bush, head buried deep inside. When she backed out, her face covered with snow and her tail wagging fiercely, she looked proud. She had found a tennis ball. She bounded toward them and Daniel laughed again. Ellen looked at her watch, then back at Daniel. He was still grinning at the dog. She took in his dimples, which she hadn't seen in months, and said, "I think breakfast will be about ready. Race you home?"

Four thirty P.M. on New Year's Eve. Ellen stood in front of her closet, perplexed. You could have said no, she told herself. Bob had called again a few days ago and Daniel had answered. Ellen had heard them chatting.

Then she'd heard Daniel in his chirpy voice say, "I'll be with my dad and grandpa for the whole weekend."

Better think of something fast, Ellen told herself when Daniel handed her the phone.

"Hello?"

"Hi, Ellen, this is Bob. About New Year's—"

"Well," she interrupted, "I won't be spending it with Daniel." She knew there was no way to use him for an excuse anymore.

"I don't know about you, but I hate big crowds on New Year's."

"Me, too," Ellen said.

"I'd like to have a little dinner party. You. Jody and her husband. Ask Anna and Sam, if you'd like. I've been wanting to meet them. I feel like I know them already."

"I don't want you to go to too much trouble or anything."

"Hey, I'd enjoy it. Why don't you come over about seven thirty?"

"Okay, sure. Can I bring anything?"

"Oh, an appetizer if you want."

Now the goat cheese, olive paste, tomatoes, and garlic toasts were packed up and ready. Anna and Sam would be here to pick her up in an hour. Ellen grabbed a long black skirt and cream-colored sweater set. This will be comfortable, she thought, but still dressy enough to be festive.

Anna had been very excited about the dinner party. She'd been wanting to meet Bob. As she kept telling Ellen, "Don't discount your feelings for this guy just because of how and when you met him."

Ellen knew it wasn't fair to Bob or to herself to ignore the attraction she felt, but she couldn't help the guilt that kept creeping into her thoughts. It is wrong, she'd think, to have anything good for me come out of James' death. She shook her head in an effort to clear away her thoughts. Glancing at the clock, she knew she'd better hurry and dry her hair and put on her makeup.

Sam helped her into the backseat.

Anna looked around and smiled as she said, "You look great, El."

"Oh, thanks." Ellen gathered her coat around her, then made sure the bag of items for the bruschetta wasn't going to tip over. "Nice outfit yourself," she added and smiled.

Anna laughed. Once again they had dressed in nearly identical outfits. Long, drapey black skirts and sweater sets.

"You both look beautiful," Sam commented, turning onto University Avenue and heading east.

Ellen gave Sam the directions to Bob's condo, which he

had dictated to her over the phone. He had a unit on the top floor of an old rehabbed school building overlooking Lake Mendota. Anna and Ellen were both eager to see his view.

"So, El," Sam asked, "how much do you like this guy?"

"Oh, I don't know."

"No, really. Want me to do some interrogation? Or will we just totally embarrass you no matter what?"

"No." Ellen laughed nervously. "I like him. You two will think he's perfect for me. But, well, I just think the timing is bad."

"El?" Sam was looking at her in the rearview mirror. Ellen saw the concern and affection in his eyes. I bet Anna told him why I don't think this should work, she thought.

"Hmm?"

"El, if it's good, that's okay, you know. You deserve a nice guy."

"Thanks, Sam. But, well, it's more than that. It's complicated."

Anna was conspicuously silent during this conversation.

"Of course it is," Sam said, "but it doesn't have to be. Don't be so hard on yourself."

Sam found a parking place on the street and then helped both of them out and around the piles of snow. They gingerly walked up the freshly shoveled sidewalk, and Anna whispered to Ellen, "Let's just have fun tonight, okay?"

"Absolutely." Ellen looked straight at Anna for a moment, then added, "Thanks."

The evening was fun and comfortable. Bob grilled salmon steaks on his gas grill, which prompted a discussion of the wonder of being able to grill out in the wintertime in Wisconsin. As midnight approached, they all stood out on Bob's balcony, looking out over the frozen lake and shivering in the light snow. Ellen looked up into the inky sky filled with glittering stars, and Sam and Bob popped champagne corks. At the stroke of twelve, they blew noisemakers and cheered. Bob reached up to touch Ellen on the cheek and she smiled and whispered "Happy New Year." He brought his face to hers and kissed her.

"I hate to sound old, but we'd better head home soon," Sam said as he stood, glanced at his watch, and began carrying a load of dishes into the kitchen.

"Let us help you clean up some before we go," Anna said, following Sam out of the living room.

"No. Don't worry about it. It won't take me long at all," Bob called after them, then, turning to Ellen, he added softly, "Would you like to stay awhile? I can take you home later."

Ellen nodded, listening to Jody and Sam talking about getting together with their kids soon. Ellen leaned back into the soft leather sofa. What a nice evening, she thought.

Anna and Sam were gathering their coats, and when Sam grabbed Ellen's out of the closet she said, "I'm going to stay and help Bob clean up. He'll take me home in a little while."

She couldn't miss Anna's grin when she said this. Ellen had tried to make it seem casual, but she and Anna both knew it wasn't.

"Have fun," Anna whispered to Ellen. "I don't know about you, but he's looking more and more like an Atticus to me."

After everyone else had left, Ellen started picking up empty plates and wineglasses. Bob allowed her one trip into the kitchen before putting out his hand to stop her.

"Hey," he said, "I didn't ask you to stay so you could clean up this mess, you know."

"Really?" Ellen teased. "I was so sure you saw the meticulous housekeeper in me waiting to spring out."

They stood together in the dim light of the hallway. Slowly, Bob took her by the hand and led her back to the sofa. He sat in the corner, and Ellen snuggled up next to him. For a long time, they sat wordlessly, staring into the fire. Finally Bob turned her toward him, and they kissed as the snow piled up outside and the wind gently rattled the windows.

Later, feeling drowsy and happy, Ellen gazed into the fire as Bob softly rubbed her shoulder and ran his fingers through her hair.

"Don't let me fall asleep," she murmured.

"Go ahead. I'm not going anywhere."

Ellen woke with a start and a cry. As she saw the dwindling fire and heard Bob's soft, slow breathing, she knew they had both slept for a few hours. Carefully and quietly, she lifted her legs off the coffee table and pulled herself out of Bob's embrace. She shook her head to try to clear out the fuzzy images. It was the same dream again. She was running. She was reaching for something or someone. She knew, in her dream, that she wouldn't get to it in time. Overlapping the dream images were bursts of memory: kissing Bob, snuggling up to him, his arm around her as she fell asleep. Dammit, she said to herself, am I ever going to be able to kiss this man without having a nightmare afterward? As she stood up, she felt Bob shift on the sofa behind her.

His hand touched her hip and he mumbled, "Come on back. You were so warm."

"I really should get home."

"Oh, El. Stay till morning. I'll take you home then."

She didn't answer, just walked to the bathroom. Splashing

water on her face, she looked at herself in the mirror. Her thoughts tumbled inside her head. I have to go home. Call a cab. Do something. How do I explain this to him? I can't even make sense of it myself.

When Ellen walked back into the living room, Bob was dozing again. She found her shoes under the sofa and went looking for a phone book.

When she turned on the light in the kitchen, Bob called to her, "El? What do you need?"

"Nothing," she called back. "Go to sleep. I'll take care of this."

Finding the yellow pages, she leafed through looking for "taxicab services," then dialed. When the dispatcher answered, she asked for a cab, then realized she didn't remember Bob's address. Since Sam and Anna had driven, she hadn't bothered to write it down. She fumbled around looking for it now. The cab dispatcher was impatient.

"Look, lady, I need to know where to send the cab."

"I know, I know," Ellen whispered tensely. "I'll find the address. Just a minute."

Ellen put the receiver down and looked for an envelope or anything nearby with Bob's address.

Her frustration increased and she could hear the dispatcher saying, "Call back when you've remembered where you are, honey."

Grabbing for the phone, Ellen's whisper grew desperate. "Look. Just give me a minute. Please."

Now Ellen grabbed the white pages, flipping to the "H's." Great, she thought, only a full page of "Hansen." As her fingers scrolled down to the "R's," she felt Bob's presence in the room.

"El."

Ellen looked up at him.

"El. What's going on?"

"Just calling for a cab."

"Hang up. I'll take you home."

Slowly, feeling like a child caught trying to run away from home, she hung up. How do I explain this, she wondered. What can I tell him that is true but doesn't make me sound nuts?

"I, uh, didn't want to wake you up. I just thought I should get home."

"It's four A.M."

"I know, but I need to let the dog out." Ellen found it hard to return his gaze when she said this. "I just need to go home."

"You okay?" Bob asked.

"Sure," Ellen answered flatly.

"You don't sound okay. Come in and talk to me."

Ellen closed the phone book and carefully pushed it back from the edge of the counter. Her hands shook as she tried to straighten the papers she had flipped through looking for Bob's address. She bit her lip and tried to conjure up words that would make sense. I should apologize, she thought, but first I have to look at him and try not to cry.

"Ellen," Bob said, "I'd really like to help you."

She stood in silence a few seconds longer, then blurted, "Do you have any tea?"

"No tea, but I do have coffee."

"That'd be great."

"So." Bob paused. "I'm guessing you're not planning to sleep anymore tonight?"

"I don't think I could get back to sleep," Ellen said, then added, "even if I wanted to."

Bob didn't say any more until the coffee finished brewing. After pouring them each a cup, he guided Ellen into the living room and once again sat on the sofa. She sat apart from

Bob at the other end, then turned sideways to face him. She sipped her coffee, then held it with both hands in front of her, feeling the steam warm her face.

"Ellen?" Bob prompted. "What's going on?"

"I don't know how to explain this," she answered, turning to look at the glowing embers of the dying fire. As if on cue, Bob got up and added another log.

"Did I do something wrong?"

"No. It's all me. You've been great."

"Then what? We fall asleep and then the next thing I know, you seem frantic to escape."

"It's just, well, I like you, Bob. I really do. But it seems wrong."

"How?"

"I feel disloyal."

"To whom?"

Ellen saw the confusion in his eyes. And the warmth and desire. He has no idea, she thought. He doesn't get it at all.

"To James."

"James?"

"Yes. If he hadn't died, I wouldn't have met you. I mean, he died, I met you, and when I'm with you it feels good. I feel happy. There's got to be something wrong about that. It can't be okay to add up that way."

Bob was quiet for several minutes before he said, "But then you're doing the reverse."

"Huh?"

"If you leave tonight, you're letting his death keep you from something that might make you happy."

Ellen thought about this. She sipped the coffee, looked at the fire and then at Bob. She reached out and took his hand. She rubbed his thumb and knuckles.

"You're right. But—" She paused and swallowed. "—that seems like the more equitable result. I'm sorry."

Ellen put the coffee mug down and reached for her coat. Bob walked her to the car, and she saw that the sky was just beginning to lighten. New Year's Day, she thought. I liked it better last night.

Bob was quiet the whole drive home. When he pulled into her driveway, he put the car in park and turned to her.

"Look. I can't say I agree with you, but I'm trying to understand."

"Thank you." Ellen reached to touch his cheek. "For this and for the legal help. You've really been a friend."

"I still am. I'll still help with the legal work. I still care. About you. And about James."

Ellen kissed his cheek before opening the door. The walk to her door seemed longer than ever.

Chapter Eleven

After Christmas vacation, Ellen once again felt relieved to start school.

The classroom became her haven—she could fall back on the patterns and behaviors of being a teacher. With the desks full of students, there was little room for her grief, the trial, or her feelings for Bob to intrude.

Ellen had even been able to evade Anna's questions about New Year's Eve and Bob because Anna and her family had spent the rest of the New Year's holiday with relatives. Once school started up, Ellen had feigned busyness with schoolwork to get out of lengthy phone conversations.

The only thing that had tripped Ellen up at all this week was when she sat down to write Bob a thank-you note for the New Year's Eve dinner party. Everything she tried to write sounded either too stiff and formal, or too shallow and vacuous. She was striving for breezy. *How do I say what I feel,*

Ellen had wondered. Can I say what I feel? And then she had chided herself with the realization that she wasn't even sure she knew how she truly felt. The note she finally dropped in the mail still left her feeling dissatisfied and guilty.

School was her solace.

At the end of the second week back, she headed to her car with a backpack full of student essays to grade when two teachers hollered to her across the parking lot. Ellen paused, adjusting the pack on her shoulder.

"Want to join us for a happy hour?"

"Oh, gee, thanks, but I doubt it," Ellen said. "I have no idea what Daniel has cooked up for tonight."

"Well, check on him, then come meet us."

"Where?"

"Delaney's. Near the mall."

"I'll see. But don't count on me. Thanks, though."

Ellen waved as they left, and had nearly forgotten about their invitation by the time she was out of the parking lot.

Daniel was playing in the snow with Stella when she got home.

"Hey, Mom," he called to her.

"How was school?"

"Pretty good. Mom?"

"Hmm?"

"Joey and his dad invited me to go skiing with them tonight. They're going to Cascade Mountain."

Ellen looked at his face, flush with excitement and the cold. She loved these moments when he seemed untouched by the tragedy that had consumed them. Just when she started to answer, he reached down and gently flicked the snow off Stella's back and head.

"Well, I guess you can go. When are they leaving? And do you have any money?"

"They wanted to try and get there by five, so I guess we'll leave pretty soon. And Grandpa gave me some money last weekend."

"Well, let's get your gear ready, then," Ellen said, walking into the house.

"Thanks, Mom! Come on, Stella, get inside, girl." Daniel rushed in after her and headed straight for the closet to assemble his hat, gloves, and other skiing paraphernalia.

Ellen listened to his preparations, checked her phone messages, and glanced through the mail. Nothing too important or interesting, she thought. She suddenly remembered the happy hour. *Maybe I could stop by for a quick drink. You don't have anything else to fill the evening,* she told herself, conveniently ignoring the essays weighing down her backpack. She didn't want to sit home alone.

"All ready, Mom," Daniel announced.

"That was pretty speedy," she said, laughing. "How about taking some snacks with you?"

Together they rummaged through the snack cupboard and selected some fruit snacks and granola bars that Daniel zipped into the various pockets of his jacket.

"Let me freshen up and then I'll drop you at Joey's."

When Ellen pulled open the heavy wooden doors of the restaurant half an hour later, she could already hear the laughter and voices of her colleagues at the bar. They saw her and waved; she found an empty chair, and a teacher handed her a beer.

"Glad you could join us."

"Me, too," Ellen replied, smiling.

And it did feel good. She had missed most of these get-togethers over the years—it had been hard to find a babysitter at first, and then, even when the boys were old enough to stay home by themselves, she usually needed to be home to oversee their activities. But when she did join her colleagues, she always felt such a nice release—they would let off steam about their week and laugh over funny stories of classroom and student antics.

"I had already told them the test was worth one hundred and fifty points. Then I mentioned that there were only four questions. This one girl raised her hand and asked, 'Is it multiple choice?' I tell you, I didn't want to laugh in her face, but it was hard," Pam, a history teacher, recounted.

"Oh, I've got one for you," Ellen joined in. "In the middle of a unit test, a girl came up and asked, in all seriousness, 'Do you want me to answer all of these or just the ones I think I know?'"

The stories were interrupted by the waitress bringing several orders of the restaurant's famed onion straws and two more pitchers of beer. Ellen relaxed into the comfortable leather chair. The fireplace nearby crackled with heat, and the tension she so regularly carried within her gradually softened with the warmth. After another beer, the edges around her began to look fuzzy. A few teachers got up to leave; several more suggested heading to the bowling alley across the street. Ellen and two others elected to stay at the bar and wait for them to come back after bowling. They ordered a few more appetizers and then were joined by some other people one of the teachers knew.

Ellen mostly observed the activity around her without saying much; it all seemed very fluid and choreographed and she found herself fascinated with watching all the steps.

"Hey, Ellen, you're not falling asleep on us, are you?"

Ellen jerked herself up straight in an effort to disprove the accusation.

"No, just very relaxed," she responded, smiling.

"I don't think we've met." It was a voice from the chair next to her. She turned, and the voice continued, "I'm Warren."

"I'm Ellen." They shook hands.

Where did he come from, Ellen asked herself, and then realized she had been off in another world for some time.

Warren, it turned out, was a friend of a friend of one of the teachers who was now bowling. Ellen couldn't follow the convoluted connection between them and knew it didn't matter. Warren worked with computers and kept refilling her beer mug. They chatted, and it gradually dawned on Ellen that he was flirting with her. He would gently touch her forearm when he was making a point, he laughed convincingly at her comments, he complimented her—and Ellen started flirting back.

At one point, Ellen looked around at the chairs and tables haphazardly pushed together and noticed that all of the teachers who had originally been there had left. She vaguely remembered telling most of them goodbye but knew that the last few must have departed while she was busy talking to Warren.

He was now suggesting they head somewhere else, and at the same time he was subtly but purposely pressing his knee into her thigh. Now she felt Warren's hand softly rubbing her back.

Ignoring the voice of reason that was calling out to her, she started punctuating her points by placing her hand on his thigh. Was it the warmth of the fire and alcohol that caused her face to flush?

"Let's go somewhere more private," Warren whispered again, leaning in close to her face.

Rather than respond, Ellen stood and, patting his shoulder, said, "Let me run to the restroom."

After using the bathroom, she checked her hair and face in the mirror. She fluffed her hair with her fingers, freshened her blush and lipstick, and dug around in her purse for a breath mint.

Ellen headed back through the bar to the table where Warren waited for her, and a voice called out to her. It was Bob, standing near the bar with two other attorneys she vaguely remembered meeting at his office. Ellen quickly tried to steady herself.

"Hey, Bob. How are you?"

"Pretty good. Surprised to see you, though. No Daniel tonight?"

"He's skiing at Cascade with a friend." Out of the corner of her eye, she saw Warren wending his way toward her, carrying her coat, which had been on the back of her chair.

"I've been trying to call you—" Bob started to say, but then stopped as Warren approached and put his arm around Ellen.

"Ready to go?"

"Uh, Bob, this is Warren. Warren, Bob." Ellen stared at the floor as she made these introductions, waiting silently while Bob introduced the two men with him.

A moment later Warren ushered Ellen through the door and out to his parked truck. Ellen couldn't help but see the hurt in Bob's face as she left with Warren. He unlocked his truck, but before opening the door, he pushed Ellen up against the side and began to kiss her.

As Ellen started to reach up and put her arms around him, he held both of her hands together behind her back with one hand, and with the other he gripped the back of her neck. She felt the cold hardness of the metal door handle as it dug into her hip bone and her feet slipped a bit on the icy blacktop as she struggled to keep her balance. That little voice of reason screamed at her now, and somehow it got through all the alcohol and finally registered. She was panting, but out of fear, not passion.

"Wait," she whispered.

He paused, then started to open the door.

"My keys. I left them in the bathroom."

"But you're not driving."

"I'll still need them eventually," Ellen said, and she maneuvered herself out of his grasp and hurried back to the bar.

Just inside the door, she saw one of the attorneys who had been with Bob.

"Is he still here?" she asked, trying not to sound too frantic.

"Yeah, he's back at the bar. Are you okay?"

She shook her head, but hurried past him to find Bob. She walked into the bar and saw him standing with his back to her. She walked up behind him and reached out and touched his arm as she said, "Bob."

He turned slowly, warily. He didn't say anything, just looked at her and waited.

"Bob," she repeated, and she started to speak, but then the tears came. He led her to an empty chair away from the bar and knelt in front of her.

"What happened? Are you okay?"

She tried to stem the tears, but couldn't. She knew people were staring at them, but she didn't care. Bob reached in his pocket for a handkerchief and handed it to her. Her tears slowed, and she dabbed at her eyes and blew her nose. She looked at him and smiled weakly.

"I'm so sorry."

"Talk to me, El. What's going on?"

"I don't want to talk here. Could we . . . do you mind if we leave? Could we go to my house?"

Bob nodded, then went to tell his friends goodbye.

They walked into the parking lot, and Ellen glanced to where Warren's truck had been parked. She sighed with relief when she saw that it was gone.

"You all right to drive?" Bob asked.

"Yeah, I think so."

He looked at her, then shook his head and said, "Ellen, you're in no shape to drive. Give me your keys; I'll grab a taxi from your house later."

Ellen shivered as Bob drove to her house. You are so stupid, she yelled to herself. She remembered how hard and cold Warren's truck door had felt. You've never allowed a guy to pick you up at a bar. You are so, so dumb. She looked at Bob as he turned the car's heater to high, and she sighed and thought, dumb, but lucky.

Once Ellen and Bob were settled on her sofa with cups of tea, she took a deep breath and started to talk. She told him about the happy hour, about Warren, about feeling afloat and unanchored.

"I'm just such a mess," she concluded. "And I'm so sorry I've dragged you into this with me."

"Look," Bob said, taking her hands in his, "quit worrying about me. I'm a big boy. I could have walked away. But you've got to be careful."

"I know. And I didn't even like that guy. I was just responding or something. I'm not like that. Really."

"I know."

They were both quiet, and Ellen pulled a quilt around her shoulders and said, "I can't stop shivering."

"Take some deep breaths," Bob soothed. "And drink your tea."

"I don't want you to think—" She paused and groped for

the right words. "I don't want you to think that I'm 'just responding' when I'm with you."

"Oh, El, I'd never think that."

"I really do like you. I just don't think I should be with anybody right now."

"Then don't be."

They sat together, sipping their tea, and Bob said, "Hey, I forgot. I told you earlier that I'd been trying to reach you. Judge Solari's ruling on your request is going to be announced Monday. I'll call you as soon as I hear anything."

"Thank you. Thank you so much."

"You're welcome. But I do need to call that cab so I can get going. Take care. Don't be so hard on yourself. We'll talk soon."

After Bob left, Ellen snuggled under the quilt, sipping tea and waiting for Daniel to get home from his ski trip.

"Ellen? Judge Solari ruled in your favor!" Bob yelled into the phone late Monday afternoon.

"You're kidding! Oh, Bob, I don't know how to thank you. Wow. Has a trial date been set?"

"Well, here's the interesting part. Not only did he rule in our favor, but he'll be setting the trial date on Friday—and at the same time he'll name the prosecutor."

"Huh?"

"He doesn't want to send it back to the same prosecutor who previously rejected the case. Seems that guy had some close ties to the family of the kid and is a Jet Skier himself."

"No way. That explains it, then. Well, so how will he assign the case?"

"Generally, he'll either choose an attorney from private practice who has a prosecutorial background and is willing, or choose a prosecutor from a nearby jurisdiction."

"And it'll be announced Friday?"

"Yes. Trial date and prosecutor. And Ellen, the word behind the scenes is that he'll name me to prosecute, since I'm already pretty familiar with the case."

"Oh, Bob, that would be too perfect, I mean, if you want it."

"I do. We'll see what finally happens. But the most important thing is, you'll have a trial; James will have his day in court."

The judge ruled as expected: the trial date was set for early May and Bob Hansen would be prosecuting. This energized Ellen. There were three months to prepare, and she found herself practically impersonating a law clerk. She became proficient at scouring the Internet for case histories in other states and forwarding them to Bob, calling later to ask him if they would help his case. Finally, overwhelmed with the calls and the mailings, Bob asked Ellen to meet for a drink.

After they sat down, Ellen blurted her question before the waitress had even taken their order. "Do you have any news? Don't you think the last case I sent you looks particularly good for us?"

"Ellen. Slow down. You need to understand some things about your case. This is not an evidence-driven case. It's all about emotion. I'm not going to win this case by spouting precedent to the judge and the jury. If I win, it'll be because the jury feels more strongly for your grief than they do for the freedom of Jet Skiers."

"But how do you prove reckless homicide, then?"

"We try to make young Mr. Buchanan out to be a bad guy. We look for other reckless acts in his past. We try to prove how inexperienced he was as a Jet Skier, which helps our argument that it was negligent and dangerous for him to be piloting around children."

"Oh. So you won't call lots of expert witnesses?"

"You will probably be my most important witness. I'll also call Anna and Sam. And Daniel if the two of you think he's up to it. Look, Ben Buchanan has a public defender, Lucy Miller. She's going to argue that it was simply an accident, a tragic accident, but that there was nothing criminal about it. I want the jury to feel bad enough for you to find it a criminal, punishable accident."

"What could I testify to? I didn't see it."

"Did you hear anything? Had the kids been in the water a long time? How far out were they? These are the types of things we'll tell the jury. Don't worry, I'll have you fully prepared for the testimony. And the deposition."

"Deposition?" Ellen was alarmed now.

"Sure. Standard procedure. The defense will question you before the trial. It will be an official, recorded proceeding. You'll be sworn in and everything. It protects your testimony."

"How?"

"So you can't get up on the witness stand and change your story. Say you testify that you saw things that you didn't. If your testimony in court differs from what you said at the deposition, they'll take it to the judge. Like I said, state what you know to be true. Don't worry about what you don't know. We'll practice beforehand."

"When does this happen?"

"Well, it's now early February. I'd think they'll want to schedule it sometime in March. That will still leave them five or six weeks before the May trial date. But relax, we've got plenty of time to prepare."

Before the deposition could be scheduled, though, a delay caused by a change in defense attorneys was announced. This change worried Ellen considerably, and the delay enraged her completely. To make it worse, Ellen learned of the change from the evening news.

Ellen was chopping vegetables for a tossed salad when James' fifth-grade picture flashed on the screen above the anchorperson's left shoulder. The paring knife Ellen was using skittered to the floor.

"The trial of Bainbridge teen Benjamin Buchanan, charged with the accidental death of young James Banks, has had a change of defense attorneys. Buchanan, who was piloting a Jet Ski on Lake Augusta when James was hit and killed, will now be defended by attorneys hired by the Jet Ski industry, Clayton Adams and Lindsay Ballwin"—at this, the picture of James disappeared and was replaced by a picture of the two new attorneys—"who have filed a motion with Judge Solari to postpone the trial, which was to have gotten under way May fourth."

Ellen heard no more of the newscast; she was unable to get the pictures of the new attorneys out of her mind. The man, Clayton Adams, was tall and regal with a thick shock of silver hair topping his tanned face. Lindsay Ballwin was petite and had sharp but pretty features. Her hair was long and dark and pulled to the side with a gold barrette. How dare they, Ellen raged to herself, and then her phone rang. Daniel hadn't come home yet, she realized, as she grabbed the phone. He's got to hear this from me, not the press.

"Hello?"

"Ellen. It's me, Bob."

"Yes." She spoke evenly, but the anger was evident in her tone.

"I promise, I didn't know about this until just now. I've been in court all day. I'll find out everything. Just let me make some calls. I'm sorry. Don't worry."

The front door burst open and Daniel's "Mom!" shattered the stillness of the house. Ellen dropped the receiver with a thud and ran to him, enveloping him in her arms.

"I was at Joey's," he gasped, "and James was on the news." He looked at her, searching for answers she didn't have.

"It just means a delay, honey, but there will still be a trial," she soothed, dredging up a calmness she didn't know she was capable of. His thin body shook in her arms and she let him sob as Stella hovered nearby, sniffing his jacket and jeans and shoes. His crying began to slow, and when he peeled himself away from her, she sensed his shyness return. He kept so much inside. She had hoped that the trial would be an opening for him to talk about the accident. He knew he would be asked to testify, and she had thought it might help them both to move on more completely. Now there was the delay.

Neither of them felt like eating the dinner she had been cooking, so they grabbed sodas from the fridge and sat on the floor in front of the fire playing Monopoly. They were reluctant to turn on the TV for fear there would be more coverage of the case, so they listened to Daniel's CDs and rolled the dice. The darkness outside swallowed the house, but the firelight seemed warm and safe. At some point, Daniel made popcorn. They tried to focus on the game, but they frequently wouldn't notice the other landing on their property and forget to collect rent. Their solitude was interrupted by Stella leaping off the couch and rushing to the front door barking viciously. Then they heard, between her barks, knocking at the door.

Ellen hurried to the front, turning lights on as she went. Peering through the door, she saw Sam's worried face.

"What's wrong?" she asked as she unlatched the door.

"That's what I came to find out."

"Huh?"

"Are you okay?" he asked.

It took Ellen a minute to remember why he would be concerned. The news. The change in lawyers.

"We will be."

"Anna has been trying to call you for hours."

"Oh my God." Ellen rushed to the kitchen, where the receiver lay facedown on a dish towel. "I dropped it here when Daniel came home. I guess I never hung it up." She laughed suddenly as the tension from the evening released, then added, "I'm sorry."

"Well, call Anna and tell her, okay? We've been trying to call you and finally she insisted I come over. Caroline's got the stomach flu or she would have come herself."

"We're fine, I promise," Ellen said while dialing Anna's number.

Bob called the next day. The trial would now begin in early June. Depositions were scheduled for mid-April. Ellen resigned herself to the delay.

"How'd these big-shot lawyers get involved?" Ellen asked.

"This case matters to the Jet Ski industry and they're pulling out all the stops."

"But why? What is it to them? My son gets killed and it becomes a major case?"

"Well, this case is getting some media coverage, and it has the potential to make the Jet Ski industry look bad. This is the season to buy them, you know. They don't need a case against them."

"But it's not like I'm suing them."

"True, but I guess they worry it could come to that. First you file criminal charges, then the civil suit comes along. That's the American way."

"But"—Ellen groped to be logical here—"I'm no lawyer, but if they find the kid guilty, doesn't that clear the manufacturer of liability? Wouldn't it be better for them if the kid bore all of the blame?"

"You've got a point there. But they're not suggesting you sue them. You've got no cause, since the equipment wasn't to blame. They're thinking of the next case down the road. And they're thinking of legislation."

"You lost me there."

"Laws to limit underage drivers. Laws to limit Jet Ski use to waterways of a certain size. Believe me, El, I don't think these lawyers are here purely because they're worried about young Buchanan's future."

"Do I need to tell you that I hate them?"

Bob just chuckled softly, and then they set up a time to prepare for the deposition.

Chapter
Twelve

The cold February days continued unabated. Ellen always believed that this was the longest and darkest month of the year even if the calendar said otherwise. The excitement and glitter of Christmas were distant memories, and not only was spring break a good six or eight weeks away, but spring itself wouldn't arrive for two to three months.

Daniel played on a school basketball team, and since his games and practices were held late in the afternoon or early in the evening, Ellen often ate dinner alone, heating up a plate for her son when he arrived later. She had always been adamant that the family eat dinner together, and even when the boys were little, she'd used place mats. They'd turned the television off and talked about their day while eating. She'd always felt that the dinner hour was part of the glue that kept them from spinning off in various directions. It rarely lived up to her Martha Stewart visions, but even if the boys' conversation consisted of verbal jabs at each other and complaints about the menu, they sat down together, held hands to say grace, and shared in the other's company.

Now, however, with Daniel's basketball schedule, Ellen found it hard to create family meals. Besides, she rationalized to herself, it was hard to cook for just two, and even Ellen could eat only so many leftovers before rebelling. She told herself it was wasteful to throw out food and convinced herself that that was a good enough reason to cut back on her cooking. She ignored the fact that she had little appetite and found it difficult to focus on planning and preparing a meal.

Daniel became adept at scrambling eggs and making sandwiches. Ellen satisfied herself by munching on fruit, carrot sticks, and crackers most evenings. That her clothes were becoming looser and looser also escaped her notice.

One cold, rainy afternoon, with a forecast of freezing rain for the next day, Ellen stopped at a gardening store on her way home. For years, she had planted a vegetable garden—it stemmed from the hidden farmer deep within her, she joked—and she liked to start with seeds. She loved watching them sprout out of the deep, dark, rich soil, and then, once the weather warmed up, she enjoyed transplanting the seedlings from their egg-carton homes into the garden in her backyard.

When the boys had been little, they had loved to help. Their pudgy fingers would pat the seeds down, and Ellen could still hear their excited laughter when the first green leaves shot through the dirt. Long after it had stopped being magical and mysterious to them, they worked with her in the garden. It had become a nice, companionable time for them all. Somehow it was easy to talk about the things most hidden in their hearts with their hands in soft, rich dirt and their eyes focused on baby green plants.

On this dreary afternoon, Ellen had the urge to buy the seeds that held the promise of the spring and summer to come.

When she walked into her dark, chilly house with the bag of seeds and potting soil, she nudged the thermostat a few degrees higher and listened for the furnace to lumber into action. There was no sign of Daniel yet, so she checked the calendar to see where he might be.

According to the schedule posted on the refrigerator, he had a late practice. She hoped he had worked on his homework before the practice started.

With the dark evening looming ahead of her, she remembered the seed packets. Her mood brightened as she changed into old jeans and pulled a flannel shirt on over a long-sleeved T-shirt. Gardening clothes, she thought. She retrieved from the basement the egg cartons she had been saving all winter and spread newspaper on the table. She hummed as she worked, patting the soil down, placing the seeds, and then covering them with a light layer of soil. Now, she thought, water lightly and wait for them to grow.

She carried the cartons full of future tomatoes, cucumbers, and peppers to the south-facing windows in the family room and admonished Boo, the cat, to leave them alone. Already spring seemed closer.

After tossing the newspapers and sweeping the kitchen floor, Ellen made tea and settled on the sofa to grade some essays. No matter how hard she tried, she always found herself falling more and more behind in her grading as the school year progressed. It was at times like this—with two class sets of *Huckleberry Finn* essays staring at her—that she envied math teachers. Why do I assign so much writing, she asked herself, but the answer was clear. I assign it because it's what the kids need, she thought. I assign it because writing is an extension of their thinking. I assign it because I love the look on a student's face when, for the first time, he gets it—gets how to prove a point, gets how to use evidence from a book to support an argument, gets to the gist of a novel by putting the pieces together himself. I just wish, Ellen said to herself ruefully, it didn't take up so much red ink and cause so much eyestrain.

Ellen was partway through the essays when she heard Daniel come in.

"Daniel? I'm in the family room," she called.

She heard his backpack land on the floor with a thud, and then he walked into the family room.

"How was practice, honey?"

"It was a game," Daniel answered, but didn't look at her.

"Oh, honey, I'm so sorry. I thought it was a practice. Sorry I missed it. How did you do?"

"Fine." Daniel's gaze was directed not at Ellen, but at the egg cartons neatly placed on the windowsills.

Ellen noticed and said, "I stopped at the seed store on the way home."

"Yeah. I can tell."

Ellen nodded and went back to work grading essays. Daniel glared at her but she completely missed his look.

Daniel walked into the kitchen and began scrounging around for a meal. He carried in a glass of milk and a plate with a roast beef sandwich and chips. He sat in a chair opposite her with his back to the window.

"You could've waited," he said.

"Huh?" Ellen asked, still marking errors with her red pen as she spoke.

"The seeds. I'd have helped."

"You're so busy. Who knows when we'd have had time to do it together."

Daniel ate his sandwich, watching her. Ellen didn't look up.

"I'll need your help, though, when it's time to plant them in the garden."

"Yeah. Well, whatever," Daniel said, then finished up his sandwich and carried his plate to the sink.

Ellen heard him getting out his books and settling in at his desk to do his homework.

When she finally grew too tired to look at another essay, she went to his door to tell him good night, but it was closed tight and no light shone through the crack at the bottom.

A few nights later, Ellen lounged on the sofa, scratching Stella's ears and finishing the wine she'd had with dinner. She was almost caught up with her grading; Daniel was in his room listening to some music with a predominantly bass beat. The dull thumping was almost relaxing, and Ellen had just started to doze off when the ringing of the phone jolted her awake.

"Hello?" Ellen tried to sound alert. She glanced at the clock and saw it was just past eight o'clock.

"Mrs. Banks?" The caller's voice sounded familiar, but Ellen couldn't quite place it. It wasn't a friend or the mom of one of Daniel's friends, Ellen thought, because they would have called me by my first name. Maybe it's the parent of one of my students.

"Yes. This is Mrs. Banks," Ellen said, as she sat up straighter. If it's a parent, she thought, I better not sound like I just sucked down two glasses of red wine.

"Hi, this is Grace Benham." There was a pause, and Ellen tried to sort through all the names in her head. The name sounded familiar, but from where? "I hope I'm not disturbing you by calling so late."

"Oh no, not at all. How are you?" Ellen faked familiarity. It was an old trick she'd honed over the years, cultivated out of necessity from running into former students and their parents all around town. Usually, if she played at pretending to know them long enough, they would eventually drop a name or some other clue, and she'd be able to click on to their identity.

"Mrs. Banks, I don't mean to intrude—"

"Please, call me Ellen."

"Okay, Ellen. I first want you to know how sorry I am about the loss of your son, and I just want to express my sincere condolences."

Ellen sucked her breath in sharply and held the phone out so she could stare at it. Who the hell are you, she wanted to yell into the receiver. What is your purpose here? Ellen heard the woman start to say something on the other end, something Ellen was certain she did not want to hear.

"Why are you calling me? Who are you?" Ellen demanded.

"I'm sorry. I should have identified myself sooner. I'm Grace Benham."

"You already told me that. Do I know you?"

"I'm with Channel Fifteen news."

"You're the press?" Ellen felt sick. That's where I know her from. Which one is she? Ellen reached for another swallow of wine to try to steady herself. Grace Benham? Oh, she's the one with normal hair, Ellen remembered. She's pretty, about my age. She looks like she could be a mom or a neighbor. "You do lots of 'found puppy' stories, don't you?"

Grace chuckled softly, then answered, "I guess you could call them that." She paused, then added, "Mrs. Banks, I'd really like to talk to you about the accident."

"Why? Why now? The accident was six months ago and the trial doesn't start until June."

"The big ski and boat show is in town this weekend."

"And?"

"And you, tragically, can put a real human spin on motorized watercraft."

"I don't know. I mean, I've been very adamant about not talking to the press through any of this. Don't take this the wrong way, but I really hate all of you. Your intrusiveness. Your insensitivity. I don't hate you personally, but, well, your kind."

"Look, Mrs. Banks, I know that a lot of reporters are just out for the big story. I know we have a reputation for not caring about the people we interview. I promise, I'm not like that."

"I still don't get why you want this interview now."

"To be real honest? I have two nephews who are badgering their parents for Jet Skis. Their dad thinks they look like fun. This area is full of kids who see only the excitement, none of the risk. You—and James—put a face on that danger. Now, on our ten o'clock news tonight we're going to have a big story on the boat show. I want to have your story, too."

"Tonight?"

"Can I come over now? It will just be one cameraman and me."

"Tonight? I'm not exactly ready."

"Please, Mrs. Banks. This is a chance for you to speak out. For James."

Ellen said nothing. She could hear Grace's patient, quiet breathing. This would give me a voice, she thought. A soapbox, almost.

"Well," Ellen started, then stopped.

"Please, Mrs. Banks. You, more than anyone I can think of, know the importance of getting this message out to parents."

Ellen heard Daniel change CDs. She pictured again the wounded look she saw so often in his eyes. She recalled the cool, smooth, wax-like appearance of James' face as he was wheeled away to have his organs removed. "Okay," she whispered. "Come over now."

After she hung up, Ellen glanced around the room. What have I agreed to, she wondered, and hurried to tell Daniel that she was about to be interviewed.

"You? Why?" Daniel muttered under his breath.

Before she could answer, Stella started barking at the news van pulling into the driveway.

"Some people from Channel Fifteen want to interview me about the boat show," Ellen answered as she walked to unlock the door.

At the door there was a brief confusing bustle as Ellen held the dog, motioned in Grace Benham and her cameraman, introduced herself, and tried to step out of the way as the cameraman hauled in his equipment.

Grace looked every bit as sincere and kind as she did on TV. She had the requisite highlighted blond hair, but it was not the standard shellacked bob that most of the newswomen sported. Grace's hair was softer and longer, and she had it tucked casually behind her ears.

"Mrs. Banks, thank you so much for letting me barge in like this." Her voice had a warm, soft cadence that exuded competence and comfort.

"Well, sure. Is there anything I should be doing? Or practicing?"

"No. We'll take care of everything." Grace smiled and

glanced around the living room. "Do you mind if I look around a little to decide where to set this up? We don't want it to look too staged."

Ellen nodded and waved her back to the family room. She heard Grace talking to the cameraman about camera angles and lighting. I guess I just wait to be summoned, Ellen thought, but then it seemed stupid to stand all by herself in the living room, so she walked back to where the others were. She noticed that Daniel had retreated to his room and closed the door.

When she turned into the family room, she was surprised to see that the camera was already set up and that the sofa had been pulled out from the wall at a slight angle. The rocking chair had been placed near it, and the coffee table pushed away to the other side of the room.

Grace looked up, mildly distracted, when Ellen walked in, but she quickly smiled at her and asked her to sit on the sofa near the rocker. "We need to get started. This really won't take very long."

"Should I put on any makeup or anything?"

"Once we get the camera going, I'll make any necessary adjustments," Grace said.

You won't need any, Ellen thought, taking in the flawless, smooth makeup Grace was wearing. She thought of her own haphazard makeup job, slapped on in less than five minutes at six thirty this morning. She hadn't done any touching up since then, with the exception of reapplying her lipstick after lunch. Great, she thought, my big TV debut and I'm going to be sitting next to Miss L'Oreal. "Can I at least freshen my lipstick?"

"Okay, but hurry. We've only got a few minutes."

Ellen quickly returned, took her seat, and the interview began.

Grace started with an intro: "We all remember the tragic accident . . ."

Ellen's mind started to blur, but then the camera was aimed at her and Grace addressed her directly.

"Mrs. Banks, tell us why you are so opposed to the use of Jet Skis."

"Well," she started, then stopped. How do I say this? Are mere words strong enough? Grace was looking at her, silently pleading with her to speak. Ellen tried to start again. "My son James was killed by a Jet Ski. People think they're toys, just safe and harmless fun, but they're not." Ellen's eyes burned, and there was a slight shake in her voice.

"Mrs. Banks, can you tell us what happened that day last August?"

As Ellen began to revisit that day, she felt herself drift back to the tranquility of the afternoon as it had been right up until the moment of impact. She felt almost removed or detached from the retelling. Grace's gentle questions prodded her narrative: the accident, the ambulance ride, the emptiness of the organ donations, the frustrations with the legal system. Then, as a last point, Grace asked, "If you could say one thing to parents who are considering the purchase of a Jet Ski, what would it be?"

Ellen took a deep breath before starting to speak. Then, looking straight into the camera, she began. "Please, consider carefully. A Jet Ski is a motorized vehicle, and you are driving it where children play. It would be like driving a motorcycle through a playground. They're not toys. I can't imagine anyone would choose to lose what I lost—my son. And if it weren't for a Jet Ski, he'd still be here."

When Ellen stopped there was a space of silence before Grace thanked her and the camera switched off.

"Mrs. Banks, you were wonderful."

Ellen nodded in response.

"You were so calm, but what you said was very poignant. Thank you."

"Well," Ellen said, "I hope my point gets across to people."

"Don't worry. We'll see that it does." Grace looked at her thoughtfully, and Ellen sensed that she wanted to say something more, but then the cameraman tapped the face of his watch, and it was as if something in Grace clicked off. She became detached, almost brusque.

"So," Ellen asked, "will this run tonight?"

"Yes, that's the plan. But we'll keep it on file, too, in case we need it some other time."

Ellen walked them to the door and told them she'd be watching for the story. Grace waved as she and the cameraman clambered into the news van. It occurred to Ellen that she hadn't heard the cameraman speak even once.

"So you're going to be on the news, huh?" Daniel was at her elbow, looking skeptical.

"That's what she said," Ellen answered, nodding at the news van retreating down their street.

"And you were wearing that?"

"What's wrong with what I'm wearing?" Ellen looked down at her ribbed red turtleneck and black jeans. Then she added, "Besides, they just filmed me from the chest up."

"It's okay, I guess." Daniel wandered back to the family room. Ellen knew that often her very existence was an embarrassment to Daniel, and she tried not to take it personally. She could still vividly remember the horror and humiliation she had felt one weekend when she was fifteen and, lacking any other plans, had deigned to go to a movie with her parents. As they had been going in to the theater, she had run into three cute boys from her high school. Never had she more wanted to disappear, to be anywhere but there. The boys had said hello and smiled at her, but Ellen had been convinced she would forever after be labeled a loser.

You look fine, she scolded herself. I just hope I don't sound like a total idiot. That was her fear. That she would sound shrill or incoherent, or, even worse, that she had made a grammatical error. She had always had a sick fascination with how people who were interviewed after disasters seemed to have IQs hovering in the mid-eighties. And now she was one of those man-on-the-street interviews. God, please don't let me come across like trailer trash.

"Hey, Mom," Daniel called to her, "the news is starting."

They watched quietly. Ellen knew the story would not appear before the first commercial break. I hope it's before the weather, though, she thought. Oh, and please don't let it be that throwaway spot after the sports right at the end of the newscast. Those are usually "feel-good" stories, though, she reminded herself, and this interview certainly wouldn't fall into that category.

"Here it comes," Daniel said, just as the anchorman turned to face Grace Benham, who was now included in the camera shot.

And there it was. Ellen's family room, Ellen's sofa, Ellen's somber story.

"You did good, Mom."

"Thanks, honey. I guess I didn't make too much of a fool of us, huh?"

Before Daniel could answer, the phone rang.

"Hello?"

"Hey, babe, you were great. How come you didn't tell us about this?" Anna asked.

"It all just came up tonight. Did I really do okay?"

"Fantastic. I'm proud of you."

Ellen talked to Anna for a few more minutes, then hung

up and went to get the coffee ready for the next morning. As she was finishing, the phone rang again. It was Bob.

"Hi. What's up?"

"What was with that interview?"

"Oh." Ellen laughed. "Did you see it?"

"Yes." Bob paused, then said, "You shouldn't do stuff like that."

"Why? This gave me a chance to be heard. To get the word out about how dangerous Jet Skis can be."

"Well, it also gave the defense ammunition to use against you and to shore up their case."

"What? How?"

"Look, Ellen, those lawyers are good. Anything you say, they can and will use against you."

"What in the world could they use from tonight's interview?"

"You said, on tape with cameras rolling, that the Jet Ski killed James. Not Ben Buchanan. Not even a machine operated by Ben Buchanan. You're helping them to cast doubt on his culpability."

"No, that's not what I said. No, Bob, nobody but you would hear it that way."

"Yes, Ellen, that's what you said. And there are plenty of people who'd hear it that way. Any good, smart lawyer out there would hear it exactly that way. And you handed it right to them."

"Oh God. Oh, Bob, I'm so sorry. Why didn't you tell me this?"

"I didn't think I needed to. You seemed to have such hatred for the press. I really didn't think it was going to come up."

"Is there anything I can do?"

"Promise me: no more interviews."

"I promise."

"And assure me that this wasn't part of a three-part series."

"Is that supposed to be a joke?"

"Not a very funny one, I guess. Sorry. Just be careful, Ellen, okay?"

Chapter
Thirteen

"Okay. Here are some of your general rules for depositions," Bob instructed. "Just answer what's asked, yes or no if possible; don't offer any explanations unless asked, and if asked, don't give more than is needed. Remember, they can ask for more info, but you can't take back something you said. Take a breath before you answer. This gives you a chance to think about your response, and it gives me a chance to object."

"Will both of them be asking me questions?"

"No. Only one attorney can question you during a depo. I'm sure it will be Clayton Adams—he's the older man you saw on the news. He's the lead attorney."

"Anything else I should know?" Ellen asked.

"Relax," Bob added as he led her down the hall to the conference room.

Ellen wasn't as nervous about her own deposition as she was about Daniel's, which would follow hers. Bob had assured her he would protect Daniel, but she was still frustrated that she couldn't be with him while he was being questioned. Even though she understood that since they were both witnesses she couldn't be in the room with him, she was adamant that he not go through this alone, and with Bob's help the defense team had agreed to allow her father to be in the room with Daniel. She was grateful her parents had been willing to help her with this; it eased her concern for Daniel somewhat. It was something she thought Tim should have offered to help with, but when he didn't, she was too stubborn to ask him for a favor. Taking a deep breath, she held her head high and entered the room. It was small with high windows that did little to add any natural light. The defense attorneys were on one side of the oblong oak table and the court stenographer at the end, still setting up her equipment. Ellen and Bob took seats facing the defense team. She was taken aback by the sheer number of them; along with the two she had seen on the news, Mr. Adams and Ms. Ballwin, there were two other men.

All four were impeccably dressed. Ms. Ballwin was wearing a teal silk suit and her hair was pulled back in a French twist. She had on what appeared to be very expensive, but simple, gold jewelry. She radiated competence and self-assurance. Ellen immediately felt rumpled. Clayton Adams was wearing a dark gray herringbone print suit. His shirt was white, perfectly starched, and his red paisley tie was complemented by a kerchief in his breast pocket. He and Lindsay are a matched set, Ellen thought. Glancing at his hands, she was sure he received regular manicures. When he saw her examining him, he gave her a smile that infuriated her. It was the smile a patient, benevolent, but uninvolved grandfather gives his toddler grandchild in the midst of a tantrum, as if to say, *Calm down now, silly one. You know I'm right, and when you've had your little fit you'll get yourself cleaned up, see things my way, and you'll apologize. Then I'll pat you on the head and send you to bed.*

Ellen didn't bother to investigate the remaining two lawyers—she knew their suits were expensive, their watches were Rolex, and they were the enemy. That was enough. Closing her eyes, she tried to relax. When she opened them and looked around the room again, she felt an incredible sense of calm. Screw all of you, she thought, looking across the table. I'm more ethical, more honorable than any of you. You make way more money than I do. I hate you and find you despicable. And I've lost something you might never, ever get. An amazing eleven-year-old son who laughed deeply from his belly, still sang made-up nonsense songs in the shower, kissed me full on the mouth except when his friends were around, and loved my spaghetti sauce. You think I'm just a mom and a teacher. Watch out.

"Let's begin, shall we?" Bob asked.

Ellen was sworn to tell the truth, reminded to answer out loud rather than by gestures, and the court reporter's machine began to hum as she tapped in their words.

Clayton Adams cleared his throat, opened his fountain pen, and sat back in his chair. "Mrs. Banks, let me first say how sorry we all are for the loss you and your family have suffered."

Ellen nodded at him warily. Bob had warned her that they might try a friendly approach, which could be disarming. He warned her not to let her guard down. "Thank you."

"Now, we just need to ask you some questions about that afternoon. Please ask for any clarification if you need it."

Again, Ellen nodded, and returned his smile with a cautious one of her own.

"Mrs. Banks, how far were you from your son when he was hit?" Clayton Adams asked softly. He was looking at her with his fountain pen poised above his legal pad.

She paused to think. She hated questions like this—she had no sense of distance or measurement. When she'd bought a phone outlet cord for her computer and modem in the hall to plug into the phone jack in her bedroom, she'd bought a cord one hundred feet long. She'd needed no more than twenty-five feet, and was amazed at all the extra cord she'd had to wind into a coil and hide behind her door. She could guess at the distance, but Bob had emphasized not to answer anything she didn't know for certain.

"I was on the dock. I don't know how far out he was."

"Fifty feet? One hundred feet?"

"I can see the exact spot in my mind, but I don't know what that distance might be."

Clayton Adams turned to one of the extra attorneys and said, "Perhaps we could go out there with Mrs. Banks to make a determination—"

"No!" Ellen blurted out. "I won't go out there."

They were startled by her outburst and began to dispute her, but Bob calmly interjected, "Those measurements are all in the police reports. No one is challenging where Mrs. Banks was, nor where the incident took place."

"Okay. Let's move on, then. Mrs. Banks, did you see the accident occur?"

Ellen again paused to try to see that day in her mind. She'd seen the Jet Skier. But had she seen the moment of impact? She wasn't sure. What she remembered most was Sam's face—and then looking out toward the children. That's when she had known something had happened.

"I don't know."

The defense lawyers looked at one another with raised eyebrows and skepticism. Lindsay Ballwin leaned over to Adams and whispered something to him. He nodded, then resumed questioning.

"Could you tell us what you do know?" The question seemed straightforward, but out of the corner of her eye Ellen thought she saw Ms. Ballwin suppress a smirk.

Look, you bitch, Ellen wanted to say to her, here's what I know: Your client mowed my son down. James had no chance. He never knew what hit him. It's a miracle your client didn't hit any of the other children. Here's what else I know: I know what it's like to sing to your child, praying and begging God with every note to let his eyelids twitch. I know what it's like to bring your thirteen-year-old into a hospital room and watch him tell his little brother goodbye, that he loves him, and that he's sorry he ever thought of him as a pain. I know what it's like to watch doctors wheel away the brain-dead but otherwise perfect body of your son to an operating room where they will cut him open and take out his organs so some other mother's child might live.

"Mr. Adams? And Miss Ballwin? Or is it Mrs.? I will tell you what I remember." Ellen spoke calmly and slowly. "The children were out in the water. They were out a good distance, but they could all still touch the bottom. Caroline was on a raft. They had been out there for at least an hour. They were diving under to retrieve things. They were playing tag. There were some ski boats on the lake, but not in the vicinity of the children. I was reading so I wasn't watching them the whole time, but I could hear them. I heard a Jet Ski approach—they make lots of noise—and I glanced up. One of us, I don't remember who, complained because it seemed awfully close to where the kids were. Then I saw the look on Sam's face just before he dove in. Then—" Ellen waited, hoping to keep her voice from breaking. "Then I looked out and saw only four heads."

Lindsay Ballwin started to whisper something else to Clayton Adams, but he cut her off, saying, "Thank you, Mrs. Banks. Bob, I believe we're done."

Ellen stared across the table at them, and out of the corner of her eye she saw the court reporter dab at her eye. Ellen pushed her chair away from the table and walked to the door.

Just before leaving, she turned to Clayton Adams and Lindsay Ballwin.

"My son, Daniel, will be in here next. Treat him kindly. Remember, he watched his little brother get killed."

Ellen waited in Bob's office while Daniel was deposed. She knew he'd be specific and detailed. He probably would know the distance from the dock to where the kids had been playing in the water. He had such a sense of accuracy about him. I'm glad he didn't see the moment of impact, Ellen thought. I wouldn't want him having to live with that memory. It was bad enough that they had the picture of Sam carrying James to the dock, the memory of James in the hospital. I don't want us to have to know the millisecond his brain went from being James to being mush.

Ellen could still recall with clarity the night Daniel had first talked to her about the accident. It had been two days after the funeral; Tim had returned to Detroit, and her parents had just left for their home in St. Louis that afternoon. Ellen and Daniel had suffered through an awkward dinner with both of them achingly aware of the empty chair at the table, but Ellen was too numb to talk about it, and Daniel seemed fearful of breaking the silence.

When Daniel had finished eating, he quietly carried his dishes over to the sink, and Ellen waved vaguely at him to signify he didn't need to help with any more cleanup. She heard him close the screen door as he went to the backyard. Then she heard the thud of the basketball as he dribbled on the driveway and began taking shots at the hoop hanging above the garage door.

How many hundreds of nights had the boys played one-on-one out there after dinner? she wondered. She could almost

hear them calling to one another, refereeing the game themselves as well as calling the play-by-play. They usually referred
to themselves in the third person, and it was always game
seven of the NBA finals. They had been good competition for
each other—James was stronger, but Daniel was quicker. The
silence that now defined Daniel's game for Ellen seemed sad
beyond words.

She was so lost in her remembering that Daniel startled
her when he came in a few minutes later. The kitchen was nearly
dark, and she caught only a glimpse of Daniel's face when
he opened the refrigerator. She had to look closely to see the
smudges of tears on his cheeks.

I should go to him, she thought. He needs a hug. He needs
to talk. But as she sat on the hard oak kitchen chair, she
thought, I don't know if I can.

Her legs and feet seemed wooden, and her tongue felt
swollen and dry, but she finally said, "Daniel? Are you okay?"

He didn't respond, just stood staring into the coolness of
the fridge, but his hand shook as he reached for the bottle of
Gatorade.

"Daniel," Ellen called to him again.

"What?" He turned to face her, and she tried to read what
was in his eyes. It wasn't the deep sadness that had been there
for days. It seemed too angry for sadness. If he hadn't looked
so tired she would have called it rage, but she knew that they
were both too exhausted for the vehemence of rage.

Finally, willing herself to get out of her chair, she got up
and walked over to him.

"Honey, what is it?" As soon as she said this, she immedi-
ately felt the stupidity of her question. It was James, of course.
Every breath, every sigh, every beat of their hearts echoed
James. "Daniel," she continued, "honey. Let's talk."

"No." He spoke softly, but he left no room for argument.

He took several big gulps from the Gatorade bottle, glared at her as if daring her to chastise him for that, screwed the lid back on, returned the bottle to the fridge, and stalked off to his room.

Ellen stood staring at the spot where he had been and shook her head. All I want to do is go to sleep, she thought. But I can't. I can't lose him to this. She walked to his room and knocked softly on the door. His reply, muffled by blankets or his pillow or both, was still decipherable.

"Leave me alone."

Where's the parenting book for this? she wondered.

"Honey?" she called through the door. "I'll be in the kitchen if you need me."

While she washed the dishes and wiped off the table and countertops, it occurred to her how inadequate language was at a time like this. We think we have so many words, she thought. We have dictionaries full of definitions. How often do I tell a student to consult a thesaurus? But words can fall so far short. I can't explain to anyone how this feels. It all sounds clichéd and trite. And there are no words that go deep enough—go all the way to the marrow of the pain. And I'm an English teacher. I'm supposed to know how our language works. If I can't put it into words, how much more frustrating must it be for Daniel? But, Ellen told herself, I have to help him try.

She went to his door again, knocked softly, but rather than wait for his dismissive response, this time she turned the knob and went on in.

He was sprawled on his bed, on his stomach, with his face turned to the wall. He hadn't invited her in, but he also didn't tell her to leave.

She sat on the bed next to him and started rubbing his back. At first, he stiffened, but, as she continued to rub, she felt him relax into her touch. His breathing grew deep and steady and slow, and just when she thought he was asleep, he rolled over on his side to face her.

Daniel looked at her for a few moments, then said, "Mom. I'm really sorry."

Ellen nodded, then wondered what exactly he was apologizing for. And she worried that if she asked for an explanation he would shut her out again.

But before she could even ask, he continued, "I'm sorry, but I wish it had been me. Or both of us, even."

At that, Ellen had to force herself to stifle a moan. God, no, she thought, I couldn't bear it to have lost both of them. But she knew how easily the Jet Ski could have hit more children.

"No, Daniel. No. Don't wish for that."

"I do, though. Then I wouldn't have to miss him."

Ah, Ellen thought. There it is. I've wished that myself. Who knows how many more times I'll wish it in the days to come. If I was dead, I wouldn't feel this.

"Oh, honey," she soothed, "we have to help each other now. We both miss James. But let's miss him together."

"Did you see it, Mom? Did you see James get hit?"

"No," Ellen said, shaking her head, remembering the sudden terror of Sam's dive into the water. "I just saw Sam bringing him to the surface. Did you see him get hit?" When Ellen asked this, she fervently hoped he hadn't.

"No. I was teasing Caroline. And she was splashing me." Daniel sighed before adding, "Maybe if I'd been watching I could have . . ." His voice drifted off.

"No, baby. Don't take that on. Nobody could have known. You couldn't have stopped it." When Ellen spoke, though, she knew that Daniel wouldn't easily let go of this.

~~~~~~

Ellen was still lost in thought when the office door opened and Bob ushered Daniel and her father inside.

"How'd it go, kiddo?" she asked.

"Kinda weird."

"How?" She looked from Daniel to Bob and back again.

"Well, I thought it might be hard to remember everything. It all happened so fast."

"Was it hard?"

"No. It was like yesterday. I was right there again."

"Oh, honey, I'm sorry."

"No, Mom. It's okay. I heard—" Daniel looked at Ellen and then at the floor. "—I heard his voice again, Mom."

Ellen felt her breath catch in her throat and she went to reach for him, but he backed away ever so slightly, stood up straight, and added, "I liked it. I was afraid I'd forgotten his voice. Talking about the lake brought it back to me."

Ellen looked up at her father. He was standing right behind her son, and Ellen sensed his desire to hug Daniel was almost as strong as her own.

"What did you think of the whole procedure, Dad?"

He coughed and tried to clear his throat before answering. "It all seemed pretty cut and dried, very business-like." He seemed very business-like himself until the crack in his voice at the end of his answer.

On the way home after the deposition, all three of them were quiet. For Ellen, as the trial grew closer, she felt both relief and fear. She had tried to make sense of it, but the most she could do was identify the emotions; she wasn't able to fully make sense of them.

In talking to Anna about it, Anna suggested that the relief and fear might stem from the same source: the finality of it all.

"Once it's over, it'll all be done with," Anna said.

"Well, I see how I'd feel relieved about that," Ellen said, "but where's the fear coming from?"

"Same thing. It'll be over. Your whole focus, at least since last fall, has been on this trial. And you're scared that when it's over you'll have to find a new focus."

Ellen had thought about that a great deal later that evening. Could that be true, she asked herself. Does the end of the trial mark the real end of James? It gave her a headache just to think about it. But she still wondered, what will get me up in the morning then? She thought of the weeks after she and Tim had finally split up. It would have been so easy to crawl under her warm covers and bemoan her life and never get up again. But mornings would come early, and the soft, high voices of her children would beckon to her, and she'd propel herself out of bed. Her day would begin by scrambling eggs and making toast—and she gradually found new patterns for her life, through her children. They had pulled her back and up at that time. Was James doing the same thing now, through the trial? And if so, then Anna was right. Who would get her up when it was all over?

Her mother was waiting for them when they returned home from the deposition. The smell of roast chicken greeted them when they walked in the house.

After hugging her mom, Ellen flopped onto the sofa, leaned back, and closed her eyes. Exhaustion and relief flooded over her. She knew today hadn't been anywhere near as intense as the trial would be, but she felt she had successfully scaled this hurdle, so that at least gave her confidence about the taller ones waiting for her up ahead.

She heard the murmured voices of her parents and Daniel

in the kitchen, and the soft rhythm of their words lulled her to sleep.

When she woke up, she realized her parents were still talking.

"Did you see the Jet Skier? That Buchanan kid?" her mother asked her dad.

"No. At least not that I know of."

"I hope this is the right thing for Ellen to be pursuing. It worries me a little."

"I don't know," her dad answered. "I guess, though, that if she thinks it'll help her, then we have to hope it will."

Their words infuriated Ellen. How could they not support her? she fumed. They'd lost a grandson, hadn't they? Didn't they want to see justice done? See somebody held accountable?

Ellen heard the chair scrape on the wooden floor when her mother got up from the kitchen table. She heard her walk to the sink, and then her mother glanced into the family room to check on Ellen.

"Hi, dear. Have a nice rest?"

Ellen gritted her teeth before responding, "Pretty good. Where's Daniel?"

Her mother, ignoring Ellen's icy tone, said, "Over at Joey's. But he should be home soon. It's nearly dinnertime."

Her father hollered in to ask if he could get her something to drink; she guessed that he was ready for his evening scotch and soda.

"Sure," she said. "I'll be right in to set the table, too."

"Don't worry," her mom said. "You just relax, I've got this all taken care of."

They don't know I overheard them, Ellen thought. They can't see how hurt and mad I am. And if I try to explain it, I'll end up in tears, and they still won't get it. They still think of me as their baby. As a child. As needing help. Like they've just taken the training wheels off my Schwinn. She remembered how they had urged her to move to St. Louis to be near them after she and Tim had split up.

"We'll be close by so we can help with everything," her mother had offered.

"Mom, our life—the boys' and mine—is here. This is the only house the boys know."

"But you'll never be able to keep it up by yourself."

Ellen ignored her mother's doubt and worry, and added, "Besides, their dad is here. I don't want to have to stick them on a plane to see him once a month or so."

"Well, I don't think you should be counting on him to stick around."

And of course, they all knew Tim hadn't stayed in Madison. Just get through the evening, she told herself; they'll be leaving in the morning.

Daniel chattered throughout dinner. Finally he asked her dad, "Will you be coming back for the trial?"

"You just let us know when it is, and we'll be here."

"That's not necessary," Ellen said.

All three of them looked at her in surprise.

"Honey, of course we'll be here," her mom protested.

"Only if you think it's 'the right thing to be doing.' "

"Ellen, you misunderstood what we said," her dad soothed.

"No, I believe that was a direct quote."

"Mom? What are you guys talking about?" Daniel looked around at all three of them, his eyes burning with concern.

"You misunderstood what we meant," her mother explained.

"Not a lot of shades of meaning there, Mom." At that, Ellen

stood up and began to gather the plates. Her mother looked worriedly at her father. Ellen went to the sink and noisily scraped the food scraps off the plates, and then she turned on the garbage disposal and let it run much longer than necessary.

When her parents left the next morning, Ellen called Anna to complain. "They're questioning the trial."

"In what way?"

"Well, I overheard them talking about if it was 'the right thing to do.' I can't believe they have any doubts about this. They saw James in that hospital room."

"Oh, El, maybe they're just worried about you and Daniel. Worried that all this is going to drain you too much."

"But can't they see how much I need this?"

"My guess, knowing your folks, is that all they can see, all they want to see, is that you're still in such pain."

The school year ended uneventfully for all of them. On the last day, as Ellen packed up some of the books in her room and took down items from her bulletin board, she heard some girls in the hallway. The voices grew closer and were soon at her door.

"Mrs. Banks?"

"Hi," Ellen said, placing some thumbtacks in a small container on her desk. "I haven't posted grades yet, if that's what you're looking for."

"No, that's okay," the two girls said in unison.

"We just wanted to give you this," one of them said, holding out an envelope.

"Well, thanks." Ellen walked toward them to accept the offering. "Can I open it now?"

The girls nodded and Ellen opened the card. While grade school teachers were usually showered with gifts at the end of the year, gifts for high school teachers were a rarity. Ellen was pleased to see a gift certificate for her favorite neighborhood bookstore.

"Thank you," she said. "This is so thoughtful."

"Well, we really loved your class. Thanks for being so fun. And for making us work so hard."

"You're very welcome. Have a great summer."

After the girls left, with smiles and promises to visit in the fall, Ellen sat back down at her desk, looking at the card and gift certificate. Fun? I didn't think I was very fun this year, she thought. She looked at the signatures on the card. Vanessa and Shelley. Ellen shook her head. I don't even know which one was which, she thought. I couldn't even say which one of my classes they were in. I truly was a robot this year. Have I been that preoccupied? That self-absorbed? What else have I missed this semester? I used to be so critical of teachers who couldn't remember names of students they'd had just the year before, and here I don't recognize kids who were in my class last week. I don't want to admit this to anybody.

Chapter
Fourteen

Ellen looked around the small, drab room she was seated in at the courthouse. She drummed her fingers on the laminate table where she sat sipping bad coffee from a Styrofoam cup. She waited. Two days ago Bob had explained, once again, why she couldn't be in the courtroom during the trial.

"You're a witness. No attorney is going to allow a potential witness to hear the testimony of other witnesses."

"But it's not like I don't talk to the other major witnesses," she argued. And she had a point. Anna, Sam, Daniel, and Sarah, Anna's oldest daughter, were all likely to be called to testify. And they had all spoken a great deal about the accident and the trial.

"I know," Bob had replied. "That's just the way it works, though. I'm sorry."

~~~~~~

During yesterday's jury selection, Ellen had been surprised when Bob came out for the lunch break and said that court was recessed until the next day, when opening arguments would begin.

"The jury is picked already?" Ellen asked.

"Sure."

"But didn't you strike a lot of them?"

"El? Let me tell you the cold, hard truth of jury selection. Most times, it's the first twelve people."

"You mean you questioned all of them and none of them is prejudiced against the case?"

Bob laughed and said, "Ellen, you watch too many lawyer TV shows. Jury selection, unless it's a huge case like OJ, is generally pretty cut-and-dried. It only becomes high drama in movies and novels."

"That's a letdown," Ellen said.

"Hey, if it makes you feel better, we had to go through fifteen to get our twelve."

"Really?" Ellen asked, her face brightening. "Why?"

"Well, one guy was scheduled for surgery and two women had child care problems."

"Oh. So, do you think it'll be a favorable jury for us?"

"Our ideal jury would have been twelve moms. All with eleven-year-old sons. We didn't get that, though."

"What did we get?"

"From what I can tell, more sympathetic parents than avid sportsmen."

Ellen thought about this for a few moments as Bob stood watching her. Finally she turned to him with a request.

"Can I see the courtroom?" Ellen asked.

"Sure."

"I just want to sit in it for a few minutes. Get a feel for it."

When Bob showed her in, the room was empty. It was

smaller than she'd expected. And less grand. She felt mildly disappointed by it. The area for family and friends was simply several rows of padded metal chairs. She had imagined pew-like rows of dark oak or pine benches, worn smooth with age. The jury box was angled behind the witness bench and was made up of the same padded metal chairs placed on risers. Where are the tall, deep windows? she thought. Where are the oak beams? The judge's bench and witness areas looked like pressed board, reminiscent of shelving systems purchased at discount department stores.

Ellen closed her eyes. In her mind she could hear the resonant voices of Gregory Peck and Spencer Tracy—the celluloid lawyers who had created her visions of what courtrooms and trials should be.

"Where's the other table?" she asked Bob.

"What other table?"

"For the defense attorneys."

There was only the single, long rectangular table placed in front of the judge's bench.

"There's only one table. They just sit at the opposite end from us," Bob explained.

Ellen shook her head and thought, nothing seems as sturdy or as sure as I had imagined. She walked up to the judge's bench and peered over. Her eyes started to fill. She turned to leave and saw Bob jotting down a note on the folded-up piece of legal paper he always had in his shirt pocket. He is sturdy. Sure. He's Atticus. She suddenly knew that it was both of them—James and Bob—who gave her the strength and the courage to be here.

For a brief moment Ellen wished her parents were here with her. She knew that their desire to be with her was stronger than their doubt about the wisdom of this trial. And as determined as she felt about this case, she wondered if she'd feel less shaky if they were with her. Once again, she tried to weigh the pluses and minuses, making two lists in her head. Her mom's hovering, which set Ellen's teeth on edge just thinking about it, versus her dad's deep, calm voice, which just in the remembering could slow her breathing. Her dad's impatient pacing, which frayed Ellen's nerves, versus her mom's scent—a blend of Dial soap, Elizabeth Arden lipstick, Oil of Olay moisturizer, and Aqua Net hair spray—which never failed to make Ellen feel cared for whenever she smelled it.

I'll see how I feel tonight, Ellen thought. They would drive up tomorrow if I want them to, she knew.

"Dad?" Ellen held the phone close to her ear but let her head fall all the way back so that it rested on the top of the sofa back.

"Hi, honey. How's the trial going?"

"Well, it'll get under way tomorrow. They just had jury selection today. Bob thought that went pretty well, I think. I'm on tomorrow after the opening arguments, and then we just wait for the verdict."

"How's Daniel holding up?"

"Fine, I think. He's pretty tough."

"I'm proud of you both."

When Ellen heard him say this, she smiled and let out a small sigh. "Thanks, Dad."

"Let me holler to your mother. I know she'll want to talk to you."

Ellen heard her dad calling her mom, and then she could hear her mother scurrying to the phone.

"Ellen, how are you doing, sweetie?"

"Well, the jury selection was today. I'm probably on tomorrow," Ellen paused, as if waiting for her mother's disapproval, but it wasn't to be found.

"Do you think it'll go well?"

"Bob seems to think so, but who knows how the jury'll hear this. It should all be over in two more days, three at the most."

"I'll be glad for you, then."

"Yeah. Me, too." Ellen rubbed her eyes and stretched out her legs. She flexed her feet then pointed her toes, trying to stretch all the muscles in her legs. Man, am I tired, she thought.

"How's Daniel doing?"

"Fine." Ellen took a deep breath before blurting out, "Can you and Dad drive up tomorrow? Then you'd at least be here for the closing arguments and the verdict."

The hesitation before her mother answered showed the surprise she must have felt at hearing Ellen's request. At least Ellen hoped it was surprise and not disapproval.

"I mean," Ellen added, "only if you guys can get away."

"Plan on it, honey. We'll leave first thing in the morning."

They said their goodbyes and already Ellen felt a prickle of regret at her invitation. She could picture her mother, bustling around, getting things packed and ready. She knew without being told that her mother would bring dinner and her sewing kit. In the two or three days her parents would be at her house, all the mending Ellen had ignored for months would be completed. And the ironing basket would soon be empty for the first time in weeks. Everything would be "shipshape"—as her mother was fond of saying. And by the end of their visit, Ellen would be completely irritated and eager for them to leave.

"So why'd you ask them to come up?" Anna asked after Ellen had reeled off her litany of complaints.

"Spur of the moment, I guess," Ellen said, stretching her neck from side to side in a vain attempt to release tension.

"I think it'll be nice for you to have them here."

"I know. I mean, I asked them. And it'll be good for Daniel. It's just that whenever we get together there's more tension than I want there to be, and I end up being really bitchy. Then, later, I feel guilty about having been so bitchy. So then, I invite them for another visit."

"One vicious circle, huh?"

"Yeah. I guess."

"Go to bed, Ellen. You're tired. And you've got to gear up for your testimony tomorrow."

"Yeah. All that and a visit from my folks."

And now Ellen sat in the witness room, drinking bad coffee and hoping Bob's opening argument had gone well. Sam had taken Sarah and Daniel out for a walk. Anna was on the stand. Bob planned to put on Anna, then the children, then Sam. He had the police scheduled for after Sam, and he wanted to close with Ellen.

"Remember," he kept telling her, "it's about emotion. We want the jury to see you trying to protect your own children as well as theirs. The defense wants the jury to see you as an intruder to the area and as an encroacher on the freedom of sportsmen. They want the jury to see you as angry and trying to place blame, rather than simply very sad and trying to prevent more tragedy."

So, Ellen thought, I can be sad, but not irate. I'm not trying to limit freedom, but ensure safety. This is like an acting job. I'm feeling all of these things, but I can't show that. Ick, she said to herself. I hate this. They keep telling me to tell the truth, but they each want me to blurt out a different truth. Bob wants the mournful, maternal truth. Adams and Ballwin want the vengeful truth. She dug in her purse looking for some gum or mints. The coffee had left an acrid taste in her mouth and her stomach was reminding her that not only hadn't she eaten, but she'd drunk too much coffee. Great, she mused, they'll call me to the stand and I'll be in the bathroom.

From where she was, she could see into the courtroom. She felt as if she were in one of those soundproof booths on a TV show. She watched Anna as she testified. Just from her body language, Ellen knew that Anna was explaining the dock and the lake. Distances, lake activity, all of that. Anna's expressive hands were busy and she knew Anna's voice, deeper than her own, and softer, would help the jury to see the lake as a place of safety and quiet recreation. She thought again about the conversation she and Anna'd had the night before last in Anna's room as they decided what to wear today. Ellen had apologized again to Anna for Sarah having to testify.

"Please, El, she's okay about it," Anna assured Ellen.

"I know, but she's only fifteen. I hate this for her."

"You know, I think she wanted to even before Bob asked her about it." Anna walked into her closet then, still talking, but her words were muffled by the clothes.

"Anna? What'd you say?"

"I said, we all wanted to testify. And—" She paused and then forged ahead. "—we never have talked about that night in the hospital. About how you felt guilty for hoping it wasn't Daniel or James."

"Oh," said Ellen. She wasn't sure she could talk about this, and she worried about what Anna would say. She'd told Anna about her prayer for the boys and Anna had been so gracious, but Ellen still felt guilty. "I think we've said it all."

"Ellie, you think you did something wrong then, don't you? You feel bad about hoping it wasn't Daniel or James. Don't."

"Well, I do."

"Look, let's get rid of the guilt, okay? Does it change anything?"

"No."

"I feel horrible, too, you know. That it was your child. That you were at our house. Even Sam has second-guessed not having buoys in place."

"None of it was your fault. It was all brought on by Buchanan."

"I know, but still . . ." Anna's voice trailed off before she continued, "As much as you have to live with your having hoped that two little boys' heads would pop up, I have to live with that instant of relief I felt when I saw three heads with long blond hair. And then—"

"And then we were in it together. We were moms grieving over one of our own."

They had looked at each other a long time then, and they both understood. And felt the relief that comes with finally saying the words.

"Ellen?"

"Hmm?" Ellen stood back and pondered two possible outfits she had spread out on the bed.

"The girls, well, all of us, were wondering if, er, hoping, you and Daniel would come out to the lake soon."

Ellen didn't respond, just kept looking at the clothes. If I pretend I don't hear her, she figured, I won't have to answer.

"El?"

"No, Anna."

"Please?"

"I said no. I can't. I'm sorry," Ellen snapped.

And now Anna was testifying. Ellen watched Anna brush her soft long curls behind her ear and knew it was a stalling tactic. Hmm, she wondered, what's being asked? She heard voices in the hall and turned toward the open door. Sam and the kids appeared and while Sarah and Daniel looked happy as they munched on bagels, Sam's face clearly showed the strain of the day. Those lines in his face were new, she thought. He looked through the window at Anna and asked Ellen, "How long has she been on the stand?"

"About twenty minutes. I have to think she'll be off soon."

"Then it's me, right?" Daniel asked.

Just then they saw Anna step down and make her way out of court. They saw Bob stand up, and then the bailiff was in the doorway asking for Daniel.

"Do great, sweetie," Ellen called after him.

He looks so small, Ellen thought as he stood before the judge, one hand on the Bible, the other raised. What must this feel like for him? When he'd been younger, she'd always been able to gauge his mood. One look at his face, or even a glance at how he stood, and she would know. She tried to read his shoulders now. They just struck her as sad. And alone. He'd be starting high school this fall; shouldn't she have helped him choose his classes? Or had she and now she couldn't remember? I know what Tim and my parents think of this trial, she thought, but I have no idea how Daniel feels about it. I should know that. And now he was on a witness stand, looking at the young man who had killed his little brother.

Ellen wondered what she would feel when she first saw Benjamin Buchanan in person. It would be sometime this afternoon, she knew. Daniel looked so earnest. She could see that when he answered he was not only saying yes or no, but nodding or shaking his head accordingly. After he'd been deposed, his only comments about the defense attorneys had been that they seemed pretty nice. Hope that holds true for you today, babe, she said to herself. Bob had assured her that Adams and Ballwin would only make the jury mad if they were rough at all with Daniel, or with her, he added.

"Remember," he had said, "if they come off like bullies, the jury'll hate them and sympathize with you. They just want to raise doubt."

"Ellen Keeler Banks." It was the bailiff standing at the door.

Numbly, she rose and followed him into the courtroom. Standing before the judge, she swore to tell the truth. Then she was seated in the witness stand. She took a deep breath, folded her hands on her lap, and directed her attention to Bob. He was looking down at his table, pulling some papers out of a file folder. A blond, tan young man caught her eye. As she looked at him, he glanced up at her with piercing blue eyes. She flinched. My God, she thought, that's him. Benjamin Buchanan. He's a child. She had imbued him with all sorts of evil. She had turned him into a monster who'd been murderously careless and reckless. He hasn't even lost all the baby fat in his face yet, she almost said out loud.

"Mrs. Banks." Bob pulled her attention back to him. "On the afternoon of August seventh, could you tell us where you and your son James were?"

"At a friend's lake house. At Lake Augusta in Bainbridge."

"Had you been there before?"

"Often. We went out frequently during the year. And every August for the past ten years we stayed out there for a full week."

"That particular afternoon, what were you and James doing just before the Jet Ski incident occurred?"

"I was on the dock with our friends. James was in the water with the other children."

"How long had he been in the water?"

"Over an hour."

"What were they doing?"

"Standing and talking. Plotting games, I suppose."

"But they were clearly visible?"

"Yes."

"Were they underwater as well?"

"One or two at a time, maybe, but there were always at least two above the surface."

"How can you be so sure?"

"Well, Caroline, my friend's youngest, was on a raft. She could just barely touch the bottom, but wasn't completely confident about it. So one of the older children was always above the surface with her."

"When did you first know something was wrong?"

"When Sam jumped in. No, actually, just before that."

"Can you explain to the jury what you mean?"

"We saw the Jet Skier drive past. He'd seemed too close to the children. We commented on that. Then I saw Sam's expression change and he dove into the water."

"Mrs. Banks. Can you tell us what happened then?"

It all flashed back. It seemed so real and close again that she could almost hear the dull whine of the ski boats and smell the gas fumes from their motors.

"Sam pulled James to the dock. Then the paramedics took him to the hospital."

"And then?" Bob asked so quietly Ellen thought the jury might have to lean forward to hear him.

"Then," she paused, remembering Bob's directions to tell it simply. Not too many medical details. Don't bore the jury, he'd warned. "Then, after he'd been transferred to University Hospital, well, by Tuesday night there was no hope. He was brain-dead. We removed him from life support."

"No more questions." Bob sat down and gave her a reassuring smile.

Lindsay Ballwin rose slowly. "Mrs. Banks? I have just a few questions for you."

Ellen nodded and tried to remember all of Bob's directions. So she's going to run this part of the trial, Ellen thought. Bob had discussed that possibility with Ellen earlier. He'd even said that if he were on the other side, he would definitely have a woman question Ellen. When she'd asked him why, his response had been that it'd even things out for the jury. When you've got two women opposing each other, he'd said, they tend to "cancel the other out" emotionally, at least for the jury.

"When you were on the dock, when did you first notice the Jet Skier?" Ms. Ballwin asked Ellen.

"Well, when he got too close to the children."

"And you were watching the children the whole time?"

"Why, yes. All three of us were."

"Not reading a book?" Ballwin queried.

"Well, that, too, but one of us was always watching and we were all listening."

"But not watching enough to warn the children they were out too deep?"

"They weren't out too deep," Ellen snapped.

"No? But they were in the way of motorized watercraft."

"Objection!" Bob stood up quickly.

"Withdrawn."

You jerk, Ellen fumed. Don't try to make me look careless. I didn't kill anybody. Ms. Ballwin paused, removed some notes from her folder, and then continued her questioning.

"Mrs. Banks, can you identify the Jet Skier who allegedly ran into your son?"

"He's right there." Ellen pointed to Buchanan. "At the table with you," she added.

"But you didn't see the actual impact, did you?"

"No, I don't believe so."

"Nor have you laid eyes on the defendant until now, have you?"

"Well, no, but I was—"

"Thank you, Mrs. Banks. The jury heard your answer. Just a few more questions."

God, I hate you, Ellen stormed to herself. I was trying to save my son, you bitch, I wasn't looking at the Jet Skier to prepare for a lineup.

"Mrs. Banks, how often do you drink?"

"What?"

"How often do you drink alcohol?" Lindsay Ballwin slowly repeated her question.

"Objection, Your Honor. Relevance?" Bob asked.

"Your Honor, if you will allow me a few more questions the relevance will be clear."

The judge nodded, then turned to Ellen and said, "Mrs. Banks, please answer the question."

"I, uh, have an occasional glass of wine."

"Every day?"

Ellen looked at Bob, the confusion and anger welling up in her. Stay calm, she told herself. Bob looked back at her with his eyebrows slightly arched. What is this all about, she wanted to ask him. Where is this coming from? He seemed to answer her unspoken question with a brief shake of his head.

"I will sometimes have a glass of wine with dinner." Ellen looked down at her clenched hands after she answered.

"Only one glass? Or is it sometimes two? Only with dinner?"

The questions came rapidly at Ellen, and she opened her mouth to answer, but didn't speak because she didn't know how to answer.

"Objection, Your Honor. Badgering. And I still am objecting to relevance."

"Ms. Ballwin," warned the judge, "let the witness answer. And get to your point."

"Mrs. Banks, how much wine had you consumed the day of the accident while you were out on the dock?"

The courtroom grew very quiet, as if they were all waiting for this one answer.

"I don't know." Ellen gripped the sides of her chair. She felt like she was going to slide right off onto the floor. Bob hadn't warned her about this. What was happening?

"You don't know?" Ms. Ballwin shook her head and gave Ellen a doubting look. "Is that because you had lost count?"

"No!" Ellen swallowed hard and tried to keep thinking straight. How should I be answering these questions?

"What did you have for dinner that day on the dock?"

"We hadn't eaten yet. It was only late afternoon." Out of the corner of her eye she saw Bob frown and rub the bridge of his nose. What, she wanted to ask him. But then she could only glare back at Lindsay Ballwin.

"So you don't just drink with dinner, do you, Mrs. Banks."

Ellen felt like she was drowning.

"Objection!"

"Your Honor." Lindsay turned to address the judge. "I am trying to show that Mrs. Banks and the other adults that day were under the influence of alcohol. They had no business supervising the children at that time. The police reports show the presence of empty wineglasses on the dock at the time of the accident. I also call into question the veracity of the rest of Mrs. Banks' testimony given that her statement about drinking just with dinner was false."

"Your Honor." Bob again addressed the judge, almost pleading with him to stop this process.

"Counsel should approach the bench."

Ellen sat back in the witness chair. She felt the jury staring at her with disapproval. She couldn't bring herself to look back at them, to face their critical eyes. She looked out at the others in the courtroom. No one would meet her gaze. Bob and the other attorneys were still whispering with the judge. Ellen tried to lean in to hear what they were discussing, but she couldn't clearly make out any of their words. As the attorneys began to back away from the bench, the judge announced that the court was adjourned until after lunch.

Ellen didn't move. She saw Bob talking to his assistant; the assistant then nodded and hurried out. Clayton Adams and Lindsay Ballwin huddled together briefly, then started gathering their documents and folders together. God, I hate them, Ellen thought. I really hate them both. She continued to glare at them as they made their way out of the courtroom. She didn't even notice Bob approaching her.

"Ellen?"

She looked up at him but failed to see the fatigue in his eyes. She started to speak, but he held his hand up to stop her.

"Let's go to one of the witness rooms. We can talk there." He paused and looked at his watch, then continued, "We have a little over an hour before we have to be back in here. I'll have some sandwiches brought in."

She followed him out of the courtroom and into the wide hallway. At the end of the hall, past the elevators, she saw Lindsay Ballwin talking to some of her associates. One of them was grinning broadly and another patted Lindsay on the back. Ellen had to fight back the urge to run screaming and clawing at them. Bob saw her staring at them and quickly ushered her into the witness room.

As soon as he closed the door, Ellen wheeled around to confront him.

"What the hell happened in there? How did I suddenly become the bad guy in all this?"

"Ellen, calm down. They're doing what they were hired to do."

"They were hired to make me look like a drunk? They were hired to focus all the blame on me?"

"In a sense, yes. They were hired to defend Benjamin Buchanan. They're good, Ellen. They can't dispute the facts of the accident, so they want to show that there is blame everywhere, not just with Ben."

"Bob, why didn't you warn me about this?"

"Why didn't you put your wineglass away before you gave that damn TV interview?" Bob shot back at her.

"What?" Ellen shook her head to try to clear away the confusion that swirled in her mind. "What're you talking about? What wineglass? What interview?"

"Ellen, sit down. Have some water."

"Don't try to 'manage' me. What do you know that I don't know?"

"The interview, El. With Grace Benham. For Channel Fifteen. The one you gave before the boat show opened."

"What about it?"

"You'd had some wine before they came over?"

"Yes. With dinner." She caught herself in the half-lie. "And a little bit after. But I wasn't drunk." She felt a hint of sheepishness creep into her answer, but shook it off. "So what?"

"Ellen. The wineglass. It's on the tape. In the background. It wasn't in the clip that made it onto the newscast, but it's on the tape." Bob's voice sounded tired.

"And how do they know that?"

"One of Ballwin's associates is friends with the cameraman, who mentioned it to her. Anyway, Lindsay knows it's on the tape. She wants to introduce it as evidence. She's got that, and the police report."

Ellen slumped at the table, then slowly looked up at Bob. "What does it say in the police report?"

"At the end of it there is a listing of what was found at the scene of the accident and what was on the dock."

"It says there were wineglasses? And you missed that? You missed that detail and let them set me up to look like a lush?"

"No. I didn't miss that detail. The report just says there were glasses on the dock. But after Ballwin learned about the wineglass on the tape from the cameraman, they went back to the officer who filed the report and asked him if he could be more specific about the type of glasses that were found."

"That can't be admissible, can it?"

"I'm sorry, but it is. So's the video."

"Oh God, the jury is going to blame me now."

"Not necessarily. Ellen, the case is still about Ben Buchanan's responsibility. I can bring the jury back to that. You've got to trust me."

"But this is bad, isn't it? This hurts us."

"Yes, it does. But it's out there now. We can't get it back. So we don't hide from it, and we try to minimize the damage as best we can."

"I'm so sorry."

The door opened, and Bob's assistant brought in some sandwiches and sodas. Ellen didn't feel like eating, so when Bob slid a sandwich her way, she shook her head.

"Ellen, you have to eat something."

"No. I can't."

"What have you had to eat today?"

"Coffee."

"Breakfast of champions."

"I wasn't hungry then, either," Ellen said and then, as a compromise, reached for a Coke. Bob reached across the table and gently grabbed her arm.

"Listen to me. You can't go back in that courtroom and get up on the stand after consuming only caffeine. You'll be shaky and jumpy. Is that what you want the jury to see?"

Ellen answered him by unwrapping the sandwich and taking a big bite out of it.

Chapter
Fifteen

"Mrs. Banks, I want to remind you that you are still under oath from this morning," the judge said as Ellen stood in the witness box.

"Yes, Your Honor."

"Mrs. Banks, before the lunch recess we were going over your alcohol consumption," Lindsay Ballwin started the questioning. "Let's briefly review for the jury, shall we?"

Ellen gritted her teeth. Remember, she told herself, stay calm. Keep your anger in check. Bob had warned her not to take the bait, not to look too defensive. The judge was less apt to let the defense introduce the Channel 15 tape if Ellen did not deny drinking.

"Now," Lindsay continued, "how many glasses of wine had you consumed that afternoon?"

"One glass."

"And what had you eaten?"

"Some fruit, some Mexican dip with chips, and some Goldfish crackers."

"And other than eating snacks and drinking wine and reading a book, you were also sunbathing, correct?"

"We were sitting on lounge chairs and they were in the sun." Ellen tried to keep her voice even.

"Were you actively working on your tan?"

"I don't believe that working on a tan takes much effort." Ellen heard a chuckle or two in the courtroom.

"Witness should answer the question," the judge warned.

"Let me rephrase," Lindsay said. "Were you lying in a prone position?"

"No. I was sitting up."

"Easier to drink and eat and read that way?"

"Possibly. But also that's the best way to watch the children."

"So between drinking wine, eating snacks, reading a book, and working on your tan, you were also acting as a lifeguard?"

"I guess you could say that."

"And from where did you receive your lifeguard certification?"

" I don't have certification."

"But you know CPR, don't you?"

"No."

"So you weren't acting as a lifeguard, were you?"

"We were all aware of the children in the water."

"Aware enough to warn them not to go out too deep?"

"Yes."

"And how would you know if they were out too deep?"

"They knew to stay where Caroline could touch the bottom."

"So you had no idea, other than relying on the judgment of children, if they were in shallow enough water."

"Miss Ballwin, we were all familiar with the lake depth. We could tell just by looking."

"And you knew that if you called them to come closer to the dock, they would do so?"

"Yes."

"What about the motorboats and Jet Skis?"

"What about them?"

"Had they been warned to make sure they were not in the path of those?"

"Of course."

"So you knew about the dangers of motorized watercraft and had passed that warning on to the children."

"Well, not to the extent that I do now, but yes, they'd been warned."

"The children knew not to get too close to them?"

"Yes."

"And you knew they were being used on the lake that day?"

"Sure. They would sometimes drown out our conversation."

"The conversation you were having on the dock while you were drinking and eating?"

"Yes."

"And the boats and Jet Skis were sometimes close enough to drown out your conversation?"

"Yes."

"Did you call to the children when that occurred?"

"No."

"Why not?"

"Because if we couldn't hear one another on the dock, then the children certainly weren't going to be able to hear us as far out as they were in the water."

"They must have been out pretty far, Mrs. Banks."

"It's a shallow lake. It's amazing how far out into the lake you can walk—" Ellen stopped. I walked right into her trap, she realized.

"So with the noise on the lake, even if you had been watching the children instead of drinking and eating and reading, they couldn't have heard you call to them, could they?"

"Objection."

"Withdrawn. No further questions." Lindsay turned and walked back to the table. Clayton leaned toward her and nodded. Ellen couldn't take her eyes off them. She was fighting to stay in control, but her cheeks burned. How dare they make me look at fault, she raged.

Bob stood then and said in his calm, steady voice, "Redirect, Your Honor."

The judge nodded, and Bob walked casually toward Ellen.

"Ellen, you stated earlier that you went to the lake regularly over the years."

"Yes."

"Your boys essentially grew up going out to the lake, did they not?"

"Yes."

"So they were as familiar with the lake depth and the motorized activity on it as you were, correct?"

"Absolutely." Ellen felt the tension in her neck and shoulders start to fade as Bob questioned her in his easy manner.

"Now, as to what you consumed on the dock that afternoon—" Bob paused and smiled at her, then continued. "—can you tell the jury a little bit more about that?"

"Sure. We'd had a big breakfast late in the morning. Eggs, bacon, hash browns, toast, the works. So we really weren't hungry again until mid-afternoon. We brought the snacks out to the dock so we could watch the kids play before we went in to start dinner."

"How long had you been on the dock?"

"A couple of hours, I guess, most of the afternoon. But we only brought the food and wine out less than an hour before James was hit."

"And how much wine had you consumed?"

"Less than a glass. And I had been eating the whole time, too."

"Ellen, were you drunk? Or even a little tipsy?"

"No. Absolutely not. I was sipping one glass of wine. I was completely aware and alert."

"And there was no warning before James was hit?"

"No. The kids had been in the same general area all afternoon. They were well in from where the motorized vehicles were. And then, from out of nowhere, the Jet Ski shot in and hit James."

"Thank you, Ellen. You may step down." Ellen nodded and began to make her way off the witness stand. "The prosecution rests, Your Honor."

Ellen walked out of the courtroom and collapsed on one of the benches lining the hallway. She leaned back against the wall and closed her eyes. She felt the cool, hard marble beneath her as she tried to gain control. What happened in there, she wondered. How did everything get so off track? She forced her breathing to slow. What now? she wondered.

She tapped her head on the wall behind her, trying to make sense of the day. Compared with the confusion and anger she felt now, the nervousness that had defined her morning looked like relaxation. She continued to slowly nod her head against the wall. Glimpses of that afternoon on the dock fluttered beneath her closed eyelids. The bright, blinding sun. The sharp, quick laughs of the children. The laziness of the day. The warm, easy, old-shoe feel of being together. The meandering thoughts and conversation. Where was the warning, she thought. The dark cloud? The ominous gust of wind? Ellen had always believed she would sense danger, smell impending doom. She'd figured she would be one of those airline passengers who would feel the prickle of fear before a fatal flight; that she'd be the one to refuse to board, and thus be saved. What arrogance, she told herself now. Not one of us really knows, really can foresee and therefore prevent. We're pawns. Surely, if there had been a warning, a threat that day, I'd have felt it and stepped in. Wouldn't I? I'd have pulled all the children close and wrapped them in my arms. Wouldn't I?

"Ellie?"

She opened her eyes. It was Sam. He sat down and put his arm around her.

"Hey, Sam." She sat forward.

"Are you okay?"

"No."

He rubbed her back. "Anything I can do?"

"Answer me this. That day, on the dock, was there any warning?"

"No. Nothing."

"See, that's what I keep telling myself. But—" Ellen swallowed hard before continuing. "But I have this nagging sense that there was a warning, and I missed it. I wasn't paying close enough attention. I'd let my guard down. I'd become careless."

"Ellen, no. None of us could've seen it coming. I grew up on that lake. Nothing like that had ever happened, not even close. We couldn't have known, couldn't have stopped it."

"I wish I could be that sure. It seems like we missed something. It can't have just been random. If it was just random, then, well, where's the point? The meaning? The importance?"

"I don't know, El. I just don't know. Let me take you home. Your parents are there with Daniel. Come on, let's go."

That evening, after dinner, Ellen sat with Daniel and her parents on the screened porch. They all tried to make small talk. True to Ellen's predictions, her mother had brought plenty of food—steaks for the grill, twice-baked potatoes, salad, and even an apple pie from her freezer. Ellen gazed out into the fading twilight, which bathed the backyard in a dreamy, soft light. Try as she might to chat aimlessly with the rest of them, her thoughts drifted to the jury and how they had heard her testimony today.

Ellen had never been called to jury duty so she had no actual experience to call on. When they were sent back to deliberate—probably tomorrow sometime—would their minds already be made up? Or would they take turns trying to sway somebody's opinion? She remembered that Bob had been confident that the jury would be sympathetic to Ellen and to James, but after today, and Lindsay's cross-examination, Ellen could no longer be sure about that. And Ben Buchanan's round, tanned face and haunted, scared expression kept floating through her mind. Would the jury find him the more compelling image? Would the jury think about the stupid, careless, maybe even negligent things they had done as teenagers? Maybe not anything serious or life-threatening, but dangerous nonetheless? Remember James, she pleaded with them in her mind. Don't lose sight of his smaller, round face, she silently begged of them.

Ellen called Bob late that night, after her parents had gone to bed. She was anxious to know how the rest of the day in court had gone. And she still couldn't shake the feeling from the other day that he had been the constant through all of this. She wanted the reassurance of hearing his voice. To her surprise, he told her that the defense had finished up their case.

"How can they be done already?"

"Their main witness was Buchanan. He wasn't on the stand more than an hour. Their other witnesses were pretty quick."

"I'd have thought they would have put more people on the stand."

"Well, the thrust of their case was you."

"Huh?"

"Lindsay's attack on you was very carefully planned and executed. Your cross-examination was Buchanan's best defense."

"Oh." Ellen sighed and rubbed her eyes. "How much did I help them?"

"Well, it's hard to judge."

"What's your gut say?"

"I think Lindsay and the rest of the defense feel pretty good. They probably feel like they raised reasonable doubt. I'm not sure the jury will buy that, though."

"Why? Or are you just trying to make me feel better? You know, talking me down from the ledge?"

"No. It's because of what I said from the beginning. This isn't an evidence-driven case. It's all about emotion. I think that while the defense might have scored some points, those same points could come back to hurt them. They came very close to looking mean, to going over the line. I still think the jury relates more to you."

"Because they're parents, too?"

"Yes. And because they know the pleasure of sitting by a lake with friends on a late-summer afternoon, having a cocktail while their kids play nearby. And they don't want that scene tarnished, don't want to think tragedy could be waiting in the wings and they'd be responsible for it. Plus, I don't think the judge liked how the defense tried to put you on trial today."

"But how does that help the jury to like me?"

"The judge will give very specific instructions to the jury in the morning. He'll tell them exactly what they need to look at and what they need to examine in order to render a guilty verdict. He'll tell them what must be proven and what they can use to do the proving. And if we're lucky, he'll remind them in no uncertain terms who is and who is not on trial."

"Okay, I'm feeling calmer now. After the judge makes his little speech, then they go deliberate?"

"First, I make my boffo closing arguments. Then they go back and find Buchanan guilty."

"Boffo?"

"You bet. Now go get a good night's sleep. See you in the morning."

"Bob?" Ellen started, then paused.

"Hmm?"

"Thank you."

The next morning was clear and cool, but the brightness of the sun hinted that it would be warm by midday. Ellen and Daniel arrived at the courthouse a little before nine, and after parking the car, Ellen suggested that they walk around the square. They'd be meeting her parents and Anna's family at the courthouse. The office workers who normally crowded these wide sidewalks were already at work, so Ellen and Daniel could stroll leisurely. Ellen had always loved walking around the Capitol. The lush green lawn and vibrantly colored flowers were immaculately kept and gave such a sense of order and serenity to a busy city. The tall elms arched gracefully overhead and mirrored the taller curved lines of the white marble dome of the Capitol.

When they neared a Starbucks, the aroma tempted Ellen to stop in.

"Daniel, I'm going to get some coffee. Do you want anything?"

He shook his head and went to sit on one of the benches ringing the square. As Ellen crossed the street, he called out to her, "Maybe a sweet roll if they have one."

She nodded and pushed her way inside the store. There were only four other customers.

"One large half coffee, half hot chocolate. No whipped cream. Please," Ellen ordered, then glanced in the glass bakery case. "Oh, and one of those apple-filled croissants, please. To go."

Fumbling with her change, she was surprised to hear that her coffee order was already done, but just as she reached for it, one of the other customers grabbed for it as well. Ellen started to say something to the woman, who glanced briefly at her and then just as quickly looked away. The clerk quickly explained to Ellen that this order belonged to the other woman and that Ellen's order was just now being prepared.

Ellen started to comment to the other woman about both of them having the same particular taste, but the woman moved toward the door without a word. She looks familiar, Ellen thought, but I can't place her. Ellen stared after her, trying to identify her. The woman looked back once, but Ellen could read nothing from her expression.

Grabbing her coffee and Daniel's pastry, she hurried back across the street.

"We better get to the courthouse, kiddo."

~~~~~~~

For the closing arguments, Ellen, her parents, Daniel, Sam, and Anna were ushered into the row directly behind the prosecution's end of the table. She knew Sean was coming as soon as he was done with surgery, and Laurie had been here yesterday.

After Ellen took her seat, she looked across the aisle and saw a woman staring intently at her. Ellen averted her eyes, but then looked back. The woman seemed frightened, but of what? She also looked very sad and quite tired—and somewhat familiar. Oh, she's the woman from Starbucks, Ellen thought, and gave her a small smile of recognition. Then, as Benjamin Buchanan was led to his seat by his attorneys, the woman reached over the railing to pat his shoulder. Her identity was suddenly clear to Ellen—she was his mother. Ellen looked at her again and watched as the woman fixed Ben's collar and smoothed invisible wrinkles on the back of his shirt. Their eyes met again briefly as the judge entered the courtroom.

Ellen listened as the judge faced the jury and began to instruct them in how to reach a verdict. She tried to keep in mind what Bob had told her last night about how the judge would delineate very specifically what they must agree on in order to find Benjamin Buchanan guilty of reckless homicide. Much of his explanation and terminology confused Ellen, but she hoped that was because she hadn't been in court for all the testimony and that the jury members weren't sharing her confusion.

Then it was time for the attorneys to make their closing arguments. Bob had explained that he would present his closing in two parts, both before and after the defense gave their close. He would have a set amount of time to restate the prosecution's position, then the defense would address the jury, then the prosecution would finish up. Ellen knew that Bob intended to save his knockout punch for the second part in hopes of watering down whatever the defense had put forth and to leave the jury with the biggest emotional impact.

"Ladies and gentlemen of the jury," Bob began, "you have before you a very simple case. James Banks is dead. The injuries that led to his death were the direct result of Benjamin Buchanan driving his Jet Ski into James. No one, not even the defense, disputes that basic fact. What you must decide is whether Benjamin Buchanan's actions constitute criminally reckless behavior. The judge has stipulated what factors must be present for such a finding.

"Now, in a few minutes, the defense will address you. They'll try to do what they did yesterday when James' mother was on the stand. They'll try to blur the picture. They'll try to spread the blame. They'll try to confuse you. Don't let them. The behavior and actions of the other adults present that day have absolutely no bearing on the facts of this case. The primary fact being that Mr. Buchanan is fully responsible for the death of young James Banks.

"Now, I'm going to ask you to do something very hard. I'm going to ask you to try to step into Ellen Banks' shoes for a minute. The defense wants you to think that because she was relaxing on the dock with her friends, she was careless. Have you ever relaxed while your children played nearby? Isn't that acceptable behavior? The defense tried to make Ellen look negligent because she was sipping a glass of wine. Think of your own summer vacations, or those relaxing weekend days with friends and family that you have enjoyed. The defense is trying to paint that innocent, bucolic behavior as something sinister or weak or reckless. You know it isn't. Something reckless and negligent and careless did occur on that lake that day, but it wasn't caused by Ellen's behavior, nor was it anything she could have prevented. Don't let them cloud your handling of the facts."

When Bob returned to his chair, Ellen reached over the railing to pat his shoulder. In response, he placed his hand over her own and gave it a quick squeeze. Then they both turned their attention to Clayton Adams, who was making his way to the front of the jury box.

"Well," he said, "to hear the prosecutor tell it, I don't even need to give a closing." A few of the jurors chuckled and then he continued, "But that's not the whole story, is it? We feel great sorrow and sympathy for Mrs. Banks and her family. But I don't think Mr. Hansen, the prosecutor, was listening as closely to us as I hope all of you were. We're not trying to blame Mrs. Banks for her son's death. We're not trying to blame anybody. That's our whole point. Of course we can't dispute the fact that James Banks is dead. And it would be so easy, and maybe, at least for some, very satisfying, to be able to point a finger at one thing or at one person and say, 'He did it. He's to blame.' That's what the prosecution wants you to do with Ben Buchanan.

"We're a society that likes to place blame. We're not always as eager to accept it, though, are we? It might seem neat and tidy and easy to point a finger at Ben and blame him. But it would be wrong. It would not be right or fair or just. James Banks died from injuries sustained in an accident. There was no criminal intent. Not only is there no clear villain here, there's no villain here at all. We know that. Just because we want to place blame doesn't always mean we should. Benjamin Buchanan cannot and should not be found guilty in the death of James Banks."

Ellen was stunned. Of course there is blame, she wanted to scream. It's the clearest thing in the world. Take Buchanan off that lake and James is still alive. Take Buchanan off that Jet Ski and I'm not in this stuffy courtroom on this summer morning; I'm at home, working in the garden or finishing a cross-word puzzle on the porch, waiting for my sons, both of them, to wake up and stumble out of their rooms to start the day. It's the most simple formula of all. James plus Ben equals death. How can anyone not see that? Ellen prayed Bob would make that clear in the rest of his closing.

"With all due respect to Mr. Adams," Bob began, "some-times it is not only possible, but also important to place blame. Imperative and responsible to place blame. This is one of those times. You've heard from the witnesses and from the defendant as well. There is no doubt as to who and what caused the fatal injuries to eleven-year-old James Banks. The only question before you is whether the actions of the defen-dant, Benjamin Buchanan, constitute criminal recklessness. Let's review the facts: One, Mr. Buchanan was driving the Jet Ski at a high rate of speed. Two, as a lifelong summer resident on Lake Augusta, Mr. Buchanan had ample knowledge of how shallow the lake was in the specific area he was traveling. Three, Mr. Buchanan testified that he was unsure of how this particular Jet Ski would handle since it was brand new. Four, he also testified that he'd seen the children playing. With all of these facts—high speed, shallow water, new Jet Ski, and aware-ness of the children—you must find that this behavior showed a callous disregard for the safety of those children and of oth-ers, and that his recklessness was criminal in its execution." Bob paused here and looked at the jury. "I am not implying that when Mr. Buchanan headed out that day on his Jet Ski, his intent was to cause harm. I'm sure everyone in this court-room agrees that this was a terrible accident. But it was a pre-ventable accident. Mr. Buchanan made numerous decisions, conscious decisions, that afternoon. And those decisions were reckless. They were negligent. And they led, one after another, to James Banks being killed.

"Please, remember James—he was playing with friends and

family. He should have been safe. Mr. Buchanan took away not only the safety of the lake. He took away James' life. Show both of them, James and Benjamin, that that's unacceptable. And punishable. Thank you."

The courtroom was quiet as Bob returned to his seat. It's over, Ellen told herself. It's all up to them now, she thought, as the jurors filed out of the courtroom.

"Lunch?"

Ellen looked at Bob and shook her head.

"Let's at least go outside then, okay?"

They walked out of the courtroom and joined the others in the hallway. Ellen wanted to say something to Bob, to thank him for his closing, to thank him for giving her grief a certain dignity, for protecting her from the defense's attacks. She didn't know if she could say anything without crying, though.

"How long do you think it'll take?" Daniel looked up at Bob, waiting for his answer and interrupting Ellen's thoughts.

"I'd hope it could be wrapped up this afternoon. I know the judge doesn't want the deliberations to stretch over into tomorrow. But we just have to wait and see."

"So what do we do now? Wait around here? Go home?" Ellen asked and looked around at her parents and Daniel, as well as at Anna and Sam. If we talk about mundane details long enough, maybe I'll be able to come up with the right words, she thought.

"They'll probably bring in lunch for the jurors. If you want to go home you can, and I'll call you when the verdict comes in," Bob said, then added, "I'll wait around here at least for a while."

"I think we're going to head home, if that's okay, but we'll have our cell phone on. Call us as soon as you hear anything," Anna said, then added, "Bob, what you said in there was wonderful. Thank you so much."

Ellen hugged her and Sam goodbye. "Thanks so much for being here for all of this," she said. Then, turning to her parents and Daniel, she added, "What works for you? I'd kind of like to hang out here, but you three don't need to stay."

"Will you call us as soon as you hear anything? We want to be here for the verdict," her dad said.

"Don't worry," Bob reassured them. "The judge will wait half an hour or so after the verdict is reached before announcing it. That gives everyone time to get back here."

"Okay, then, we'll see you later," her dad said, and then as he started to turn away, he stopped and added, "Bob, we want to thank you, too. I don't know how the jury could decide anything but for us after what you said in there. Thanks."

"You're very welcome. This case, and all of you, mean so much to me. I'm glad you felt I did a good job," Bob said, reaching out to shake hands with Ellen's dad and patting Daniel on the back. Then he turned to Ellen and said, "Let's walk outside."

The streets and sidewalks around the courthouse teemed with office workers on their lunch breaks. Bob maneuvered Ellen to an empty bench and they sat down. Ellen gazed up at the clear blue sky crinkling through the deep green leaves of the trees. Then she turned to Bob. "Thank you."

"For what?"

"For sticking with me through all this. For believing so much in this case. For putting up with me. For all the times you talked me down." As she said this, she lightly touched his arm with her hand.

"Ellen, it's been my pleasure."

"Oh," she said with a small laugh, "I don't think that's always been the word you used to describe it."

He took her hand in his before he answered.

"Well, you might be right about that, but I'd say at least

ninety percent of the time I've been glad I got to meet you, glad I got to work with you."

"I know I must seem like such a mess to you. I just wish we'd met under different circumstances."

"But you know what? We didn't. This is how we met. Through James. Because of James. Maybe you could try looking at it a bit differently."

"Ah, I don't know, Bob. I'm not sure I can."

"You could try."

"You mean rather than think that we only met because my son died, I should instead consider that in his dying he brought us together?"

"Something like that, El."

Ellen looked up into the trees again, closed her eyes, and shook her head, as if she could mix up all the floating variables into new arrangements. What new patterns would emerge? she wondered.

Bob's beeper went off then, and he glanced at it and saw the message.

"The jury's back," he told her.

She reached for her cell phone and dialed her parents and Anna. When they answered she blurted out the same short message to both of them, "The jury's returned. I'll see you at the courthouse."

She and Bob were quiet on their short walk back. This is it, Ellen thought. A decision has been made and I can't do anything about it. I wonder how I'll react, either way. She had been so focused on this for so long, and now, in a few minutes, it would be over. What then? she wondered.

The jury filed in. Ellen couldn't look at anyone else. She just clasped her hands tightly and stared at the jury foreman. She had once asked Bob if it was true that a jury never looks at the side they have decided against. At the time, she had been embarrassed to ask, sure that it was a phenomenon found only in movies or books to increase the drama. But he had surprised her by saying that he and his colleagues had found it to be quite accurate and true. She had promised herself at the time that she would watch for it when the jury returned in this trial. But when she saw the foreman hand the small slip of white paper to the judge, she realized that her heart had been pounding so hard and her vision had been so narrow that she'd missed who the jury members were not looking at. All she had seen was the small gesture and the piece of paper with the verdict on it. For a brief moment, while the judge looked at the slip and then handed it back to the foreman, she considered asking Bob if he had noticed, but then she heard the judge asking for the verdict to be read aloud.

Ellen's ears started to buzz and she was afraid she was going to collapse. She heard nothing else except the word "guilty" and a gasp and cry from Ben Buchanan's mother. Around her, Sam and Anna hugged and Daniel shot his right arm up and said, "Yes!" Her parents embraced and then reached for Daniel. Anna put her arm around Ellen, and Bob turned around to embrace her as well.

It's over, she thought, and then she heard the judge state, "Sentencing hearing in four weeks. Court adjourned."

She was rushed out of the courtroom in a wave of excitement, but not without catching a glimpse of Benjamin Buchanan stoically hugging his mother before being led from the courtroom.

Bob deftly ushered them through and around the reporters who were yelling questions at her. Ellen was surprised at how immune she had become, over the past year, to their intrusiveness. She was no longer stunned at their abrasiveness or at their inability to understand her craving for privacy. This is my pain, she wanted to tell them. Mine and Daniel's. And those around us. You can't report that, she wanted to tell them. You can't photograph that. She caught a glimpse of Grace Benham among the reporters but made no effort to make eye contact with her. It was a relief to know that once the sentencing hearing took place, James would fade from newsworthiness.

On their way to the car, Daniel walked ahead of her with Sam and talked to him excitedly. Ellen's parents, after quick hugs in front of the courthouse, had hurried ahead of the others to their car. Her mom wanted to get home to fix dinner for all of them, including Sam, Anna, and their girls. Ellen and Anna walked quietly, both deep in thought. Daniel ran back, panting, and said, "Mom, Sam said we could go to the lake this weekend, okay?"

"Wait, kiddo," Sam interrupted, "give your mom a little time now, okay?"

"Please, Mom. We haven't been—"

"No." Ellen spoke precisely and without emotion.

"Huh?" Daniel stopped dead in his tracks.

"I said no."

"No, yourself," Daniel shot back.

Ellen was stunned. "Excuse me?"

"I want to go to the lake. You can't keep me from there forever," Daniel yelled at her. Ellen couldn't even hear his words anymore. She just saw his angry face. When did his face lose the baby curves, she found herself wondering. Sam led him away. She and Anna got in the car. The silence after Daniel's outburst stung.

"El?"

"Hmm?" she answered distractedly, then said, "You know, I'm almost glad to see him explode. He keeps so much in."

"Would you let us take him out there this weekend?"

Before she answered, Ellen looked out the car window at Sam walking with Daniel. She could see that Sam was talking while Daniel fought to catch his breath.

"You know I can't go with you."

"I know, but let us take him."

Ellen didn't answer but kept looking through the car window at Daniel. She hadn't seen him this emotional in months. When had they stopped talking to each other? she wondered. She tried to remember. Somehow, since late winter and through the spring, a numbness or distance had crept between them. They were polite to each other but not friendly. How often had Ellen asked him about his day and then stopped listening before he'd even started to answer? This was the first time in months she'd done more than simply notice him.

Daniel and Sam headed back to the car. Sam opened the door for him, and when he got in he glanced up at Ellen.

"I'm sorry, Mom. I shouldn't have yelled."

"I know. It's okay."

"I'm really sorry."

Ellen reached out to rub his hair. "Dan, if you'd like, you can go with Sam and Anna and the girls. Just for the weekend."

"Really?" His whole face brightened. "But only if it's really okay."

"Just be careful," Ellen said as she brushed her lips against his forehead. Please God, she prayed, help me to let him do this.

After dinner, Ellen's father and Sam went out to look at some branches that were worrying Ellen. Daniel and the girls wandered out after them. Ellen's mother started clearing dishes, but Ellen motioned for her to sit down and relax.

"Those won't take long anyway, Mom."

After one more trip carrying dishes from the table, her mom sat down and asked, "So what happens at the sentencing hearing?"

"Bob said it was pretty simple. The judge has a range of options and both sides try to sway his decision."

"What're you hoping for, honey?"

"The maximum for this charge is three years, but given that this kid is a first-time offender, we'll be lucky to get eighteen months."

"Lucky? Hmm."

Anna had been quietly watching the two of them during this exchange, and when she heard this last comment, she held her breath, waiting for the fallout.

"What's that supposed to mean, Mom?"

"How is it 'lucky' to put that kid in prison?"

"Mother, he killed James."

"Honey, I know that. But, well, your dad and I have talked about this so much."

"And?" Ellen challenged.

"We were never convinced the trial was the best way to go, but we wanted whatever was going to help you and Daniel through this."

"Right. And the trial did that for us."

"I know. You were able to have your say. I can't imagine anybody who has heard or read about this will ever look at Jet Skis the same way again."

"And that's a good thing," Ellen argued.

"Right. But wasn't that the point?"

"Huh?"

"Look at what the public has seen and learned through James' death. What more is there to prove?"

"What do you mean?"

"What more do you want from this? You've shown people the dangers of Jet Skis. What else is left?"

Ellen folded and refolded her napkin. She straightened the edges of her place mat and took a sip of her iced tea.

"I want Benjamin Buchanan to lose something, too," she said, looking down at her now-shredded napkin.

"Don't you think he has?" Her mother's voice was soft.

Ellen shook her head before answering, "Not enough. Not yet."

Chapter
Sixteen

Since I'm not having any luck finding cute sandals on sale, I deserve a Cinnabon, Ellen told herself as she neared the food court. The sweet, sugary scent had been wafting into the mall, growing stronger as she made her way from store to store.

The food court was starting to fill up with an early lunch crowd, so Ellen grabbed the first table she could—one partially hidden behind plants, which was fine with her.

As she savored the sweet roll and her coffee, she put her head back and closed her eyes. She heard some women sit down at a table behind her, on the other side of the plants, and their conversation sparked Ellen's imagination.

"It's just so sad," the first woman said. "I know he's lonely and scared and not eating well."

"I know, dear," a gravelly smoker's voice answered, "but this is just something we have to help him get through. You can't let him see that you're all upset about it, too. He needs to know you believe in him."

"I guess."

Hmm, Ellen thought. It's too early for them to be talking about a homesick college freshman. Maybe the kid is away at overnight camp for the first time.

"He's losing weight, too, I think, and he says he exercises all the time."

"Well, dear, like I said, this isn't something he can get out of just yet."

Sounds like a mom and grandma, Ellen thought. But not a very fun camp. The voices got quieter and although Ellen strained to hear, she didn't want to appear too obvious. Ellen loved eavesdropping on conversations. It was a game she'd taught the boys, too. When they were little and getting restless in restaurants, she'd let one of them pick a table of people and they would start making up lives and problems for them. Daniel had lost interest in this a few years ago, but James had still been a willing partner. Most of his story lines revolved around spies or terrorists so his plots had a certain predictability to them, but it had still been a fun pastime.

Ellen's coffee was nearly gone, but just as she started to get up from the table, the conversation behind her began again, so she stayed in her seat.

"I don't know, Mom. Every time I talk to him he seems younger and sadder. It just kills me not to be able to protect him better."

Ellen was starting to worry about this kid, whom she was now convinced was at a military boot camp. She knew two of her students were headed to a boot camp this summer and wondered if one of them was the subject of this painful conversation behind her.

"Honey," the gravel voice said, "I do know how helpless

you feel. It's how I feel about you and your anguish through all of this."

"I know," the younger voice murmured, "I know."

Ellen felt a bond of mothering. Do fathers have this same emotional yoke, she wondered. She'd always felt this way, even before James' death, although that had certainly amplified it. What a strange phenomenon, she thought. Get a group of mothers together, and we always have that in common. No matter what our differences are in every other area, mothers can always connect on that visceral level. Here I am, she thought, worried about this kid in basic training, probably in Georgia somewhere, with a mean drill sergeant yelling at him, and my inclination is to get his address and send him cookies. If I intrude on their conversation, though, to tell them I'm worried about this kid, too, they'll think I'm a total nut. Just finish your coffee and get back on the quest for new sandals that make your size nine feet look like sevens.

She heard the women gathering their shopping bags, so she told herself to stay seated and at least get a glimpse of them before getting up. As they passed her, she felt a tug of recognition. Was it one of her students they had been talking about? Then the younger of the two women spoke again and Ellen knew who she was immediately.

"The sentencing hearing is the week after the Fourth. Then I'll really know how much to worry about Ben."

"Anna, it was so strange," Ellen said as they drank iced tea on the porch. "Here I am, not three feet from Ben Buchanan's mother and grandmother. And this after I saw his mother in Starbucks the other day."

"Did they see you?"

"No, thank God. As they were leaving, though, before I

knew it was them, I nearly turned to smile at them. I almost told them to hang in there and that things would get better."

They sipped their tea and looked out into the late-afternoon light.

"I know he's only a kid, Anna," Ellen began, "but I still think I need to go through with this."

"I know you do."

"You 'know I do' what? Know I need to do this, or know I think I need to do this?"

"Both, maybe," Anna answered.

"Sometimes it seems so clear," Ellen explained. "Most times it does. But then, today, just for a minute, I was an outsider, and for a second I was sympathetic. But . . ." Her voice trailed off.

"But what?"

"But then I always come back to James."

"Mrs. Banks? Hey, Mrs. Banks."

Ellen turned and looked for who had called her in this throng of revelers. Fourth of July. Fireworks in Elver Park. Who was that waving at her? Melanie? Ellen waved and waited as Melanie rushed over.

"Do you have a minute?" Melanie panted, then added in a rush, "You've got to meet my little brother."

Ellen smiled and walked with her.

"He's so cute. And really smart. He's three months old already. Wait. You'll see," Melanie said as they walked, carefully stepping around blankets. "Right over here." Melanie picked up her brother, who beamed as she nuzzled his neck. "This is Charlie," she said proudly.

Ellen reached out to hold him, but he gripped his sister.

"C'mon, pumpkin," Melanie cooed, "let's walk with Mrs. Banks for a minute."

"What a cutie," Ellen said, trying to reorient herself to where her blanket was located.

"I love him so much," Melanie confided. "I can't believe how much."

"Of course you do. He's your brother."

"You were so right."

"About what?" Ellen asked.

"That whole conversation we had about how I needed to consider things from all angles."

"Well," Ellen said, "I hope I didn't sound like I thought I was an expert or anything. I'm muddling along through life just like you are, only I have the benefit of a few more years behind me."

"You sounded like a mom," Melanie said with a laugh.

"Well, I am that."

"But you were a mom I could talk to when I didn't think I could talk to my own."

"I'm glad." Ellen paused as she looked around for Daniel and Anna's family. "How are your mom and Stan?" she finally asked, directing her attention back to Melanie.

"Good. We talk a lot more now. Which is kinda funny because I thought she'd be too busy with everything else."

"Yeah, but sometimes when you have so much going on you're more careful to make time for what really matters."

"True. But it's still pretty weird. I guess it's one more example of nothing being black and white, like you told me."

"What?" Ellen asked. But Charlie had started to fuss, and Melanie needed to head back.

"Feeding him is the one thing my mom is the only expert at. Thanks again, Mrs. Banks. See you around."

Ellen waved absently and took a few steps before stopping to look in all directions for her blanket. She finally saw Daniel laughing with Sam and made her way to them just as the park lights dimmed for the fireworks.

Ellen waited for the fireworks to begin and thought back to previous Fourth of July celebrations. When James had been three, he'd been terrified; not of the noise, but of the lights. She'd found a bench for them, away from the crowds and the fireworks, and they had snuggled and whispered and listened to the oohs and aahs from the crowd.

How did I learn to be a mother, she wondered. Was it all instinct? How did I know what they needed? What would comfort them? She thought back to her conversation with Melanie last summer when Melanie had so wanted to believe her mom was replacing her and starting over. Her mom hadn't realized, until almost too late, how Melanie had really felt. How little control we have over our children's lives. Is that one of the things that binds us as mothers, she wondered as the first light displays splintered down from overhead. I couldn't keep James safe from harm, Melanie's mother couldn't protect her daughter, even Ben Buchanan's mother can't shelter him now that he'd been convicted.

As the colors showered down over them against the dark, velvety sky, she thought once again of what Melanie had thanked her for. What had she told Melanie more than a year ago? That nothing is black and white, just all shades of gray? But that limit to our power to protect or control, that's pretty black and white. And surely there are absolutes when it comes to right and wrong, Ellen thought now. She wanted to ask Anna, but the noise and fireworks precluded it. She watched the greens and blues and reds shoot up and out like a waterfall, and the last stray embers tumbled down and down and down. See, nothing up there is gray, she told herself. Of course, nothing is black and white, either.

Bob had explained to her that the judge decides on the sentence. The jury convicts; the judge sentences. At the sentencing hearing, though, the victims and their families, as well as the family of the person convicted, would all have a chance to speak. Even Benjamin Buchanan could address the judge. Ellen planned to speak, and she'd told Daniel that if he wanted to he could as well.

He wanted to. So did Brian, James' best friend. When Brian's mom, Diane, had asked Ellen about it, Ellen had been surprised and touched. Brian still came by to play with Daniel at times, but Ellen missed the daily contact she'd had with both Brian and Diane before James had died. Bob told them all to speak honestly to the judge about their loss and about why they believed Buchanan should serve time—probably eighteen months, according to Bob—rather than probation.

To Ellen, the sentencing hearing seemed like her last chance to speak out about James. She was eager for the hearing in the weeks leading up to it. It was important, she thought, for people to recognize the danger of Jet Skis. And to be held accountable. They weren't toys.

As the hearing drew closer, Daniel seemed to retreat inside himself more. After the outburst about the lake following the verdict, he'd become more lighthearted. Ellen had hoped the burdens he'd carried for almost a year—James' accident and death, her grief, his desire for family routines and traditions—were finally starting to ease. They laughed more easily in remembering James now, and although Ellen had no desire to go back to the lake, Daniel was free to go whenever he was invited.

A week before the hearing, Daniel had gone with Joey and his family up to their cabin. Ellen had enjoyed the time alone, and she had been glad Daniel could get away for some fun as well.

Upon his return, he reported he'd had fun, then scooted outside to shoot baskets. Some of the neighborhood kids stopped by, and through the open windows she heard them laughing and talking. Ellen was busy making jam, and between sterilizing the jelly jars and preparing the strawberries, she paid no attention to what the kids were saying in her driveway.

Suddenly, though, the words "the Jet Skiing was awesome" permeated through to her consciousness. She limply dropped the knife she'd been using to slice the berries and shook her head as if to gain a better perception of the words. That couldn't have been Daniel, she told herself.

But then she heard it again, and it was Daniel's voice. He was saying, "Those things go so fast. But you bounce a lot."

Mechanically, Ellen walked through the house and to the front door. The kids were all huddled on the driveway near an open window. Daniel was the center of attention.

"It was so cool." Daniel spoke with authority.

"Daniel." Ellen's voice cracked in the air.

Daniel's head shot up in her direction.

"What?"

"Come inside, please."

He glanced at the others, shrugged, then made his way to where she was standing. Control yourself, Ellen thought. Don't lose it, yet. Take slow breaths, she warned herself.

When Daniel came in, he stood quietly, facing her. He's nearly as tall as I am, she thought. When did that happen?

"Were you on a Jet Ski?" Ellen demanded.

She watched as the expression on his face closed down and retreated from her. He looked at the floor, started to answer, then stopped and glared right back at her.

"Yes." His voice shook when he answered her, although whether from fear or defiance she didn't know.

"How could you? What were you thinking?" Ellen fought to keep control. She wanted to lash out at him, and she wanted to hug him close.

"Mom." Daniel paused, then continued. "It was safe, okay. We all had on life jackets. Everyone was doing it."

"Oh, like that's a good reason. Don't you know—"

"Of course I know," Daniel interrupted her, practically spitting the words out at her.

"Oh, Daniel. After what happened to James . . ." Ellen's words trailed off.

"I know what happened, Mom. I was there, too, remember?"

Where is all this anger coming from? Ellen asked herself. Why can't he see why I am so upset?

Daniel stopped and tried to catch his breath. He was breathing heavily and his eyes, while filling with tears, burned with anger.

"Honey, I know you were there. We all were," Ellen soothed. "They, those Jet Skis, they're just so dangerous."

"Mom, they're fun. Fun!" he yelled at her, and then added, his voice barely above a whisper, "James would've loved it."

She shook her head. "No," she said. "Don't."

"You can't keep me from doing things. You can't use James to do that."

Use James, she thought. My God, he's not an excuse or a reason.

"Look, Daniel. I'm your mother. I set the rules and the limits. Jet Skis are off limits. If I can't trust you—"

"Then what? What are you going to do?"

"Go to your room!" Ellen yelled. "That's what I'm doing first." She knew it was a feeble response, but for now it was the best one she had.

~~~~~~~~

Later, while Ellen ladled strawberry jam into the prepared jars, Daniel walked into the kitchen.

"Hi," Ellen said, concentrating on not spilling the hot strawberry mixture.

"Sorry, Mom."

"Me, too."

"But, Mom? It *was* fun."

"Oh, honey. Let's not fight."

"I don't want to, either. But, well, I'm just tired of all of this."

"All of what?" Ellen asked.

"The trial. The sentencing. The way you are."

Ellen stopped mid-scoop. The thick, hot red mixture glistened as it dripped onto the counter. Carefully, she put the ladle back into the pot and then turned toward Daniel.

"What?" Ellen asked slowly.

"I'm sorry. I shouldn't have said that." Daniel turned to walk out of the room.

"No. Wait. It's okay. Come sit down."

They each edged toward the table, then sat down on opposite sides.

"It's just, well, I feel like you don't even see me anymore. Everything is about James."

"Oh, honey."

"It's true, Mom. The only time you ever talk to me is about James. The only time I ever get noticed is when he's the conversation. He's more here than I am."

Ellen fumbled to reach Daniel's hands across the table. Could this be true? she asked herself. When was the last time they had sat here for a family dinner? she wondered. Those used to be so important to her.

"Daniel, I'm sorry. I didn't mean for it to be that way."

"I know. And I won't Jet Ski anymore, not if you don't want me to."

"This will be over soon, honey, I promise."

"I hope so," Daniel said. But he didn't sound convinced.

The night before the hearing, Ellen marinated and grilled a flank steak. They had salad and corn.

"Hey, this looks good!" Daniel said, sitting down at the table.

Since their argument about his Jet Skiing, Ellen had made more of an effort to have family dinners.

"Glad you think so. Do you know what you're going to say to the judge tomorrow?"

"I guess I'll know when I get up there," Daniel told her. "How many of us are talking?"

"I think just three of us. Not counting the Buchanans. You, me, and Brian."

"Do you know what you're going to say?" Daniel asked.

"Still working on it, but I have it pretty well outlined."

After dinner, Daniel retreated to his room, and she could hear him playing video games. She still caught herself listening for the banter between the boys. She hadn't known how comforting she had found that until it was gone. She'd loved reading in bed and listening to the rise and fall of their voices down the hall. They often slept in the same room, and while she usually hadn't been able to make out the words they said, she loved the rhythms of their voices. She had always been glad they had each other—believed it had helped them weather the divorce and liked that they shared things with each other that she was not privy to. Now Daniel had only his own noises.

Lying in bed, with the house dark, Ellen went over again what she wanted to say to the judge. She hoped for the right combination of what she'd lost and what she'd never have. James as a baby and child, and James the adult she'd never know. Who would he have become? She tried to imagine how he would've looked in five or ten years. What angles would have become clear in his face once the child in him was gone? She couldn't get a clear picture, just fuzziness.

That night for the first time in months, she dreamed about the lake. And she saw the accident all over again. She awoke with a start, afraid she might have cried out loud. Trying to get rid of the disturbing images from her dream, she rubbed her eyes. She knew now, with a clear certainty, that she could not have stopped the accident, could not have prevented it unless she had held James back from everything in his life; unless she had shaped a very different and lesser existence for him. She had been powerless to keep him safe from all harm.

But she also recognized that she still had a power when it came to shaping other lives.

Becoming more awake, she finally knew what she needed to do later that day. She got up, narrowly missing stepping on Stella, and gathered the things she'd need after the sentencing. She put her things in her backpack and carried it out to the car. Dawn was just beginning to break. She looked up and watched the last of the stars disappear, hurried into her closet, dug deep in the back of it, and brought one last thing out to the car. Then she went in, turned on the coffee, and started her shower.

The courtroom seemed smaller this time. She was surprised by how many friends had shown up to support her, and she'd been most surprised, and very pleased, by the arrival of her parents. When Brian, James' friend, walked up and sat at the table before the judge, Ellen reached around to hold his mom's hand. He spoke so softly the judge had to lean forward to hear him.

But his last words rang out clearly. "He was my best friend," Brian stated, "for four years. I still miss him." Brian walked back to his mom and Ellen's arms ached to hold him. She had loved watching the two of them saunter off together. And now it was just Brian.

Ellen turned her attention to Daniel.

"James was my little brother. Even though he was bigger than me. Now that he's gone, our family seems empty. I know we used to fight a lot, and he could make me really mad. But he was my brother. When my mom used to get mad at our fighting, she'd tell us we needed to remember how lucky we were to have a brother. Not everybody gets one, she'd say. So be nice. She'd also say that we'd be glad to have each other when she was old and dotty. Well, I'll never know. It'll just be me.

"She was right, not everybody gets a brother," Daniel finished, looking intently at the judge.

Oh, Daniel, Ellen thought, you sweet, brave boy. And then she took a deep breath and approached the judge.

"Your Honor. You have heard James' brother and best friend. Now it's my turn.

"I've been so angry and so sad for almost a full year. I think about James and I remember so much—but some of it fades. I can still see his small, sturdy back on his first day of school as he climbed aboard the school bus. He straightened his shoulders and never looked back. He was so scared, but he forged ahead. I can sometimes still hear his deep laugh. And if I close my eyes just right I can feel him snuggle up against my shoulder like he used to when I would read to him.

"And I'm glad he didn't suffer. I know children all over the world suffer more painful deaths than he did. And I know there are mothers who suffer unspeakable sorrow and grief over their children." Ellen paused, took a deep breath, and continued. "But I'll never get to see James as a father. I'll never get to know which career he ended up with—hockey star or math teacher. I'll never get to meet his wife or help him when some girl has broken his heart.

"I've spent a lot of time wondering who he'd have become in five or six years. I try to picture his adult face, and all I can see is—" Ellen paused and looked around the room. Her eyes met Benjamin Buchanan's, who was staring intently at her. "All I can see is Ben Buchanan."

Ben flinched as if she had slapped him, and nearly everyone in the courtroom gasped and looked at Ben before looking back at Ellen. Her mother's and father's attention never wavered from her, however.

"Your Honor, Ben seems like the kind of young man James might have grown up to be." And now Ellen turned and spoke directly to Ben. "For all of this year, I have hated you. I wanted you to pay for hitting and killing James. I kept telling myself that if I could help send you to jail, I'd be able to begin healing. I was wrong. When I think about James at sixteen or seventeen, I know that he would've jumped at the chance to ride a Jet Ski. And he'd have driven it too fast. And he'd have been sorry for doing so. But that's what kids do.

"I wanted you to be a monster. You're not. You're a scared kid who made a terrible mistake. And you have to live with that mistake forever." Ellen saw that even though Ben was biting his lip, tears streamed down his face. Out of the corner of her eye she saw her dad put his arm around her mother. Her mother nodded at her, and Ellen thought she saw tears in her mother's eyes.

"Your Honor, I would ask you to sentence Ben to community service or probation, but no jail time. Putting him in jail won't bring James back. And I don't want another mother to lose her son. Even for a short time. I know what James would say if he were here. He'd say, *Mom, it was an accident. He didn't mean to hurt me.*"

As Ellen went to her seat, the woman she had recognized as Ben's mother rose to face her. The two of them embraced. "I'm so sorry," they murmured over and over. It was the only sound in the courtroom.

When Ellen finally got back to her seat, Daniel and her parents were the only ones who would look at her. Everyone else seemed stunned. Can't you all see, Ellen wanted to yell. It's not an equation. Even if I help send Ben Buchanan to jail, I don't get James back.

The judge sentenced Ben Buchanan to probation and two hundred hours of community service.

Slowly, Ellen turned to all of her friends. "Can you understand?" she said. "It just didn't make any sense." She shook her head softly as she stood to leave. "Daniel," she said, holding her hand out to him, "I need your help with something." On their way out the door, she hugged her parents, and her father kissed her on the forehead.

Daniel looked at her carefully as she pulled the car out of the parking garage, then said, "You were right, Mom."

"Oh, honey, I'm so glad you understand."

They drove in silence for ten minutes before it dawned on Daniel that they were not headed home.

"Where are we going?"

Ellen didn't answer but pointed with her thumb to the backseat.

"Huh?" Daniel said, then spotted the backpack she used for the lake and her towel. He smiled softly and relaxed into the seat. "Are you sure?"

"Yes."

Ellen felt her breathing quicken as they entered the city limits of Bainbridge. It was only thirty minutes from Madison, but it seemed galaxies away.

"Won't the others worry?" Daniel asked.

Leave it to him, Ellen thought, to be thinking of everybody else.

"I left messages this morning."

"Then you planned this?"

"Well, since the middle of last night."

Ellen eased the car into the driveway of the lake house. She felt the tears at the back of her throat. It's okay, she thought, go ahead and come. She handed Daniel her backpack and flipped open the rear door. She reached in and pulled out a package about the size of a shoe box, which was deceptively heavy. Daniel had started walking toward the lake, then paused and waited for Ellen to catch up. She was crying, but he sensed that it was okay this time. While they walked, his eyes filled, but they kept walking, on to the dock and out to the edge. Ellen took off her shoes and hiked her skirt up over her knees. She sat then and dangled her feet in the water. Daniel pulled off his shoes and socks and rolled up his pants. They sat together looking out over the lake and twirled their toes in the cold, dark water.

"I can still see the spot where it happened," Ellen said.

"Me, too."

Then she gazed back at the dock. That's where his body was, she thought, sprawled out right there. But it was only his body. His spirit was already gone.

"I love it here." Ellen spoke quietly, almost talking just to the lake.

"He did, too, you know." Daniel peered up at her. "He'd told me. Just that day."

"Told you? Told you what?"

"James and I were talking that morning. You'd already gone out with your coffee. It was before he went out to scare you, and I went back to sleep."

"What did he tell you?"

"He said that you were right about the lake. About it being our happiest place."

Ellen looked out to the water. She felt the anger and rage flowing away from her. She'd never stop missing James. She'd always have an emptiness deep within her core. But putting Benjamin Buchanan in jail wouldn't have filled it. And not donating James' organs wouldn't have lessened her grief; it just would have created more elsewhere.

She reached next to her for the box. Slowly, she unsealed the wrapping.

"Daniel," she said softly, "I think this is the right place for this."

He nodded and reached to help her with the corners. Inside were James' ashes. They stood then, put the box on a table, and, holding hands, began to toss the ashes into the lake. She heard footsteps on the dock but didn't look up until she saw Anna's hand reach in for a handful and felt Sam's arm around her shoulder. All of them, the girls, Daniel, Anna, Sam, Ellen, and her parents, tossed the ashes into the water and watched the wind and the current take them in every direction. They sparkled and glittered in the air, some landing in the water like fine dust, others wafting and rising and twirling in the breeze. Ellen looked up toward the house and saw Bob standing under a tree. He smiled, and she answered back by nodding, smiling softly, and letting another handful of ashes flutter away. "Rest well," she whispered to the last handful in the wind. "All the numbers."

All the
Numbers

Judy Merrill Larsen

A READER'S GUIDE

A Conversation with
Judy Merrill Larsen

During the summer of 2005, Judy Larsen was invited to New York to the Random House Publishing Group offices, and while visiting there, she was introduced to Bev Marshall, author of Walking Through Shadows, Right as Rain, *and* Hot Fudge Sundae Blues. *After Bev said how much she loved* All the Numbers, *she asked Judy if she'd answer a few questions about her novel over a cup of coffee. Here are a few bits and pieces of their conversation.*

Bev Marshall: I've already told you how much I loved *All the Numbers*, but I didn't tell you that I actually stayed up until three A.M. reading it. I just couldn't go to sleep until I knew what was going to happen to poor Ellen.

Judy Merrill Larsen: Well, I'd say I'm sorry you lost sleep, but I'm not. What a thrill to know you couldn't put it down.

BM: I'd bet I wasn't the only reader you kept up late, and I'd also wager that I wasn't the only one who wants to know if this was an account of a personal experience. Have you suffered the loss of a child?

JML: Thank God, no. But I think most parents have had those scary trips to the emergency room when you hope your child just needs a few stitches or those moments of terror when your toddler is lost in a crowd, and you try to remember what he was wearing. As a mother, one of the most frightening moments I had was when my first grader was hit by a car. I was frozen for a few seconds. I didn't want to run out and check on him because I was so scared of what I might have to face. He turned out to be fine, but of course I didn't know that yet.

BM: Thank God for that! So was your son's accident the inspiration for *All the Numbers*?

JML: Not exactly. I think I'd been dreaming it up for years—ever since I became a mother and learned that overwhelming, awful truth of how much I loved my sons, how much I wanted to protect them, and how in so many ways I was powerless.

BM: I'm a mother, too, so I know exactly what you mean. What was so very chilling to read was the contrast between this idyllic scene at the lake and the horror that followed. I could visualize that scene, hear the Jet Ski approaching. I'm guessing you've spent some time on a lake yourself. Am I right?

JML: Yes. Just like Ellen, I'm lucky enough to have a best friend who has a lake house and we go there often. The story came to me one summer day on her dock in Lake Ripley in Wisconsin. We sat there, sipping wine and talking as her daughters and my sons played in the lake. A Jet Skier went by. And I started to think, what if? What if one of the children had been a bit farther out? What would that do to me as a mother? To our friendship? To the other children? The story flowed from there.

BM: Speaking of flowing, I think you should give out boxes of tissues with your book to wipe all the tears that your readers will shed. I used up an entire box myself.

JML: You know, I hear that from everyone who reads this. Even men. And I find it very gratifying that I am able to elicit that kind of emotional connection with my words. I still catch myself tearing up when

I reread certain parts of the book, and it's good to know I'm not the only one sniffling.

BM: Like most authors, I have great empathy for my characters, and I'm sure that you do, too. We live inside their bodies as we write, so how on earth did you manage to survive writing about Ellen's pain?

JML: Well, it was hard because I did relate to Ellen so closely. There were days I was just exhausted for and with her. And my poor sons— they were the same ages as Daniel and James the summer I wrote the first draft, and they'd be headed to the pool and I'd be hollering after them, *Don't go in too deep, and be careful,* when what I really wanted was for them to sit inside where I knew they'd be safe and sound.

BM: I know what you mean. I feel the same way about my grandson every time he goes to our pool.

JML: So there never comes a point when we get to relax? I hadn't even thought about worrying about future grandbabies, Bev.

BM: Nope, you never stop worrying. Motherhood is a lifetime profession. But besides understanding the fears of us mothers (and grandmothers), you seemed to know so much about the stages of grief and all of the complex emotions a mother would feel after the death of her child. How did you know this, Judy? Did you consult professionals or do other kinds of research about the subject?

JML: Again, I think the only research I did was forcing myself to imagine the very worst. I think that's how I cope with fears—try to go all the way through to what I would do. Who would I call? I wanted Ellen to have honest reactions. That's what always intrigues me when I hear or read about real-life accidents and tragedies. I always want to ask the survivors, *What's your new normal? How long did it take you to get there?* I remember reading an article about Elizabeth Edwards, and she said how after her sixteen-year-old son was killed she just watched the weather channel day after day after day. And I thought, yeah, that sounds about right, I could see myself becoming almost catatonic.

BM: I think that's so brave of you, to vividly imagine the worst happening. That's probably why I thought this novel was a personal experience. You also captured exactly how I think a teenage boy would react to all of the events that occur in the novel. I know that, like me, you are a teacher, and I'm wondering if your perceptions of Daniel were based on your interactions with your students?

JML: I think it was based on both my students and my sons. I really find those early teenage years, especially with boys, to be such a fascinating time. They aren't little boys anymore, but they don't have the confidence and swagger they'll have in a few years. There is such a sweetness there, but also a coolness or distance. I always describe my ninth-grade students (mainly the boys) as being like puppies. They mean well, but their feet are too big. And for Ellen, Daniel is becoming someone she doesn't know—partly because she's so wrapped up in her pain, but also because that's part of the growing-up process.

BM: I love that analogy of the boys' feet and puppy paws. And while we're on the topic of students and school, I noticed numerous references to numbers and the Capitol throughout the novel that seemed to me to have symbolic significance. Did you consciously work these references into the text, and if so, how did you perceive their significance?

JML: Did my English students feed you this question, Bev? I love symbolism, but I know there are always a few of them who sit and shake their heads, thinking, "She is so making this stuff up." What's funny is that with the references to numbers, that was very intentional, but the references to the Capitol were not conscious at all. I thought the idea of numbers might tie in to things making sense— you know $x + y = z$. And of course, for Ellen, those familiar patterns have been completely destroyed—what she is looking for are new patterns, new rules. Now that I think about it, the Capitol references kind of tie in to the same idea—you know, structure, order, rules.

BM: Well, now I have to ask you if you were consciously conveying a message about organ donation to your readers. I was really surprised by Ellen's reaction to donating James' organs.

JML: Let me say right off I am a huge believer in organ donation. My card is signed. I want to encourage everyone to become an organ donor. But I also think that, at least for me, donating organs in the face of losing a child wouldn't bring relief right away. It certainly wouldn't prevent me from offering my child's organs, but it wouldn't lessen my agony. That just fit with how I thought Ellen would react. She's not noble in her grief. She just hurts, and there's not a thing in the world that's going to lessen that hurt other than time.

BM: And I suspect that even time can't heal the grief but only lessen the pain one must feel after losing a child. As I read the novel, I saw that Ellen's reaction to that pain was to focus her thoughts and actions on revenge. She directs her rage toward Ben Buchanan and the manufacturers of Jet Skis. But Ellen experiences a complete turnaround in her sympathy for the Buchanan family. Did you foresee this happening, and if so, did you view this "epiphany" as part of the healing process?

JML: What I liked was how Ellen, initially so stuck in her grief and rage, gradually is able to look outward. I think that's how she heals, and probably how we all heal. When all we can see is our own pain, that's a very narrow vision. As Ellen sees things more broadly—through Daniel, through Ben's mom and others, she is able to forgive and move on. So yes, all that is part of her healing.

BM: And Ellen's healing is revealed beautifully in the last scene. Oftentimes I'm disappointed by the endings of novels, but the ending of *All the Numbers* was just perfect. Did you know the outcome of the trial and the denouement for Ellen when you began writing or was this ending a surprise to you?

JML: I knew she would ultimately forgive Ben, but I didn't know all the specifics of how that would come about. That's one of the things I love about writing: my characters let me know who they are as I write. It's fun to have those moments where as I'm writing I am also thinking, "Hmmm, I sure didn't see that coming."

BM: Oh, I know, I know. Oftentimes my characters surprise and delight me. I think they're all a lot smarter than I am. So you didn't know what the final scene would be?

JML: I did know what the final scene would be—Ellen and the others, standing on the dock, spreading James' ashes to the wind. The challenge was getting her to that point. I knew there would be a trial; I knew that Ellen would lose her "blood thirst" for Ben Buchanan. What I didn't know was how she would get drawn into the mud—how she would be made to look guilty. That came in one of the later revisions.

BM: Speaking of revisions, are you hard at work on another novel?

JML: Yes—and it is completely different from this book. I promise you won't need any Kleenex.

BM: I don't mind buying another box, but what is the new novel about?

JML: It's a romantic comedy about a woman in her thirties who has had it with dating—and with shaving her legs. So she decides if she quits one she can quit the other, too. Then of course she meets a great guy—but she's taken a stand and doesn't want to back down.

BM: One final question: My readers are always curious about my writing habits, and I'm sure that your readers want me to ask you about yours. What's a typical writing day like for you? How often and where do you write? Do you have a special talisman or ritual that helps you write?

JML: I don't know how typical it is, but a good writing day for me starts with me taking a long walk with my dog—often I'm the first one up, and this not only gets us some exercise, but it's some time I can think about where my characters and I might be going that day. It's a way for me to focus and get inside my characters' heads. Once everyone in the house is off to work or school, I try to write for a few hours. This is my most productive time. I write my first draft (and make most of my revisions) in longhand—preferably sitting on my front porch with a cup of coffee, so my talismans would be a stack of new legal pads and some good ink pens (not ballpoint). I really like writing in longhand—it seems more intimate.

BM: I knew you had a dog! Judy, thanks so much for sharing all of this with me. I know you have to go back home, but I've had so much fun I hate to leave. Let's plan to meet again somewhere soon. I have a feeling we're going to become good friends.

JML: Absolutely, just tell me where and when. And even more, I think our characters (and maybe even our dogs!) would be buddies, too.

Reading Group
Questions
and Topics for
Discussion

1. In the interview with Bev Marshall, Judy Larsen discusses the use of symbolism in *All the Numbers* (page 276). Did you notice references to numbers in the book? Were they effective as symbols, in your opinion?

2. Discuss some examples of effective symbolism in your favorite novels. When has an author successfully used symbols, and when have you felt an author's use of symbols was ineffective?

3. One of the surprising moments in *All the Numbers* is Ellen's internal debate about organ donation. Were you surprised by her reaction when organ donation was suggested? Do you feel her reaction was realistic?

4. In the interview with Bev Marshall, Judy and Bev discuss the ending of the book. Was the ending satisfactory to you?

5. What constitutes a strong ending for a novel, in your opinion? Have you been disappointed by a novel's ending in the past? How much bearing did that have on your opinion of the novel as a whole?

6. In the novel, Ellen is criticized for giving an interview to the media before the trial. Did you agree that she should have remained silent or did you feel the interview was appropriate? How influential do you feel the media is in our justice system?

7. Ellen clearly struggles with her romantic interest in Bob. Do you think she is unfair to him? Both Bob and Ellen recognize that they met because of James' death. Whose argument seems more convincing to you—Bob's or Ellen's?

8. Who or what do you think is most responsible for Ellen's change of heart regarding Ben Buchanan? Her mother's words seem to fall on deaf ears throughout most of the book—do they finally get through to her or is it seeing Ben's mom or running into Melanie? Or something else?

9. Does Ellen's position as a single mother make her more vulnerable? Does any of her anger with Ben Buchanan seem to get mixed up with her anger at Tim, her ex-husband?

10. The lake house is first introduced as Ellen's "happiest place"— and even the boys see it that way. Does that increase the horror of James' accident both for the reader and for Ellen? Do you think she would have the same desire for revenge if the accident had happened elsewhere?

11. When the defense attorneys first throw accusations at Ellen, she is stunned and mad at Bob that he didn't see it coming. Did you have any sense that she would be blamed? Do you fault her or feel that she has to bear some of the responsibility?

12. Ellen is very lucky to have good friends who have clearly sustained her over the years, and that continues with James' accident and death. What do you think their view of the trial is? Anna espe-

cially seems to stay out of the argument—do you get any hints as to whether she agrees with Ellen's mother that Ellen is being too punitive or aggressive with Ben? Do you think she is?

13. The relationship between Ellen and her son Daniel goes through some real changes. How do you imagine their relationship six months after the final scene?

14. How do you think Daniel would feel about Bob and Ellen dating? How did Ellen's grief affect her relationship with Daniel? What other factors were affecting their relationship? How did you feel about Ellen's treatment of Daniel after James' death?

About the Author

JUDY MERRILL LARSEN teaches high school English in Saint Louis, where she lives with her husband and their five children. She has a master's degree from Washington University. *All the Numbers* is her first novel.

About the Type

The text of this book is set in Loire, which was created by the French type designer Jean Lochu. In 1968, Lochu met Albert Hollenstein, who recognized Lochu's talent and gave him the opportunity to design his own typefaces at Hollenstein Studios, where, ever since, he has been creating original fonts especially suited for elegant text typography. Lochu, whose training as a designer is rooted in the classical tradition, is said to have designed the Loire typeface "with the Garamond spirit."